POPULAR PUBLICATIONS   FACSIMILE EDITIONS

Black Mask #129
(September 1929)

Quite simply, *Black Mask* magazine is the most important Detective fiction magazine ever published, printing the most significant works of Dashiell Hammett, Raymond Chandler, and Erle Stanley Gardner, among others over its 20-year life. This facsimile of the September 1929 issue represents *Black Mask* at its peak with the first installment of *The Maltese Falcon* by Dashiell Hammett, along with stories by Erle Stanley Gardner, Horace McCoy, Frederick Nebel, and Raoul Whitfield.

Authors:

*Dashiell Hammett, Horace McCoy, Erle Stanley Gardner,
Frederick Nebel, Henry Wallace Phillips, Lester Reynard,
Raoul F. Whitfield, Eugene Cunningham*

Illustrators:

Arthur Rodman Bowker, Henry C. Murphy, Jr.

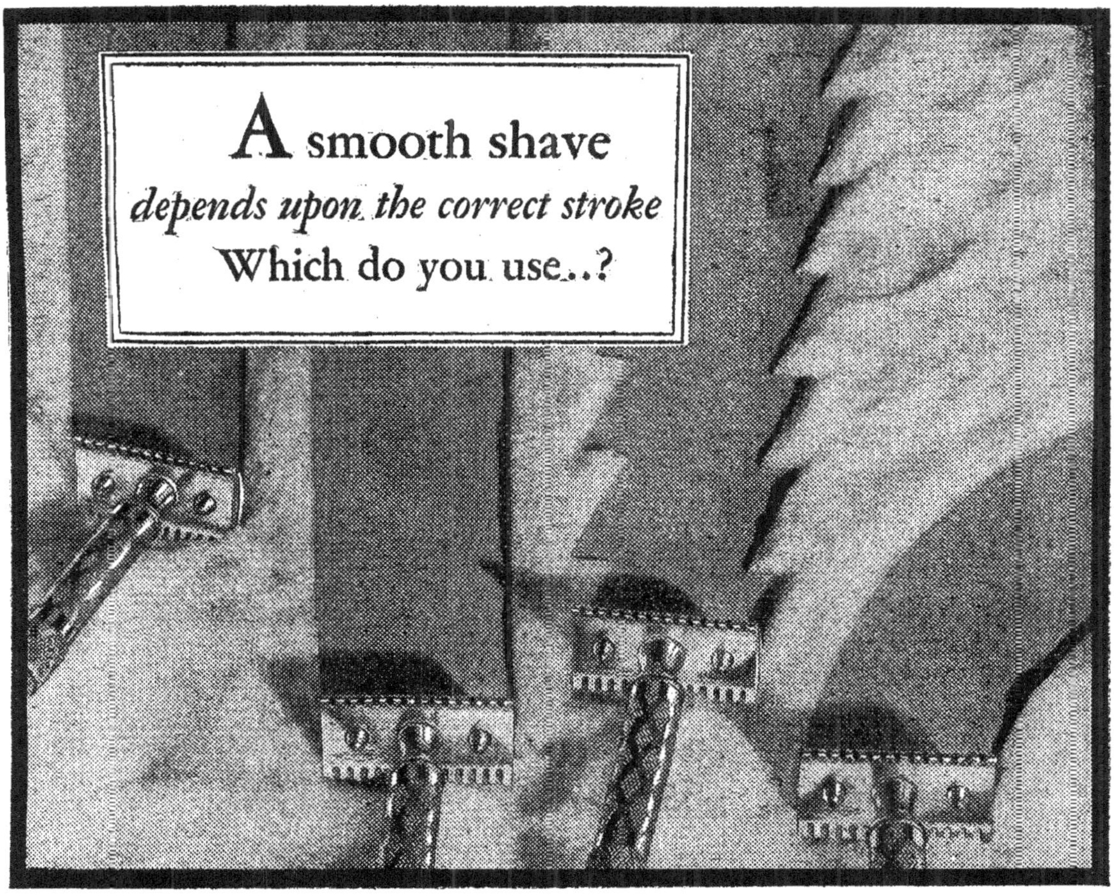

A smooth shave
depends upon the correct stroke
Which do you use...?

EIGHT out of ten American men shave with a Gillette Razor, and probably not more than half of them use the correct diagonal stroke shown at the extreme left.

But they all judge a shave on its face value, and they find the value *there* in every Gillette Blade, no matter what stroke they happen to use. Gillette has put it there — designed the blade to meet all possible changing conditions.

In the past ten years the Gillette plant has invested $12,000,000 in blade improvements alone. Today the work is done by amazingly skilful machines — adjusted to one ten-thousandth of an inch. And the product of these machines is tested and re-tested by a long line of inspectors who get a bonus for every blade they discard.

Tomorrow morning slip a fresh Gillette Blade into its holder. Lather well and use the correct diagonal stroke. Let the world's best blade in the world's best razor give you the best of all possible shaves. Gillette Safety Razor Co., Boston, U. S. A.

King C. Gillette

THE only individual in history, ancient or modern, whose picture and signature are found in every city and town, in every country in the world, is King C. Gillette. This picture and signature are universal sign-language for a perfect shave.

Gillette

Black MASK

A MAGAZINE OF DETECTIVE, ADVENTURE, AND WESTERN STORIES
The entire contents of this magazine are protected by copyright and must not be reprinted.
JOSEPH T. SHAW, Editor

VOL. XII. No. 7

SEPT, 1929

Contents

Cover painting by Henry C. Murphy, Jr.   Headings by Arthur Rodman Bowker

A. W. SUTTON, President   P. C. CODY, Vice-President and Circulation Director

Issued Monthly by PRO-DISTRIBUTORS PUBLISHING COMPANY, Inc., 578 Madison Avenue, New York, New York
YEARLY SUBSCRIPTION $2.00   SINGLE COPIES 20 CENTS   IN CANADA, 25 CENTS
Entered as second class mail matter, March 1, 1920, at the Post Office at New York, N. Y.
under act of March 3, 1879. Printed in U. S. A.
Member Newsstand Group—Men's List. For advertising rates address B. R. Crowe & Company, Inc.
25 Vanderbilt Avenue, New York, or 225 North Michigan Avenue, Chicago, Ill.

Amazingly Easy Way
to get into ELECTRICITY

Don't spend your life waiting for $5 raises in a dull, hopeless job. Now ... and forever ... say good-bye to 25 and 35 dollars a week. Let me teach you how to prepare for positions that lead to $50, $60 and on up to $200 a week in Electricity—NOT by correspondence, but by an amazing way to teach that makes you a Real Electrician in 90 days! Getting into electricity is far easier than you imagine!

Learn Without Books in 90 DAYS

LACK of experience—age, or advanced education bars no one. I don't care if you don't know an armature from an air brake—I don't expect you to! It makes no difference! Don't let lack of money stop you. Most of the men at Coyne have no more money than you have. That's why I have worked out my astonishing offers.

Free Employment Service

I will allow your railroad fare to Chicago, and assist you to part time work while training. Then, in 12 brief weeks, in the great roaring shops of Coyne, I train you as you never dreamed you could be trained ... on one of the greatest outlays of electrical apparatus ever assembled ... real dynamos, engines, power plants, autos, switchboards, transmitting stations ... everything from door-bells to farm power and lighting ... full-sized ... in full operation every day!

No Books—No Classes

No dull books, no baffling charts ... all real actual work ... building real batteries ... winding real armatures, operating real motors, dynamos and generators, wiring houses, etc., etc. That's a glimpse of how we help to make you

H. C. LEWIS, President

Prepare For Jobs Like This

Here are a few of hundreds of positions open to Coyne-trained men. Our free employment bureau gives you lifetime employment service.

Armature Expert
    up to $100 a Week
Substation Operator
    up to $65 a Week
Auto Electrician to $60 a Week
Inventor - - - Unlimited
Maintenance Engineer
    up to $75 a Week
Service Station Owner
    $60 a Week and up
Radio Expert $60 a Week and up

Students wiring and checking ignition on one of the late type Radial Aircraft Engines in our aviation electrical department

a master electrician, teaching you far more than the average ordinary electrician ever knows and fitting you to hold big jobs after graduation.

Jobs, Pay, Future

Don't worry about a job. Coyne training settles the job question for life. Our employment department gives you lifetime service. Two weeks after graduation, Clyde F. Hart got a position as electrician with the Great Western Railroad at over $100 a week. That's nothing unusual. We can point to many Coyne men making up to $600 a month. $60 a week is only the beginning of your opportunity. You can go into radio, battery or automotive electrical business for yourself and make up to $15,000 a year.

Get the Facts

Coyne is your one great chance to get into electricity. Every obstacle is removed. This school is 28 years old—Coyne training is tested—proven beyond all doubt—endorsed by many large electrical concerns. You can find out everything absolutely free. Simply mail the coupon and let me send you the big, free Coyne book of 150 photographs ... facts ... jobs ... salaries ... opportunities. Tells you how many earn expenses while training and how we assist our graduates in the field. This does not obligate you. So act at once. Just mail coupon.

Get this FREE Book

Mr. H. C. Lewis, Pres.
COYNE ELECTRICAL SCHOOL, Dept. 69-66
500 S. Paulina St., Chicago, Ill.
Dear Mr. Lewis:
    Without obligation send me your big free catalog and all details of your Railroad Fare to Chicago offer. Free Employment service, Aviation, Radio and Automotive Courses without extra cost, and how I can "earn while learning."

Name_____

Address_____

City_____ State_____

COYNE ELECTRICAL SCHOOL
500 S. Paulina St., Dept. 69-66, Chicago

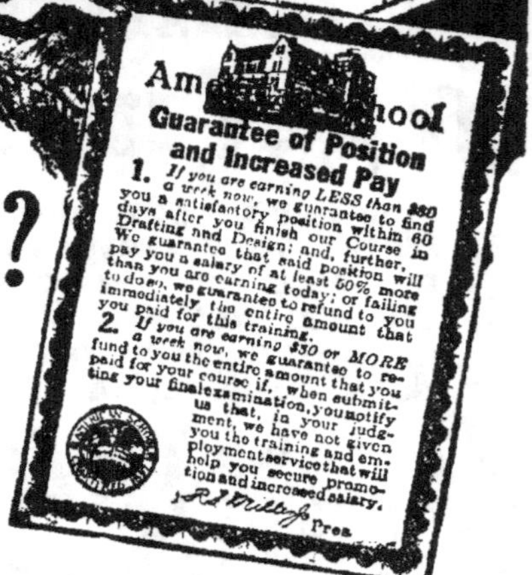

BLACK MASK

The Maltese Falcon

By DASHIELL HAMMETT

Spade and Archer.

AMUEL SPADE'S jaw was long and bony, his chin a jutting V under the more flexible V of his mouth. His nostrils curved back to make another, smaller, V. His yellow-gray eyes were horizontal. The V *motif* was picked up again by thickish brows rising outward from twin creases above a hooked nose, and his pale brown hair grew down, from high, flat temples, in a point on his forehead. He looked rather pleasantly like a blond Satan.

He said to Effie Perine: "Yes, sweetheart?"

She was a lanky, sunburned girl whose tan dress of thin woolen stuff clung to her with an effect of dampness.

Her eyes were brown and playful in a shiny, boyish face.

She finished shutting the door behind her, leaned against it, and said:

"There's a girl wants to see you. Her name's Wonderly."

"A customer?"

"I guess so. You'll want to see her anyway; she's a knockout."

"Shoo her in, darling," said Spade. "Shoo her in."

Effie Perine opened the door again, following it back into the outer office, standing with a hand on the knob while saying:

"Will you come in, Miss Wonderly?"

A voice said, "Thank you," so softly that only the purest articulation made the words audible, and a young woman came through the doorway. She advanced slowly, with tentative steps, looking at Spade with cobalt-blue eyes that were both shy and probing.

She was tall. She was pliantly slender. Her erect, high-breasted body, her long legs, her narrow hands and feet, had nowhere any angularity. She wore two shades of blue that had been selected because of her eyes. The hair curling from under her blue hat was darkly red, her full lips more brightly red. White teeth glistened in the crescent her timid smile made.

Spade rose, bowing and indicating with a thick-fingered hand the oaken armchair beside his desk. He was quite six feet tall. The steep, rounded slope of his shoulders made his body seem almost conical, no broader than it was thick, and kept his freshly pressed gray coat from fitting very well.

Miss Wonderly murmured, "Thank you," softly as before, and sat down on the edge of the chair's wooden seat.

Spade sank into his swivel-chair, made a quarter turn to face her, and smiled politely. He smiled without separating his lips. All the V's in his face grew longer.

The tappity-tap-tap and the thin bell and muffled whir of Effie Perine's typewriting came through the closed door.

Somewhere in a neighboring office a power-driven machine vibrated dully. On Spade's desk a limp cigarette smoldered in a brass tray filled with the remains of limp cigarettes. Ragged gray flakes of cigarette ash dotted the yellow top of the desk and the green blotter and the papers that were there. A buff-curtained window, eight or ten inches open, let in from the court a current of air faintly scented with ammonia. The ashes on the desk twitched and crawled in the current.

Miss Wonderly watched the twitching and crawling gray flakes uneasily. She sat stiffly on the very edge of her chair, her feet flat on the floor, as if she were about to rise. Her hands in dark gloves clasped a flat, dark handbag in her lap.

Spade rocked back in his chair and asked:

"Now what can I do for you, Miss Wonderly?"

She caught her breath and looked at him. She swallowed and said hurriedly: "Could you—? I thought—I —that is—" Then she tortured her lower lip with glistening teeth and said nothing. Only her dark eyes spoke now, pleading.

Spade nodded and smiled as if he understood her, but pleasantly, as if nothing really serious were involved. The same assurance was in his voice when he spoke.

"Suppose you tell me all about it, and then we'll know what needs doing. Better begin as far back as you can, as near the beginning."

"That was in New York," she said.

"Yes," he said.

"I don't know where she met him. I mean I don't know where in New York. She's five years younger than I, only seventeen, and we didn't have the same friends. I don't suppose we were ever as close as sisters should be. Mama and Papa are in Europe. It would kill them. I've got to get her back before they come home."

"Yes."

"They're returning the first of the month."

Spade's eyes brightened. "Then we've two whole weeks," he said.

"I didn't know what she had done until her letter came. I was frantic." Her lips trembled. Her hands mashed the dark handbag in her lap. "The fear that she had done something like this kept me from going to the police, and the fear that something had happened to her kept urging me to go. There wasn't anyone I could go to for advice. I didn't know what to do. What could I do?"

"Nothing, of course," Spade said amiably, "but then her letter came?"

"Yes, and I sent her a telegram asking her to come home. I sent it to General Delivery here. That was the only address she had given me. I waited a week, but no answer came, not a word from her. And Mama and Papa's return was drawing nearer and nearer. So I came to San Francisco to get her. I wrote her I was coming. I shouldn't have done that, should I?"

"Maybe not. It's not always easy to know what to do. Then you haven't found her?"

"I haven't found her. I wrote her that I would go to the St. Mark, and I begged her to come and let me talk to her even if she didn't intend going home with me. But she didn't come. I waited there three days, and Corinne didn't come, didn't even send me a message."

Spade nodded his blond Satan's head slowly, frowning sympathetically, his lips tightened together.

"It was horrible," she said, trying to smile. "I couldn't sit there like that and wait and wait, not knowing what had happened to her, what might be happening to her." She stopped trying to smile, and shuddered. "The only address I had was General Delivery. I wrote her another letter, and yesterday afternoon I went to the Post Office. I stayed there until dark, but I didn't see her. I went there again this morning,

and still didn't see Corinne, but I saw Floyd Thursby."

Spade nodded again, but his frown had vanished. In its place was a look of sharp attentiveness.

"He wouldn't tell me where Corinne is," she went on, hopelessly. "He wouldn't tell me anything, except that she is well and happy. But how can I believe him? That is what he would tell me anyhow, isn't it?"

"Exactly," Spade agreed, "but it might be true."

"I hope it is. I do hope it is," she exclaimed. "But I can't go back home like this, without having seen her, without even having talked to her on the phone. He wouldn't take me to her. He said she didn't want to see me. I can't believe that. He promised to tell her he had seen me, and to bring her to see me if she would come—this evening at the hotel. He said he knew she wouldn't. He promised to come himself if she wouldn't. He—"

She broke off with a startled hand to her mouth as the office door opened.

THE man who had opened the door came in a step, said, "Oh, excuse me," hastily took his brown hat from his head, and backed out.

"It's all right, Miles," Spade told him. "Come in. Miss Wonderly, this is Mr. Archer, my partner."

Miles Archer came into the office again, shutting the door behind him, ducking his head and smiling at Miss Wonderly, making a vaguely polite gesture with the hat in his hand.

He was of medium height, solidly built, wide in the shoulders, thick in the neck, with a jovial, heavy-jawed red face and some gray in his close-trimmed hair. He was apparently as many years past forty as Spade was past thirty.

Spade said:

"Miss Wonderly's sister ran away from New York with a fellow named Floyd Thursby. They're here. Miss Wonderly has seen Thursby, and has a date with him tonight. Maybe he'll bring her sister with him. The chances are he won't. Miss Wonderly wants us to help her find her sister and get her away from him and back home." He looked at Miss Wonderly. "Right?"

"Yes," she replied indistinctly.

The embarrassment that had gradually been driven away by Spade's ingratiating smiles and nods and assurances was pinkening her face again. She looked at the bag in her lap and picked nervously at it with a gloved finger.

Spade winked solemnly at his partner.

Miles Archer came forward to stand at a corner of the desk. While the girl looked at her bag he looked at her. His little brown eyes ran their bold, appraising gaze from her lowered face to her feet and up to her face again. Then he looked at Spade and made a silent whistling mouth of appreciation.

Spade raised two fingers from the arm of his chair in a brief warning gesture and said:

"Well, that should be easily enough managed. It's simply a matter of having a man at the hotel this evening to shadow him away when he leaves, and to keep on shadowing him till he leads us to your sister. If she comes with him, so much the better."

Archer said: "Yeh." His voice was heavy, coarse.

Miss Wonderly looked up quickly, at Spade, puckering her forehead between her eyebrows.

"Oh, but you must be careful." Anxiety quivered in her voice. Her lips shaped the words with little nervous jerks. I'm deathly afraid of him, and of what he might do. She's so young, his bringing her here from New York is such a serious— Mightn't he— mightn't he do—something to her?"

Spade smiled and patted the arms of his chair.

"Just leave that to us," he said. "We'll know how to handle him."

"But mightn't he?" she insisted.

"There's always a chance." Spade nodded judicially. "But you can trust us to take care of that."

"I do trust you," she said earnestly, "but I want you to know he's a dangerous man. I honestly don't believe he'd stop at anything. I don't believe he'd hesitate to—to kill Corinne if he thought it necessary to save himself. Mightn't he do that?"

"You didn't threaten him with arrest, did you?"

"I told him all I wanted was to get Corinne home before Mama and Papa came, so they'd never know what she had done. I swore to him that I'd never say a word to them about it if he'd help me do that, but that if he didn't Papa would certainly have him punished. I— I don't suppose he believed me, altogether."

"Can he cover up by marrying her?" Archer asked.

The girl blushed and said in confusion:

"He has a wife and three children in England. Corinne wrote me that, to explain why she'd gone off with him."

"They usually do," Spade said, "though not always in England." He leaned forward to reach for a pencil and pad of paper lying on the desk. "What does he look like?"

"He's thirty-five, perhaps, and as tall as you, and either naturally dark or quite sunburned. His hair is dark, too, and he has thick eyebrows. He talks in a rather loud, blustery way, and has a nervous, irritable manner. He gives an impression of being—of violence."

Spade, scribbling on the pad, asked without looking up: "What color eyes?"

"They're bluish gray, and watery, though not in a weak way. And—oh, yes—he has a marked cleft in his chin."

"Thin, medium, or heavy built?"

"Quite athletic. He's broad-shouldered and carries himself erect, what you would call a decidedly military carriage. He had on a light gray suit and a gray hat when I saw him this morning."

"What does he do for a living?" Spade asked as he pushed the pad back and laid down the pencil.

"I don't know," she said. "I've never had the slightest idea."

"When's he coming to see you?"

"At eight this evening."

"All right, Miss Wonderly. We'll have a man there. It'll help if—"

"Mr. Spade, could either you or Mr. Archer?" She made an appealing gesture with both hands. "Could either of you look after it personally? I don't mean that the man you send wouldn't be capable, but, oh! I am so afraid of what might happen to Corinne. I'm afraid of him. Could you? I'd expect to be charged more, of course." She opened her handbag with nervous fingers and put two hundred-dollar bills on Spade's desk. "Will that be enough now?"

"Yeh," Archer said, "and I'll handle it myself."

Miss Wonderly stood up, impulsively holding a hand out to him.

"Thank you. Thank you," she exclaimed, and then gave Spade the hand, repeating, "Thank you."

"Not at all," Spade said over it. "Glad to. It'll help some if you either wait for Thursby downstairs or come down with him when he leaves."

"I will," she promised, and thanked the partners again.

"And don't look for me," Archer cautioned her. "I'll see you all right."

SPADE went to the outer door with Miss Wonderly. When he came back to his desk Archer nodded at the hundred-dollar bills there, growled complacently, "They're right enough," picked one up, folded it, and tucked it in a vest pocket. "And they had brothers in her bag."

Spade pocketed the other bill before he sat town. Then he said:

"Well, don't dynamite her too much. What do you think of her?"

"She's a sweet job. And you telling me not to dynamite her." Archer guffawed suddenly, without merriment. "Maybe you saw her first, Sam, but I spoke first." He put his hands in his pants pockets and teetered back on his heels.

"You'll play hell with her, you will." Spade grinned wolfishly, showing the edge of teeth far back in his jaw. "You've got brains, yes you have." He began making a cigarette.

CHAPTER II

Death in the Fog

 TELEPHONE bell rang in darkness. The third time it rang bedsprings creaked, fingers fumbled on wood, something small and hard thudded on a carpeted floor, the springs creaked again, and a man's voice said:

"Hello. . . . Yes, speaking. . . . Dead? . . . Yes. . . . Fifteen minutes. Thanks."

A switch clicked and a white bowl, hung on three gilded chains from the ceiling's center, filled the room with light.

Spade, barefooted in green and white checked pajamas, sat on the side of his bed. He scowled thoughtfully at the telephone on the table while his hands took from beside it a packet of brown papers and a sack of Bull Durham tobacco.

Cold, steamy air blew in through two open windows, bringing with it half a dozen times a minute the Alcatraz foghorn's dull moaning. A tinny alarm clock, insecurely mounted on a corner of Duke's *Celebrated Criminal Cases of America*, which lay face down on the table, held its hands at five minutes past two.

Spade's thick fingers made a cigarette with deliberate care, sifting a measured quantity of the tan flakes down into curving paper, spreading the flakes so that they lay equal at the ends with a slight depression in the middle, thumbs rolling the paper's inner edge down and up under the outer edge as forefingers pressed it over, thumbs and fingers sliding to the paper cylinder's ends, holding it even while tongue licked the flap, left forefinger and thumb pinching their end while right forefinger and thumb smoothed the damp seam, right forefinger and thumb twisting their end and lifting the other to Spade's mouth.

He picked up the pigskin and nickel lighter that had been knocked off the table, worked it, and with the cigarette burning in a corner of his mouth stood up.

He took off his pajamas. The smooth thickness of his arms, legs and body, the sag of his big, rounded shoulders, made his body look like a bear's. It looked like a shaved bear's; his chest was hairless. His skin was childishly smooth and pink.

He scratched the back of his neck and began to dress. He put on a thin white union suit, gray socks, black garters, and dark brown shoes. When he had laced his shoes he picked up the telephone, called Graystone 4500, and ordered a taxicab. He put on a green-striped white shirt, a soft white collar, a green necktie, the gray suit he had worn that day, a loose tweed overcoat, and a dark gray hat.

The street door bell rang as he switched off the light.

WHERE Bush Street roofed Stockton before slipping downhill to Chinatown, Spade paid his fare and left the taxicab. San Francisco's night fog, thin, clammy and penetrant, blurred the street. A few yards from where Spade had dismissed the taxicab a small group of men stood looking up an alley. Two women stood with a man on the other side of Bush Street, looking at the alley. There were faces at windows.

Spade crossed the sidewalk between iron-railed hatchways that opened above bare, ugly stairs, went to the parapet, and, resting his hands on the damp coping, looked down into Stockton Street.

An automobile popped out of the tunnel beneath him with a roaring swish, as if it had been blown out, and ran away. Not far from the tunnel's mouth a

man was hunkered on his heels before a billboard that held advertisements of a moving picture and gasoline across the front of a gap between two store buildings. The hunkered man's head was bent almost to the sidewalk so he could look under the billboard. A hand flat on the sidewalk, a hand clenched on the billboard's green wooden frame, held him in this grotesque position.

Two other men stood awkwardly close together at one end of the billboard, peeping through the few inches of space between it and the building at that end. The building at the other end had a blank gray sidewall that looked down on the lot behind the billboard. Lights flickered on the sidewall, and the shadows of men moving among lights.

Spade turned from the parapet and walked up Bush Street to the alley where men were grouped. A uniformed policeman, chewing gum under an enamel sign that said *Burritt St.* in white against dark blue, put out an arm and asked:

"What do you want here?"

"I'm Sam Spade. Tom Polhaus phoned me."

"Sure you are." The policeman's arm went down. "I didn't know you at first. Well, they're back there." He jerked a thumb over his shoulder. "Bad business."

"Bad enough," Spade agreed, and went up the alley.

Halfway up it, not far from the entrance, a dark ambulance stood. Behind the ambulance, on the left, the alley was bounded by a waist-high fence, three strips of rough boarding. From the fence dark ground fell away steeply to the billboard on Stockton Street below.

A ten-foot length of the fence's top rail had been torn from a post at one end, and hung dangling from the other. Fifteen feet down the slope a flat boulder stuck out. In the notch between boulder and slope Miles Archer lay on his back. Two men stood over him. One of them held an electric torch's beam on the dead man. Other men with lights moved up and down the slope.

One of them hailed Spade, "Hello, Sam," and clambered up to the alley, his shadow running up before him. He was a barrel-bellied tall man with shrewd, small eyes, a thick mouth, and carelessly shaven dark jowls. His shoes, knees, hands and chin were daubed with brown loam.

"I figured you'd want to see it before we took him away," he said as he stepped over the broken fence.

"Yes. Thanks, Tom," Spade said. "What happened?"

He put an elbow on a fence post and looked down at the men below, nodding to those who nodded to him.

Tom Polhaus poked his own left breast with a dirty finger.

"Got him right through the pump, with this." He took a fat revolver from his coat pocket and held it out to Spade. Mud inlaid the depressions in the revolver's surface. "A Webley. English, ain't it?"

Spade took his elbow from the fence post and leaned down to look at the weapon, but he did not touch it.

"Yes," he said. "Webley-Fosbery semi-automatic revolver. That's it. Thirty-eight, eight shot. They don't make them any more. How many gone out of it?"

"One shot." Tom poked his breast again. "He must've been dead when he cracked the fence." He raised the muddy revolver. "You've seen this before?"

Spade nodded.

"I've seen Webley-Fosberys," he said indifferently, and then spoke rapidly: "He was shot up here, huh? Standing where you are, with his back to the fence. The man that shot him stands here." He went around in front of Tom and raised a hand breast-high with leveled forefinger. "Let's him have it and Miles goes back, taking the top off the fence and going on through and down till the rock catches him. That it?"

"That's it," Tom replied slowly, working his brows together. "The shot burnt his coat."

"Who found him?"

"The man on the beat, Shilling. He was coming down Bush, and just as he got here a machine turning around threw headlights up here and he saw the top rail off. So he came up and found him."

"What about the machine that was turning around?"

"Not a damned thing about it, Sam. Shilling didn't pay much attention to it, not knowing anything was wrong. He says nobody didn't come out of here during the time it took him to come down from Powell, or he'd've seen them. The only other way out would be under the billboard on Stockton. Nobody went that way. The fog's got the ground soggy, and the only marks are where Miles slid down and where this here gun rolled."

"Didn't anybody hear the shot?"

"For the love of God, Sam, we only just got here. Somebody must've heard it, when we find them." He turned and put a leg over the fence. "Coming down for a look at him before he's moved?"

Spade said: "No."

Tom halted astride the fence to look back at Spade with surprised, small eyes.

Spade said: "You've seen him. You'd see everything I could."

Tom, still looking at Spade, nodded doubtfully and withdrew his leg over the fence.

"His gun was tucked away on his hip," he said. "It hadn't been fired. There was a hundred and sixty-some bucks in his clothes. Was he working, Sam?"

Spade, after a moment's hesitation, nodded.

Tom asked: "Well?"

"He was supposed to be tailing a fellow named Floyd Thursby," Spade said, and described Thursby as Miss Wonderly had described him.

"What for?"

Spade put his hands into his overcoat pockets and blinked sleepy eyes at Tom.

Tom repeated impatiently: "What for?"

"He was an Englishman, maybe. I don't know what his game was, exactly. We were trying to find out where he lived." Spade grinned softly and took a hand from his pocket to pat Tom's shoulder. "Don't crowd me." He put the hand in his pocket again. "I'm going out to break the news to Miles's wife." He turned away.

Tom, scowling, opened his mouth, closed it without having said anything, cleared his throat put the scowl off his face, and spoke with a husky sort of gentleness:

"It's tough, him getting it like that. Miles had his faults same as the rest of us, but I guess he must've had his good points, too."

"I guess so," Spade agreed in a tone that was utterly meaningless, and went out of the alley.

IN an all-night drug store on the corner of Bush and Taylor Streets Spade used a telephone.

"Precious," he said into it some time after he had given central a number, "Miles has been shot. . . . Yes, he's dead. . . . Now don't get excited. . . . Yes. . . . You'll have to break it to Iva. . . . No, I'm damned if I will. You've got to do it. . . . That's a good girl. . . . And keep her away from the office. Tell her I'll see her—uh—some time. . . . Yes, but don't tie me up to anything. . . . That's the stuff. You're an angel. Bye."

SPADE'S tinny alarm clock said three-forty when he turned on the light in the suspended bowl again. He dropped his hat and overcoat on the bed and went into his kitchen, returning to the bedroom with a wineglass and a tall, dark bottle of Bacardi. He poured a drink and drank it standing. Then he put bottle and glass on the table, sat down on the side of the bed facing them, and rolled a cigarette.

He had drunk his third glass of Bacardi and was lighting his fifth cigarette when the street door bell rang. The hands of the alarm clock stood at four-thirty.

He sighed, rose from the bed, and went to the telephone box beside his bathroom door. He pressed the button that released the street door lock. He muttered, "Damn her," and stood scowling at the black telephone box, breathing irregularly while a dull flush grew in his cheeks.

The grating and rattling of the elevator door being opened and closed came from the corridor. Spade sighed again and moved toward the corridor door. Soft, heavy footsteps sounded on the carpeted floor outside, the footsteps of two men. Spade's face brightened. His eyes were no longer harassed. He opened the door quickly.

"Hello, Tom," he said to the barrel-bellied tall detective with whom he had talked in Burritt Street, and, "Hello, Lieutenant," to the man beside him. "Come in."

They nodded together, neither saying anything, and came in. Spade shut the door and ushered them back into his bedroom. Tom sat on an end of the sofa by the window. The lieutenant sat on a chair beside the table.

The lieutenant was a compactly built man with a round head under short-cut grizzled hair and a square face behind a short-cut grizzled mustache. A five-dollar gold piece was pinned to his necktie, and there was a small, elaborate diamond-set secret society emblem on his lapel.

Spade brought two wineglasses in from the kitchen, filled them and his own with Bacardi, gave one to each of his guests, and sat down with his on the side of the bed. Spade's face was placid and incurious. He raised his glass, said, "Success to crime," and drank it down.

Tom emptied his glass, set it on the

floor beside him, and wiped his mouth with the back of a muddy finger. He stared at the foot of the bed as if he were trying to remember something of which it vaguely reminded him.

The lieutenant looked at his glass for a dozen seconds, took a very small sip of the rum, and put the glass on the table at his elbow. He examined the room with hard, deliberate eyes, and then looked at Tom.

Tom moved uncomfortably on the sofa and without looking up asked:

"Did you break the news to Miles's wife, Sam?"

Spade said: "Uh-huh."

"How'd she take it?"

Spade shook his head. "I don't know anything about women."

Tom said softly: "The hell you don't!"

The lieutenant put his hands on his knees and leaned forward. His greenish eyes looked at Spade with a peculiarly rigid stare, as if their focus was a matter of mechanics, to be changed only by pulling a lever or pressing a button.

"What kind of a gun do you carry?" he asked.

"None. I don't like them much. There are some in the office, of course."

"I'd like to see one of them," the lieutenant said. "You don't happen to have one here?"

"No."

"You sure of that?"

"Look around." Spade smiled and waved his empty glass a little. "Turn the dump upside-down if you want. I won't squawk, if you've got a search warrant."

Tom protested: "Oh, hell, Sam!"

Spade put his glass on the table and stood up facing the lieutenant.

"What do you want, Dundy?" he asked in a voice hard and cold as his eyes.

Lieutenant Dundy's eyes had moved to maintain their focus on Spade's. Only his eyes had moved.

Tom shifted his bulk on the sofa again, blew a deep breath out through his nose, and growled plaintively:

"We're not wanting to make any trouble, Sam."

Spade, ignoring Tom, said to Dundy:

"Well, what do you want? Talk turkey. Who in hell do you think you are, coming in here trying to rope me?"

"All right," Dundy said in his chest. "Now sit down and listen."

"I'll sit or stand as I damned please," said Spade, not moving.

"For God's sake be reasonable," Tom begged. "What's the use of us having a row? If you want to know why we didn't talk turkey, it's because when I asked you who this Thursby was you as good as told me it was none of my business. You can't treat us that way, Sam. It ain't right, and it won't get you anywheres. We got our work to do."

Lieutenant Dundy jumped up, stood close to Spade, and thrust his square, pink face up at the taller man's.

"I've told you before your foot was going to slip one of these days."

Spade made a deprecative mouth, raising his eyebrows.

"Everybody's foot slips sometime," he said with derisive mildness.

"And maybe this is your time?"

Spade smiled and shook his head.

"No. I'll do nicely, thank you." He stopped smiling. His upper lip, on the left side, twitched over his eyetooth. His eyes became narrow and sultry. His voice came out deep as the lieutenant's. "I don't like this. What are you sucking around for? Tell me, or get out and let me go to bed."

"Who's Thursby?" Dundy snapped.

"I told Tom what I knew about him."

"You told Tom damned little."

"I knew damned little."

"Why were you tailing him?"

"I wasn't. Miles was, for the swell reason that we had a client who was paying good United States money to have him tailed."

"Who's the client?"

Placidity came back to Spade's face and voice.

"Now, now," he said reprovingly. "You know I can't tell you that until I've talked it over with the client."

"You'll tell it to me or you'll tell it in court," Dundy said hotly. "This is murder, and don't forget it."

"Maybe. And here's something for you to not forget, sweetheart. I'll tell it or not as I damned please. It's a long while since I burst out crying because policemen didn't like me."

Tom came over and sat on the foot of the bed. His carelessly shaven mud-smeared face was tired and lined.

"Be reasonable, Sam," he pleaded. "Give us a chance. How can we turn up anything on Miles's killing if you won't give us what you've got?"

"You needn't get a headache over that," Spade told him. "I'll bury my dead."

Lieutenant Dundy sat down and put his hands on his knees again. His eyes were warm green discs.

"I thought you would," he said. He smiled with grim content. "That's just exactly why we came to see you. Isn't it, Tom?"

Tom groaned, but said nothing articulate.

Spade watched Dundy warily.

"That's just what I said to Tom," the lieutenant went on. "I said, 'Tom, I've got a hunch that Sam Spade's a man to keep the family troubles in the family.' That's just what I said to him."

Spade put the wariness out of his eyes. He made them look bored. He turned his face to Tom and asked with great carelessness:

"What's itching your boy friend now?"

Dundy jumped up and tapped Spade's chest with the ends of two bent fingers.

"Just this," he said, taking pains to make each word very distinct, emphasizing them with repeated taps: "Thursby was shot down in front of his hotel just thirty-five minutes after you left Burritt Street."

Spade spoke, taking equal pains with his words:

"Keep your — damned dirty paws off me."

Dundy withdrew the tapping fingers, but there was no change in his voice.

"Tom says you were in too much of a hurry to even stop for a look at your partner."

Tom growled apologetically: "Well, damn it, Sam, you did run off like that."

"You didn't go to Archer's house to tell his wife," the lieutenant's accusing voice went on. "We called up and that girl in your office was there, and said you sent her."

Spade nodded. His face was stupid in its blankness.

Lieutenant Dundy raised the two bent fingers toward the private detective's chest, quickly lowered them, and said:

"I give you ten minutes to get to a phone and do your talking to the girl. I give you ten to fifteen minutes to get to Thursby's joint—Geary near Leavenworth—you could do it easy in that time. And that gives you ten or fifteen minutes of waiting before he showed up."

"I knew where he lived?" Spade asked. "And I knew he hadn't gone straight home after killing Miles?"

"You knew what you knew," Dundy replied stubbornly. "What time did you get home?"

"Twenty minutes to four. I walked around thinking things over."

The lieutenant wagged his round head up and down.

"We knew you weren't home at three-thirty," he said. "We tried to get you on the phone. Where'd you do your walking?"

"Out Bush Street a way and back."

"Did you see anybody that—?"

"No. No witnesses," Spade said and laughed, but pleasantly now. "Sit down, Dundy. You haven't finished your drink. Get your glass, Tom."

Tom said: "No, thanks."

Dundy sat down, but paid no attention to his glass of rum.

Spade filled his own glass, drank, put the empty glass on the table, and resumed his seat on the side of the bed.

"I know where I stand now," he said, looking with friendly eyes from one police detective to the other. "I'm sorry I got up on my hind legs. But you birds made me nervous, coming in and trying to put the work on me. Having Miles knocked off bothered me, and then you birds cracking foxy. That's all right now, though, now that I know what you're up to."

Tom said: "Forget it."

The lieutenant said nothing.

Spade asked: "Thursby dead?"

While the lieutenant hesitated Tom said: "Yes."

Then the lieutenant said angrily: "And you might just as well know it—if you don't—that he died before he could tell anybody anything."

Spade was rolling a cigarette. He asked, without looking up:

"What do you mean by that? You think I did know it?"

"I meant what I said," Dundy replied bluntly.

Spade looked up at him and smiled, holding the finished cigarette in one hand, his lighter in the other.

"You're not ready to pinch me yet, are you, Dundy?" he asked.

Dundy shook his head, no.

"Then," said Spade, "there's no particular reason why I should give a damn what you think, is there?"

Dundy looked at Spade with hard green eyes and said nothing.

Tom said: "Aw, be reasonable, Sam."

Spade put the cigarette in his mouth, set fire to it, and laughed smoke out.

"I'll be reasonable, Tom," he promised. "How'd I kill this Thursby? I've forgotten."

Tom grunted disgust. Lieutenant Dundy said:

"He was shot four times in the back, with a .44 or .45, from across the street, when he started to go into his hotel. That's the way it figures, though nobody saw it."

"And he was wearing a Lüger in a shoulder holster," Tom added. "And it hadn't been fired."

"What do the hotel people know about him?" Spade asked.

"Nothing except that he'd been there a week."

"Alone?"

"Alone."

"What did you find on him? or in his room?"

Dundy drew his lips in and asked:

"What'd you think we'd find?"

Spade made a careless motion with his limp cigarette.

"Something to tell you who he was, what his store was. Did you?"

"We thought you could tell us that."

Spade looked at the lieutenant with yellow-gray eyes that held an almost exaggerated amount of candor.

"I've never seen Thursby," he said, "dead or alive."

Lieutenant Dundy stood up looking dissatisfied. Tom rose yawning and stretching.

"We've asked what we came to ask," Dundy said, frowning over eyes hard as green pebbles. He held his mustached upper lip tight against his teeth, letting his lower lip push the words out. "We've told you more than you've told us. That's fair enough. You know me, Spade. If you did or you didn't you'll get a square deal out of me, and most of the breaks. I don't know that I'd blame you a hell of a lot for dropping him, but that won't keep me from nailing you."

"Fair enough," Spade agreed evenly. "But I'd feel better about it if you'd drink your drink."

Lieutenant Dundy turned to the table, picked up his glass, and slowly drained it. Then he said, "Good night," and held out his hand. They shook hands with marked formality. Tom and Spade shook hands with marked formality. Spade let them out. Then he undressed, turned off the lights, and went to bed.

CHAPTER III

Three Women

HEN Spade reached his office at ten the following morning Effie Perine was at her desk opening the morning mail. Her boy's face was pale under its sunburn. She put down the handful of envelopes and the paper-knife she held, and said: "She's in there." Her voice was low and warning.

"I asked you to keep her away," Spade complained irritably, though he too kept his voice low.

Effie Perine's brown eyes opened wide and her voice was sharp as his: "Yes, but you didn't tell me how." Her eyelids went together a little, and her shoulders drooped. "Don't be cranky, Sam," she said wearily. "I had her all night."

Spade came over and stood beside the girl, putting a hand on her hair, smoothing it away from the part.

"Sorry, angel, I haven't—"

He broke off as the inner door opened.

"Hello, Iva," he said to the woman who had opened it.

"Oh, Sam!" she said.

She was a blonde woman of a few years more than thirty. Her facial prettiness was perhaps five years past its best moment. Her body, for all its sturdiness, was finely modeled and exquisite. She wore black clothes from hat to shoes. They had as mourning an impromptu air.

Having spoken, she stepped back from the door and stood waiting for Spade. He took his hand from Effie Perine's head and entered the inner office, shutting the door.

Iva came quickly to him, raising her face for his kiss. Her arms were around him before his held her. When they had kissed he made a little motion as if to release her, but she pressed her face to his chest and began to sob.

He stroked her round back, saying: "Poor darling."

His voice was tender. His eyes, squinting at the desk that had been his partner's, across the room from his own, were angry. He drew his lips back over his teeth in an impatient grimace and turned his chin aside to avoid contact with the crown of her hat.

"Did you send for Miles's brother?" he asked.

"Yes. He came over this morning." The words were blurred by her sobbing and his coat against her mouth.

He grimaced again and bent his head for a surreptitious look at the watch on his wrist. His left arm was around her, the hand on her left shoulder. His cuff was pulled back far enough to leave the watch exposed. It showed ten-thirteen.

The woman stirred in his arms and raised her face again. Her blue eyes were wet, round, and white-ringed. Her mouth was moist.

"Oh, Sam," she moaned, "did you kill him?"

Spade stared at her with bulging eyes. His bony jaw sagged. He took his arms from around her and stepped back out of her arms. He scowled at her and cleared his throat.

She held her arms up as he had left them. Anguish clouded her eyes, partly closed them under eyebrows pulled up at the inner ends. Her soft damp red lips trembled.

Spade laughed a harsh syllable. "Ha," and went to the buff-curtained window. He stood there with his back to her, looking through the curtain into the court, until she started toward him. Then he turned quickly and went to his desk. He sat down, put his elbows on the desk, his chin between his fists, and looked at her. His yellowish eyes glittered between narrowed lids.

"Who," he asked coldly, "put that bright idea into your head?"

"I thought—" She put a hand to her mouth and fresh tears filled her eyes. She came to stand beside the desk, moving with easy sure-footed grace in black slippers whose smallness and heel-height were extreme. "Be kind to me, Sam," she said humbly.

He laughed at her, his eyes still glittering. "You killed my husband, Sam, be kind to me." He clapped his palms together and said: "Great God!"

She began to cry audibly, holding a white handkerchief to her face.

He got up and stood close behind her. He put his arms around her. He kissed her neck between ear and coat collar. He said: "Now, Iva, don't." His face was expressionless.

When she had stopped crying he put his mouth to her ear and murmured: "You shouldn't have come here today, precious. It wasn't wise. You can't stay. You ought to be home."

She turned around in his arms to face him, asking:

"You'll come tonight?"

He shook his head gently.

"Not tonight."

"Soon?"

"Soon."

"How soon?"

"As soon as I can."

He kissed her mouth, led her to the door, opened it, said. "Good-bye, Iva," bowed, shut the door, and returned to his desk.

He took tobacco and cigarette papers from his vest pockets, but did not roll a cigarette. He sat holding the papers in one hand, the tobacco in the other, and looked with brooding eyes at his dead partner's desk.

EFFIE PERINE opened the door and came in. Her brown eyes were uneasy. Her voice was careless. She asked: "Well?"

Spade said nothing. His brooding gaze did not move from his partner's desk.

The girl frowned and came around to his side.

"Well," she asked in a louder voice, "how did you and the widow make out?"

"She thinks I shot Miles," he said, only his lips moving.

"So you could marry her?"

Spade made no reply to that.

The girl took his hat from his head and put it on the desk, then leaned over and took the tobacco sack and the papers from his inert fingers.

"The police think I shot Thursby," he said.

"Who is he?" she asked, separating a paper from the packet, sifting tobacco into it.

"Who do you think I shot?" he asked.

When she ignored the question he said: "Thursby's the guy Miles was supposed to be shadowing for the Wonderly girl."

Her thin fingers finished shaping the cigarette. She licked it, smoothed it, twisted the ends, and placed it between Spade's lips.

He said, "Thanks, honey," put an arm around her slim waist and rested his cheek wearily against her hip, shutting his eyes.

"Are you going to marry Iva?" she asked, looking down at his pale brown hair.

"Don't be silly," he muttered. The unlighted cigarette bobbed up and down with the movement of his lips.

"She doesn't think it's silly. Why should she, the way you've played around with her?"

He sighed and said: "I wish to God I'd never seen her."

"Maybe you do now." A trace of spitefulness came into the girl's voice. "But there was a time."

"I never know what to do or say to women, except that way," he grumbled. "And then I didn't like Miles."

"That's a lie, Sam," the girl said. "You know I think she's a louse, but I'd be a louse too if I could have a body like that."

Spade rubbed his face impatiently against her hip, but said nothing.

Effie Perine bit her lower lip, wrinkled her forehead, and, bending down for a better view of his face, asked:

"Do you suppose she could have killed him?"

Spade sat up straight and took his arm from her waist. He smiled at her. His smile held nothing but amusement. He took out his lighter, snapped it on, and lit his cigarette.

"You're an angel," he said tenderly through smoke, "a nice rattle-brained angel."

She smiled a little wryly.

"Oh, am I? Suppose I told you that your Iva hadn't been home very many minutes when I arrived to break the news at three o'clock this morning?"

"Are you telling me?" he asked. His eyes had become alert, though his mouth continued to smile.

"She kept me waiting at the door while she undressed or finished undressing. I saw her clothes where she had dumped them on a chair. Her coat and hat were underneath. Her singlette, on top, was still warm. She said she had been asleep, but she hadn't. She had wrinkled up the bed, but the wrinkles weren't mashed down."

Spade took the girl's hand and patted it.

"You're a detective, darling, but"— he shook his head—"she didn't kill him."

Effie Perine snatched her hand away from him.

"That louse wants to marry you, Sam," she said bitterly.

He made a careless gesture of dismissal with one hand.

She frowned at him and demanded: "Did you see her last night?"

"No."

"Honestly?"

"Honestly. Don't act like Dundy, sweetheart. It ill becomes you."

"Has Dundy been after you?"

"Uh-huh. He and Tom Polhaus stopped in for a drink at four o'clock."

"Do they really think you killed this what's-his-name?"

"Thursby."

He dropped what was left of his cigarette into the brass tray and began to roll another.

"Do they?" she insisted.

"God knows." His eyes were on the cigarette he was making. "They did have some such notion. I don't know how far I talked them out of it."

"Look at me, Sam."

He looked at her and laughed so that for the moment merriment mingled with the anxiety in her face.

"You worry me," she said, seriousness returning to her face as she talked. "You always think you know what you're doing, but you're too slick for your own good, and some day you're going to find it out."

He sighed mockingly and rubbed his cheek against her arm.

"That's what Dundy says, but you keep Iva away from me, sweet, and I'll manage to survive the rest of my troubles." He stood up and put on his hat. "Have the *Spade & Archer* taken off the door and *Samuel Spade* put in its place. I'll be back in an hour, or phone you."

SPADE went through the St. Mark's long purplish lobby to the desk and asked a blond dandy if Miss Wonderly was in. The dandy turned away from Spade, and then back to him shaking his head.

"She checked out this morning, Mr. Spade."

"Thanks."

Spade walked past the desk to an alcove off the lobby, where a plump young-middle-aged man in dark clothes sat at a flat-topped mahogany desk. On the edge of the desk facing the lobby was a triangular prism of mahogany and brass inscribed *Mr. Freed*.

The plump man got up from his chair and came around the desk holding out his hand.

"I was awfully sorry to hear about Archer, Spade," he said in the tone of one trained to sympathize readily but without intrusiveness. "I've just seen it in the *Call*. He was in here last night, you know."

"Thanks, Freed. Were you talking to him?"

"No. He was sitting in the lobby when I came in early in the evening. I didn't stop. I thought he was working and I know you fellows like to be let alone when you're busy. Did that have anything to do with his—?"

"I don't think so, but we don't know yet. Anyway, we won't mix the house up in it if we can help it."

"Thanks."

"That's all right. Can you give me some information about an ex-guest, and then forget I asked for it?"

"Surely."

"A Miss Wonderly checked out this morning. I'd like to know the details."

"Come along," Freed said, "and we'll see what we can learn."

Spade stood still shaking his head.

"I don't want to show in it," he said.

Freed nodded his sleek head and went out of the alcove. In the lobby he halted suddenly and returned to Spade.

"Barriman was the house detective on duty last night," he said. "He's sure to have seen Archer. Shall I caution him not to mention it?"

Spade looked at Freed from the corners of his eyes.

"Better not, Freed. That won't make any difference as long as there's no connection shown with this Wonderly. Barriman's all right, but he likes to talk, and I'd rather he didn't think there was anything to be kept quiet."

Freed nodded again and went away. Fifteen minutes later he returned.

"She came here last Tuesday, registering from New York. She hadn't a trunk, only some bags. There were no phone calls charged to her room, and she doesn't seem to have gotten much mail, if any. The only visitor I could learn about was a tall dark man of thirty-six or so. They seem to have been together a lot. She went out at half-past nine this morning, came back an hour later, paid her bill, and had her bags carried out to a car. The boy who carried them says it was a Nash touring car, probably a hired car. She left a forwarding address: The Ambassador, Los Angeles."

Spade said: "Thanks a lot, Freed," and left the St. Mark.

WHEN Spade returned to his office Effie Perine stopped typing a letter to tell him: "Your friend Dundy was in. He wanted to look at your guns."

"And?"

"I told him to come back when you were here."

"Good girl. If he comes back let him see them."

"And Miss Wonderly called up."

"It's about time. What did she say?"

"She wants you to come to see her." The girl picked a slip of paper up from her desk and read the memorandum penciled on it: "She's at the Coronet, on California Street, apartment 1001. You're to ask for Miss Leblanc."

Spade said, "Give me," and held out his hand. When she had given him the memorandum he took out his lighter, snapped on the flame, applied it to the slip of paper, held the paper till all but one corner was curling black ash, dropped it on the linoleum floor, and mashed it under his shoe-sole.

The girl watched him suspiciously.

He grinned at her, said, "That's just the way it is, dear," and went out again.

CHAPTER IV

The Black Bird

MISS WONDERLY, in a belted green crêpe silk dress, opened the door of apartment 1001 at the Coronet. Her face was flushed. Her dark red hair, parted on the left side, swept back in loose waves over her right temple, was somewhat tousled.

Spade took off his hat and said: "Good morning."

His smile brought a fainter smile to

her face. Her eyes, of blue that was almost violet, did not lose their troubled look.

She lowered her head, and said in a hushed, timid, voice: "Come in, Mr. Spade."

She led him past open kitchen, bathroom and bedroom doors into a cream and red living-room, apologizing for its confusion: "Everything is upside down. I haven't even finished unpacking."

She laid his hat on a table and sat down on a walnut settee. He sat on a brocaded oval-back chair facing her.

She looked at her fingers, working them together, and said:

"Mr. Spade, I've a terrible, terrible confession to make."

Spade smiled a polite smile, which she did not raise her eyes to see, and said nothing.

"That—that story I hold you yesterday was all—a story," she stammered, and looked up at him now with miserable frightened eyes.

"Oh, that," Spade said lightly. "We didn't exactly believe your story."

"Then—?" Perplexity was added to the misery and fright in her eyes.

"We believed your two hundred dollars."

"You mean—?" She seemed to have no idea of what he meant.

"I mean that you paid us more than if you'd been telling the truth," he explained blandly, "and enough more to make it all right."

Her eyes lighted up suddenly. She lifted herself a few inches from the settee, settled down again, smoothed her skirt, leaned forward, and spoke eagerly:

"And even now you'd be willing to—?"

Spade stopped her with a palm-up motion of one hand. The upper part of his face frowned. The lower part smiled.

"That depends," he said. "The hell of it is, Miss— Is your name Wonderly or Leblanc?"

She blushed and murmured: "It's

O'Shaughnessy, B r i g i d O'Shaughnessy."

"The hell of it is, Miss O'Shaughnessy, that a couple of murders"—she winced—"coming together like this get everybody stirred up, make the police think they can go the limit, make everything and everybody hard to handle, and expensive. It's not—"

He stopped talking because she had stopped listening and was impatiently waiting for him to finish.

"Mr. Spade, tell me the truth." Her voice quivered on the verge of hysteria. Her face had become haggard around desperate eyes. "Am I to blame for—for last night?"

Spade shook his head.

"Not unless there are things I don't know about," he said. "You warned us that Thursby was dangerous. Of course you did lie to us about your sister and all, but that doesn't count: we didn't believe you." He shrugged his sloping shoulders. "I wouldn't say it looked like your fault."

She said, "Thank you," very softly, and then moved her head from side to side. "But I'll always blame myself." She put a hand to her throat. "Mr. Archer was so—so alive yesterday afternoon, so solid and hearty and—"

"Stop it," Slade commanded. "He knew what he was doing. They're the chances we take."

"Was—was he married?"

"Yes, with ten thousand insurance, no children, and a wife who didn't like him."

"Oh, please don't!" she whispered.

Spade shrugged again. "That's the way it was." He glanced at the watch on his wrist, and moved from his chair to the settee beside her. "There's no time for worrying about that now." His voice was amiable but firm. "Out there a flock of policemen and reporters and assistant district attorneys are running around with their noses to the ground. What do you want to do?"

"I want you to save me from—from all of it," she said in a thin, tremulous voice. She put a hand timidly on his forearm. "Mr. Spade, do they know about me?"

"Not yet. I wanted to see you first."

"What—what would they think if they knew about the way I came to you, with those lies?"

"That wouldn't mean anything to the police except guilt. That's why I've been stalling them till I could see you. I thought maybe we wouldn't have to let them know it all. We ought to be able to fake a story that will rock them to sleep, if necessary."

"Mr. Spade, you don't think I had anything to do with—the murders—do you?"

He grinned at her and said: "I forgot to ask you that. Did you?"

"No."

"That's good. Now what are we going to tell the police?"

She squirmed on her end of the settee and her eyes wavered between heavy lashes, as if trying and failing to free their gaze from his. She seemed smaller, and very young and oppressed.

"Must they know about me at all?" she asked. "I think I'd rather die than that, Mr. Spade. I can't explain now, but can't you somehow manage so that you can shield me from them altogether, so I won't have to answer their questions? I couldn't stand being questioned, Mr. Spade. I would rather die. Can't you?"

"Maybe," he said, "but *I'll* have to know what it's all about."

She went down on her knees at his knees. She held her face up to him. Her face was wan, taut, and fearful over tight-clasped hands.

"I haven't lived a good life," she cried. "I'm bad—worse than you could know—but I'm not all bad. Look at me, Mr. Spade. You know I'm not all bad, don't you? You can see that, can't you? Then can't you trust me a little? I'm so alone and afraid, and I've got nobody to help me if you won't help me. I know I've no right to ask you to trust me if I won't trust you. I do

trust you, but I can't tell you. I can't tell you now. Later I will, when I can. I'm afraid, Mr. Spade. I'm afraid of trusting you. I don't mean that. I do trust you, but—but I trusted Floyd, and —I've nobody else, nobody else, Mr. Spade. You can save me. You've said you can save me. If I hadn't believed you could save me I would have run away today instead of sending for you. If I thought anybody else could save me would I be down on my knees to you? I know this isn't fair of me. But be generous, Mr. Spade. Don't ask me to be fair. You're strong, you're resourceful, you're brave. You can spare me some of that strength and resourcefulness and courage, surely. Help me, Mr. Spade. Help me because I need help so badly, and because if you don't where will I find anyone who can, however willing? Help me. I've no right to ask you to help me blindly, but I do ask you. Be generous, Mr. Spade. You can save me. You can. Won't you?"

Spade, who had held his breath throughout much of this speech, now emptied his lungs with a long sighing exhalation between pursed lips and said:

"You won't need much of anybody's help. You're good. You're very good. It's chiefly your eyes, I think, and that throaty sob you get into your voice when you say things like, 'Be generous, Mr. Spade.'"

She jumped up on her feet. Her face crimsoned painfully, but she held her head erect and she looked Spade straight in the eyes.

"I deserve that," she said. "I deserve it, but—oh!—I did want your help so much, and I do want it so much, and the lie was in the way I said it, Mr. Spade, and hardly at all in what I said." She turned away from him, no longer holding herself erect. "It's my own fault that you can't believe me now."

Spade's face reddened and he looked down at the floor, muttering:

"Now you are dangerous."

Brigid O'Shaughnessy went to the table and got his hat. She came back and stood in front of him holding the hat, not offering it to him, but holding it for him to take if he wished. Her face was white and thin.

Spade looked at his hat and asked: "What happened last night?"

"Floyd came to the hotel at nine o'clock, and we went out for a walk. I suggested that, so Mr. Archer could see him. We stopped at a restaurant in Geary Street, I think it was, for supper and to dance, and got back to the hotel at about half-past twelve. Floyd left me at the door, and I stood inside and watched Mr. Archer follow him down the street, on the other side."

"Down? You mean toward Market Street?"

"Yes."

"Do you know what they'd be doing in the neighborhood of Bush and Stockton, where Archer was shot?"

"Isn't that near where Floyd lived?"

"No. It would be a dozen blocks out of his way if he was going from your hotel to his. Well, what did you do after they left?"

"I went to bed. And this morning when I went out for breakfast I saw the headlines in the paper and read about both of them being killed. Then I went up to Union Square, where I had seen automobiles for hire, and got one and went to my hotel for my luggage. After I found my room had been searched yesterday I knew I would have to move, and I had found this place yesterday afternoon. So I came up here and then phoned your office."

"Your room at the St. Mark was searched?" he asked.

"Yes, while I was in your office." She bit her lip. "I didn't mean to tell you that."

"You mean by that that I'm not to question you about it?"

She nodded timidly.

He frowned.

She moved his hat a little in her hands.

He laughed impatiently and said:

"Stop waving my hat in my face. Haven't I promised to do what I can?"

She smiled contritely, returned the hat to the table, and sat beside him on the settee again.

He said: "As for trusting you blindly, I've got nothing against that except that I won't be able to do much if I haven't some idea of what's going on. For instance, I've got to know something about your Floyd Thursby."

"I met him in the Orient." She spoke slowly, looking down at a pointed finger that traced 8's on the seat of the settee between them. "We came here together from Hongkong, last week. He was—he had promised to help me. He took advantage of my helplessness and dependence on him to—to betray me."

"Betray you how?"

She shook her head and said nothing.

Spade frowned impatiently and asked: "Why did you want him shadowed?"

"I wanted to know how far he had gone. He wouldn't even tell me where he was staying. I wanted to find out what he was doing, who he was meeting, things like that."

"Did he kill Archer?"

She looked up at him, surprised.

"Yes, certainly," she said.

"He had a Lüger in a shoulder-holster. Archer wasn't shot with a Lüger."

"He had a revolver in his overcoat pocket," she said.

"You saw it?"

"Oh, I've seen it often. I know he always carried it there. I didn't see it last night, but I know he never wore an overcoat without it."

"Why all the guns?"

"He lived by them. There was a story in Hongkong that he had come out there, to the Orient, as bodyguard to a gambler who had had to leave the States, and that the gambler had since disappeared. They said Floyd knew about his disappearance. I don't know. I do know that he always went heavily armed, and that he never went to sleep without covering the floor around his bed with crumpled newspapers, so nobody could come silently into his room."

"You picked a nice sort of playmate."

"Only that sort could have helped me," she said simply, "if he had been loyal."

"Yes, if." Spade pinched his lower lip between finger and thumb and looked gloomily at her. The vertical creases over his nose deepened, drawing his brows together. "How bad a hole are you actually in?"

"As bad," she said, "as could be."

"Physical danger?"

"I'm not heroic. I don't think there's anything worse than death."

"Then it's that?"

"It's that as surely as we're sitting here"—she shivered—"unless you help me."

He took his fingers away from his mouth and ran them through his hair.

"I'm not Christ," he said irritably. "I can't work miracles out of thin air." He looked at his watch. "The day's going and you've given me nothing to work with. Who killed Thursby?"

She put a crumpled handkerchief to her mouth and said, "I don't know," through it.

"Your enemies or his?"

"I don't know. His, I hope, but I'm afraid—I don't know."

"How was he supposed to be helping you? Why did you bring him here from Hongkong?"

She looked at him with frightened eyes and shook her head in silence. Her face was haggard and pitifully stubborn.

Spade stood up, thrust his hands into his jacket pockets, and scowled down at her.

"This is hopeless," he said savagely. "I can't do anything for you. I don't know what you want done. I don't even know if you know what you want."

She hung her head and wept.

He made a growling animal noise in his throat and went to the table for his hat.

"You won't," she begged in a small choked voice, not looking up, "go to the police?"

"Go to them!" he exclaimed, his voice loud with rage. "They've been running me ragged since four o'clock this morning. I've made myself God knows how much trouble standing them off. For what? For some crazy notion that I could help you. I can't. I won't try." He put his hat on his head and pulled it down tight. "Go to them? All I've got to do is stand still and they'll be swarming all over me. Well, now I'll tell them what I know, and you'll have to take your chances."

She rose from the settee and held herself straight in front of him though her knees were trembling, and she held her white panic-stricken face up though she couldn't hold the twitching muscles of mouth and chin still. She said:

"You've been patient. You've tried to help me. It is hopeless and useless, I suppose." She stretched out her right hand. "I thank you for what you've tried to do. I—I'll have to take my chances."

Spade made the growling animal noise in his throat again and sat down on the settee.

"How much money have you got?" he asked.

The question startled her. Then she bit her lip and answered reluctantly:

"I've about five hundred dollars left."

"Give it to me."

She hesitated, looking timidly at him. He made angry gestures with eyebrows, mouth, hands and shoulders. She went into her bedroom, returning almost immediately with a thin sheaf of paper money in her hand.

He took the money from her, counted it, and said:

"There's only four hundred here."

"I had to keep some to live on," she explained meekly, putting a hand to her breast.

"Can't you get any more?"

"No."

"You must have something you can raise money on," he insisted.

"I've some rings, a little jewelry."

"You'll have to hock them," he said, and held out his hand. "The Remedial's the best place, Mission and Fifth."

She bit her lip, looking pleadingly at him. His yellow-gray eyes were hard and implacable. Slowly she put her hand inside the neck of her green dress, brought out a slender roll of bills, and put them in his waiting hand.

He smoothed the bills out and counted them, four twenties, four tens, and a five. He returned two of the tens and the five to her. The others he put in his pocket. Then he stood up and said:

"I'm going out and see what I can do for you. I'll be back as soon as I can. with the best news I can manage. I'll ring four times—long, short, long, short—so you'll know it's me. You needn't go to the door with me. I can let myself out."

He left her standing in the middle of the room looking after him with dazed blue eyes.

SPADE went into a reception room whose door bore the legend *Wise, Merican & Wise.* The red-haired girl at the switchboard said: "Oh, hello, Mr. Spade!"

"Hello, darling," he replied. "Is Sid in?"

He stood beside her with a hand on her plump shoulder while she manipulated a plug and spoke into the mouthpiece: "Mr. Spade to see you, Mr. Wise." She looked up at Spade. "Go right in."

He squeezed her shoulder by way of acknowledgment, crossed the reception room to a dully lighted inner corridor, and passed down the corridor to a frosted door at its far end. He opened the door and went into an office where a small olive-skinned man with a tired oval face under thin dark hair dotted. with dandruff sat behind an immense desk on which bales of paper were heaped.

The small man waved a cold cigar stub at Spade and said:

"Push a chair around. So Miles got his last night?" Neither his tired face nor his rather shrill voice held any emotion.

"Uh-huh. That's what I came in about." Spade frowned and cleared his throat. "I think I'm going to have to tell a coroner to go to hell, Sid. Can I hide behind the sanctity of my client's identity and secrets and whatnot, like a priest or a lawyer?"

Sid Wise lifted his shoulders and lowered the ends of his mouth.

"Why not?" he said. "An inquest is not a court trial. You can try, anyway. You've gotten away with more than that before now."

"I know, but Dundy's getting snotty, and it's a little bit thick this time. Get your hat, Sid, and we'll go see the right people. I want to be safe."

Sid Wise looked at the mass of papers on his desk and groaned, but he got up from his chair and went to the closet by the window.

"You're a son of a gun, Sammy," he said as he took his hat from its hook.

SPADE returned to his office at ten minutes past five that evening. Effie Perine was sitting at his desk reading *Time.* Spade sat on the desk and asked:

"Anything stirring?"

"Not here. You look like you'd swallowed the canary."

Spade grinned contentedly.

"I think we've got a future. I always had an idea that if Miles would go off and die somewhere we'd stand a better chance of thriving. Will you take care of sending flowers for me?"

"I did."

"You're an invaluable angel. How's your woman's intuition today?"

"Why?"

"What do you think of Wonderly?"

"I'm for her," the girl said without hesitation.

"She's got too many names—Wonderly, Leblanc, and she says the right one's O'Shaughnessy."

"I don't care if she's got all the names in the phone book. That girl is all right, and you know it."

"I wonder." Spade blinked sleepily at Effie Perine. Then he chuckled. "Anyway, she's given up seven hundred bucks in two days, and that's all right."

Effie Perine sat up straight and said:

"Sam, if that girl's in trouble, and you let her down, or take advantage of it to bleed her, I'll never forgive you, never have any respect for you, as long as I live."

Spade smiled unnaturally. Then he frowned. The frown also was unnatural. He opened his mouth to speak, but the sound of someone coming in at the corridor door stopped him.

Effie Perine rose and went into the outer office. Spade took off his hat and sat in his chair. The girl returned with a card: *Mr. Joel Cairo.*

"This guy is queer," she said.

"In with him, then, darling," said Spade.

MR. JOEL CAIRO was a small-boned dark man of medium height. His hair was black and smooth and very glossy. His features were Levantine. A square-cut ruby, its sides paralleled by four baguette diamonds, gleamed against the deep green of his cravat. His black coat, cut tight to narrow shoulders, flared a little over slightly plump hips. His trousers fit his round legs more snugly than was the current fashion. The uppers of his patent leather shoes were hidden by fawn spats. He held a black derby hat in a chamois-gloved hand and came toward Spade with short mincing, bobbing, steps. The fragrance of *chypre* came with him.

Spade inclined his head at his visitor and then at a chair, saying: "Sit down, Mr. Cairo."

Cairo bowed elaborately over his hat, said, "I thank you," in a high-pitched thin voice, and sat down. He sat down primly, crossing his ankles, placing his hat on his knees, and began to draw off his yellow gloves.

Spade rocked back in his chair and asked: "Now what can I do for you, Mr. Cairo?" The amiable negligence of his tone, his motion in the chair, were precisely as they had been when he had addressed the same question to Brigid O'Shaughnessy on the previous day.

Cairo turned his hat over, dropped his gloves into it, and placed it bottom-up on the corner of the desk nearest him. Diamonds twinkled on the second and fourth fingers of his left hand, a ruby that matched the one in his tie even to the surrounding diamonds on the third finger of his right hand. His hands were soft and well cared for. Though they were not large, their flacid bluntness made them seem clumsy. He rubbed his palms together, and said over the whispering sound they made:

"May a stranger offer his condolences for your partner's unfortunate death?"

"Thanks."

Cairo bowed.

"May I ask, Mr. Spade, if there was, as the newspapers inferred, a certain—ah—relationship between that unfortunate happening and the death a little later of the man Thursby?"

Spade said nothing in a blank-faced definite way.

Cairo rose and bowed. "I beg your pardon." He sat down and placed his hands side by side, palms down, on the corner of the desk. "More than idle curiosity made me ask that, Mr. Spade. I am trying to recover an—ah—ornament that has been mislaid. I thought —I hoped—you could assist me."

Spade nodded with eyebrows lifted to indicate attentiveness.

"The ornament is a statuette," Cairo went on, selecting and mouthing his words carefully, "the black figure of a bird."

Spade nodded again, with courteous interest.

"I am prepared to pay, on behalf of the figure's rightful owner, the sum of five thousand dollars for its recovery." Cairo raised one hand from the desk and touched a spot in the air with the broad-nailed tip of an ugly white forefinger. "I am prepared to promise that —what is the phrase?—no questions will be asked." He put his hand on the desk beside the other and smiled blandly over them at the private detective.

"Five thousand is a lot of money," Spade commented, looking meditatively at Cairo. "It—"

Fingers drummed lightly on the door.

When Spade had called. "Come in," the door opened far enough to admit Effie Perine's head and shoulders. She had put on a small dark felt hat and a dark coat with a gray fur collar.

"Is there anything else, Mr. Spade?" she asked.

"No. Good night. Lock the door when you go, will you?"

"Good night," she said, and disappeared behind the closing door.

Spade turned his chair to face Cairo again, saying:

"It interests me some."

The sound of the corridor door closing behind Effie Perine came to them.

Cairo smiled and took a short compact flat black pistol out of an inner pocket.

"You will please," he said, "clasp your hands together at the back of your neck."

(Continued in October issue)

From PART II of THE MALTESE FALCON in OCTOBER BLACK MASK

"All right, Spade, we're going." Dundy buttoned up his overcoat. "We'll be in to see you now and then. Maybe you're right in bucking us. Think it over."

"Uh-huh," Spade said, grinning. "Glad to see you any time, Lieutenant, and whenever I'm not busy I'll let you in."

A voice in Spade's living room screamed:

"Help! Help! Police! Help!"

The voice was high and thin and shrill.

Lieutenant Dundy stopped turning away from the door, confronted Spade again, and said decisively:

"I guess we're going in."

The sounds of a brief struggle, of a blow, of a subdued cry, came to the men.

Spade's face twisted into a smile that held little of joy.

He said, "I guess you are," and stood out of the way.

When the police detectives had entered, he shut the corridor door and followed them back to the living room. . . .

Dirty Work

By

HORACE McCOY

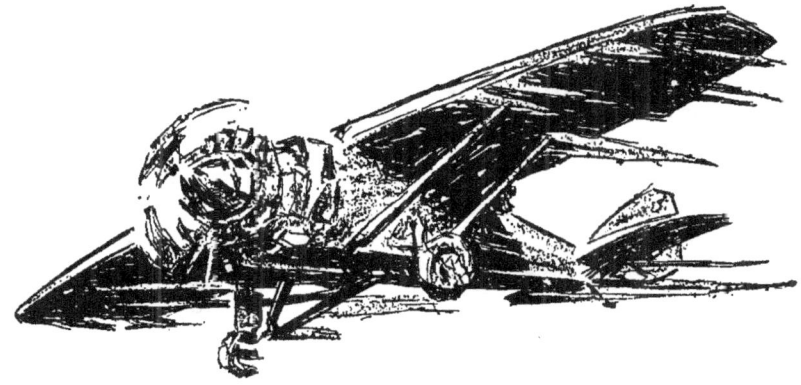

The Rangers take to the air.

 APTAIN JERRY FROST walked through the rotunda of the Texas State capitol, past the oils of Crockett and Houston and Hogg, and into the deep-toned offices of the Adjutant-General.

"What's on your mind, General?" he said, dropping himself into a chair and stretching his long legs.

"This Jamestown business." The Adjutant-General drummed on the desk with his incredibly long fingers. "It's quite a mess." Plainly he was just a little irritated.

Frost grinned. "Yes, sir. It's quite a mess." But the Adjutant-General didn't think it was so funny. He was quite serious.

"Jerry, for the life of me I can't understand why all police act so stupidly. This purely is a local case, but they can't handle it. They bump their heads against the wall and cry for the Rangers. I'm sometimes sorry we've got such a thing. Now the bigwigs are kicking." He held up a small packet. "Know what these are? Got any idea what they mean?"

Captain Frost confessed he hadn't.

"They're clippings from newspaper editorials in which the people who sit in the offices of the daily gazettes tell us how to run our great commonwealth. The robbery is up to us. I'm sorry, of course, you had to be ordered off leave. You know what that means, don't you?"

Jerry nodded. Did he know what that meant? Indeed! And since when had the Adjutant-General become so obtuse? He was tempted to laugh. Did he know what that meant? Hell, of course he knew. What did trips to this office usually mean? Dirty work —that's what. Dirty work.

He was not offended; he was too much of a soldier for that. It was that he just didn't have any illusions about the romance of criminal work. That was a lot of applesauce that looked good in print and nowhere else. He had spent two months in the Border Patrol on some tough work and had been promised a week's leave. He had

29

got but two days of it. Two days on the Galveston beach, and when the messenger boy found him with that fatal telegram from the Adjutant-General he was waiting on a fair young person who would be due in ten minutes.

That annoyed him no end. He had earned a rest, why couldn't he get it? Now there was more dirty work to be done. That's all he had ever done, it seemed. God knows, there had been plenty of it in the old Lafayette Escadrille, where he won his wings, and that crazy hitch with the Kosciusko Squadron over in Poland hadn't been any pink tea. And those four years down in the Guatemalan banana country hadn't made a dilettante out of him.

Go into any Latin-American country and mention Captain Jerry Frost and nobody would have the slightest idea of whom you spoke. But mention El Beneficio to any *soldado* and he was all attention. In those countries where men still die for illusions and assume musical names, they tell you that El Beneficio was a bold, roistering Americano who could handle women and a machine-gun like nobody's business.

No, he was no stranger to dirty work.

"Well," the Adjutant-General interrupted his reveries, "you can take the pick of the staff. You can do anything you want to. Forty years ago a train robbery in Texas might have been ordinary, but this is 1929. This infernal publicity is bothering me. It's up to you and the men you name."

"I'd rather look around a bit first," Frost said, as he rose to go. "If I need anybody, I'll let you know."

"Good luck to you."

He accepted the hope with a nod of his head and walked out.

CAPTAIN FROST expected little information from the chief of police of Jamestown, and he was not disappointed. The chief pointed out that he and his men were after all merely humans, and that they were doing everything humans could do. That this had availed nothing was not his fault. Captain Frost could see that?

Very frankly, Captain Frost said he couldn't. "It beats me," he said. "Here it is, the high-powered twentieth century—a scientific age. And a gang of bandits stick up a passenger train in orthodox Wild West manner and get away clean with a fortune. Every copper in North Texas is caught flat-footed. I'd like to have the opportunity sometime to get in on top of a case instead of waiting two or three weeks. I sure would."

"Well," the chief observed pointedly, "maybe we can arrange that just for *you.* It's a funny thing, but criminals never invite us to their parties. However, they might make an exception for the Rangers."

"Never mind the wisecracks! Didn't anybody in North Texas make any reports or anything after the robbery? It looks to me like a correspondence school sleuth could have done that."

"Ain't I been telling you they didn't? There wasn't nothing to report! My God, don't say that any more to me! It makes me sore all over. Every newspaper in this town has been plastering stories all over their front pages about it. It's got me goofy!

"Now, listen while I go over it again. Then you'll know as much as we do— or anybody else does. That train carried $300,000 in torn money that was going back to Washington. It left Jamestown, going East, at 8:45 and when it got to Reddy, about eight miles out, it was flagged down by a man on the track with a lantern. A moment later the engineer and fireman looked into the muzzle of a sub-machine-gun held by a masked robber.

"While this one kept the engineer and fireman covered, another went in the express car, blowed open the safe and got the coin. They slipped in on the messenger, tied him up, but when Cummings, the brakeman, ran through the door, they dropped him with a slug of lead in the forehead. Before anybody else knew what it was all about, the train started. It stopped a little farther on, but the bandits had disappeared.

"It happened right beside the highway but they had put red lights half a mile apart to stop the traffic. It's the general opinion that they are hiding out somewhere, but we've got the numbers of some of the bills and sooner or later we'll nab the men. Nobody can beat the law!"

It was the sort of a preachment Frost could expect from the chief. He was a man who had been in the chair for twenty years, and was slightly antiquated. One of the old school, as the newspaper boys liked to say.

"Now you know as much as we do."

"So that's all, eh?"

"All? Ain't it enough? It's been plenty to keep these newspapers in copy. It ought to be enough for you."

"Are you worried about what they think?"

The chief glared. "Ain't you?"

"Not particularly."

"Well *I* am; you're damn well right I am. We got an election coming off here next month and unless the right guy gets in, I go back to pounding a beat. Damn if these crooks can't pick fine moments to pull big jobs! So, you see how much I'm for you. Personally, I'll let you have my moral support and hope you have a lot of luck. *But I don't think you will!*"

OMEBODY once wrote that clever crime detection is one-third luck, one-third hard work and one-third intuition. Great detectives rate luck and intuition as a stand-off, which is to say they reckon one as important as the other.

Jerry Frost was not a scientist, he was not a criminologist, he was not,

in the technical sense of the word, a detective at all. But he had had a fair amount of luck thus far, he was perfectly willing to work hard, and he knew his intuition had stood him in good stead before.

And he was going to be able to use it this time. He realized that an hour after he had left the Jamestown chief of police.

He saw something that clicked in his mind—and would not be shaken. The very incredibility of the thing was what sold him.

He had dropped into the Secret Service offices of the government in the Federal Building, for, after all, it was their case. His conversation with the inspector had not been especially productive. But his eye caught a picture on the desk. It was a wrecked airplane, and he naturally was interested.

"This was a sweet one," he said. "Where'd it happen?"

"That," replied the inspector, "is an old one. It happened about a year ago. I was rummaging around my desk the other day and found it."

"Nasty spill."

"Yea, Charlie Cox got killed in it. You ought to remember that. The air-mail pilot. He crashed up in the Red River country. We lost a registered pouch in it."

"Oh, said Frost. "I do remember now. Never got anything on that case, did you?"

"Nope, never did. None of the bonds ever showed up."

"Ever have any ideas about it?"

"Well, not exactly. Charlie just crashed, that was all. Somebody came along and took the pouch. Anybody'd know the difference between registered mail and ordinary mail. We figured some farmer had got it, but we watched that county for a long time. None of the bonds ever showed up. Just another one of those mysteries."

It was at that moment that Jerry got his idea. But then it was too ridiculous. His intuition kept trying to tell him something, but he wouldn't listen. The voice was too faint. A little later the idea came bounding back again. And he couldn't lose it. The air-mail job. What made him think it was connected with the train robbery?

He wondered. Still, there had been innumerable baffling crimes solved by leads much more absurd than this. The air-mail job. Well, the idea was there to stay. He couldn't get rid of it.

He slept on it all night. Or tried to. Writing people and artists know how that is. You can't tear those things out of you. They weigh you down like an anvil. Sometimes you can't breathe comfortably. You think of it for hours and then very suddenly it comes, clear and clean, like big handwriting. All you have to do then is sit down and copy it.

Frost was like that. In the morning, it took definite form. It wasn't nebulous any longer. That air-mail job hadn't been an accident. It was premeditated. Everybody thought it was just one of those things that have to be a part of any new field of endeavor when man pits his brain and brawn against nature. But Jerry was willing to bet his life it had been premeditated.

Once, down south, when they were having a lot of fun with Salazar and Madero, a grizzled veteran had said, "Kid, when you get a hunch— *ride it!*" Well, that wasn't always so easy. The odds were big. No matter if you had a strong body, the odds were big. But Jerry Frost had a hunch. And he was going to ride it.

It all depended on one thing, and he went out to see about that. He wasn't the least bit surprised when he discovered the spot where the train had been held up was but a few hundred yards from Withers Field, the municipal airport. He had expected it.

He telephoned the Secret Service chief and the Jamestown chief and made the same request of both. It was for them to forget they had seen him.

Irrespective of the theories of the investigators, and their verdicts, Jerry was convinced the mail plane had been tampered with. To do that required cold nerve and daring that not every criminal possessed. Find the man who conceived that idea and you had the brains behind the train robbery. And he was a man who would need and who would have, a sound knowledge of airplanes.

That afternoon he reported to the hangar of the Mid-West Air Transport Company at Withers Field with a letter of introduction to Captain Eads. An hour before Captain Eads had been telephoned that one, Thomas Femrite, a name Jerry adopted for obvious reasons, was to be given employment as a mechanic and test pilot.

He knew, of course, that there was little chance of any of the bandits being at the Field now. But that flying field once had been the center of their operations. That wasn't much to work on, but it was something. It was considerably more than anybody else had decided.

"Captain Eads?" Jerry asked.

A man seated at the inside desk turned and looked. Before him in the door stood a man six feet tall and as brown as a nut. He had long arms, long legs, and good eyes. He looked every inch a flyer. There is something about a new man who comes to a flying field that compels attention. You immediately size him up and wonder how much stuff he's got, and whether he's going to be a heel or a good fellow, and whether or not he can fly. Captain Eads decided this lad would do.

"Mr. Femrite reporting for duty."

"Come in, Mr. Femrite. An old army man?"

"Yes, sir."

"I thought so. What outfit?"

"The Forty-seventh."

Captain Eads lifted his eyebrows. "Oh, yeah? Pretty good gang of cratebusters. The downtown office telephoned me about you. How many hours have you had."

"Oh, six or seven thousand."

"Whoosh! That's plenty. Well, you've come to the right place if you're a seven-thousand hour man. We need men who can assemble motors and who aren't afraid to fly those same motors. Know what I mean?"

"Yes, sir."

"All right. Red!"

An oily individual who escaped being a dwarf by a few inches, shoved his auburn head through the door.

"Take Mr. Femrite around and make him acquainted. He's going to work for us."

Getting acquainted with the Mid-West crew was the work of but a few moments. Red was short, Jerry learned, for Fred Walker, and apart from him the only other veteran was Slimmer King. There were a couple of youngsters but they didn't count. They hadn't passed the prop-spinning stage.

Going over big was simple with Red and Slimmer. Jerry spoke their language. The kids were aloof, but after he had stunted one of the rickety Travelairs one afternoon, they warmed up and immediately made him a model.

Nor had his maneuvers hurt his prestige with the old-timers. Jerry had all but knocked the knob off St. Peter's gate. That particular day he went crazy. What he didn't do with that old bus hadn't been invented.

"Gee, you looked great!" Red beamed. "But I thought once or twice we oughta kissed you good-bye before you left the ground."

"Stop kidding, Red. I bet you can do things with a crate I've never thought of."

"Naw," Red confessed. "I ain't much of a stunter. I can get 'em up there and get 'em down and that lets me out. I wasn't born to kick no rudder bar. My head belongs in a motor."

After that, things came easier for Jerry. The ice had been broken. He came to know something of the other fellows on the Field. He was particularly attracted to the bunch in the No. 6 hangar. They were commercial men.

He sensed a sort of rivalry between the Mid-West fellows and the bunch in No. 6. There was no particular reason for it, but he did. Ostensibly, they just about had the commercial business at the field sewed up. The Mid-West wasn't in competition with them, yet they growled and glared every time Jerry got close. He spoke to Red about it.

"They're just a gang of five-dollar-a-lick boys," Red said. "Don't pay them any attention. They haul passengers, but personally, I wouldn't let one of 'em push me in a wheelbarrow. I just don't crave their company."

"There's no reason for them to be sore at me," Jerry said.

"That's their way. They're sore at everybody. The farther away from those guys you stay the better off you'll be."

But he had no intention of staying away. He was curious. So the next day under the pretext of borrowing a porcelain, he invaded their hangar. He went up to the fellow who had been pointed out as Casey.

Casey gave him the porcelain. He was stocky and careless in his personal appearance, even for an airplane mechanic. "Where you come from, feller?"

"Oh, all over," said Jerry.

"I saw you yesterday doing some fancy flying. Looked like you'd wobbled a stick before."

"Yep—I've wobbled 'em before."

"You a new air-mail pilot?"

"Nope, just a mechanic."

"Well, there ain't many mechanics can fly like that."

"Oh, I dunno."

"A guy like you is wasting his time meddling with spark plugs and pushing a gasoline truck over a flying field. You'd ought to get in the big money. Commercial stuff."

"Sounds pretty good."

"It is good." Casey was positive. "Any guy what can bust clouds like you can is wasting his time drawing two hundred bucks a month. Interested?"

"Maybe. Much obliged for the porcelain."

THAT night Captain Jerry Frost reported to the Adjutant-General by telephone. He reported that he had become established and that the outlook was promising and that something possibly would happen soon.

The Adjutant-General, still annoyed, retorted that something would happen soon—to the entire force. "They're still raising hell," he said bluntly. "Let me send you some help."

"Now, listen," said Jerry firmly. "Any outside interference will gum the whole works. You sit tight and stop worrying. And don't send anybody! Forget all about it."

The Adjutant-General grumblingly agreed, and then told himself he was glad Frost was on the job. If anybody could do it, Jerry could.

Jerry was convinced the gang in No. 6 hangar wasn't all everybody thought it was. He had been made an overture, and he expected another. To bring it about, he spent the next few days in direct defiance of all the laws of flying. He was either a plain damn fool or the sweetest pilot who ever brought a bus down on one tire. He almost tore the ships to pieces. All this time the gang in No. 6 looked on.

One night Casey and another man, of a distinct continental air, visited the Transport hangar.

"Meet Mr. Crouch," said Casey. "He's the boss of our outfit."

Jerry shook hands with him.

"I'm glad to know you," Crouch said. "I saw you the other day and I wanted to congratulate you. I've seen a lot of flying in my time, but I don't think I ever saw the equal of that."

The man spoke with a slight accent, and a high voice. It was an unusual tone. Something in Jerry's memory stirred. He looked into the face closely. Gray mustache. Black eyes, sharp and deep-set. A small mouth and thin lips.

He had seen that face somewhere before. But where? The panorama of his life passed swiftly. It produced nothing.

"Thank you, sir," Jerry said. "I sometimes think I was born with my feet on a rudder bar."

"You were," Crouch agreed; "and that's just the point. You are the type of man commercial flying needs. Would you consider a change?"

"Well," said Jerry, "a fellow always needs—"

"Exactly. And you're worth just twice as much to us as you are to the air-mail people."

Jerry debated for a moment. He had no idea of refusing; he just didn't want to be too anxious.

"I'll take it."

"Good! When can you leave?"

"When do you want me?"

"Tomorrow. We're opening a hangar at Waco. You'll be on hand in the morning?"

"Yes, sir. I don't think they'll hold me."

"Of course they won't! If necessary, tell 'em to go to hell!"

Getting his release was simple. He merely got in touch with the home office, where the officials knew his mission and identity, and explained the situation. They in turn notified the Field. There was little comment. There seldom is. Young flying men are notorious nomads.

Waco was but an hour's hop from Jamestown, and as Jerry was eager to get there he left at once. During that hour he rolled his memory before him, seeking to pull from its kaleidoscope the face of the man called Crouch. That high voice rang in his ears above the drone of the motor; and gradually the years fell away.

Flying now, as he was flying then,

the slender threads of memory were picked up more easily.

Once more he was in the air over Bapaume with the 47th. This was Richthofen's old stamping ground and the Boche knew it like birds. Jerry was flying a Camel at 8,000 feet. They were climbing in close formation. He looked ahead and to the right. There was Bapaume in all its raggedness, half-obscured in the mist. On his left were a couple of youngsters. They waved. They were going through the agony of their first patrol. He had gone through it two months before. But it hadn't wrecked him. He hadn't a lot of imagination. He was sure of himself. But he knew it must be hell on the youngsters. He thought he'd better keep an eye on the eaglets.

There were clouds above—g r a y blanket clouds that came together in a solid roof, with only a gaping hole here and there to reveal the blue. Bad stuff. The squadron leader knew. He kept them climbing. Jerry glanced again at the youngsters. It bucked him up a bit to think about them. They were green. He squinted his eye and put up his thumb to have a look around the sun. They were up above now. He warmed his guns. The chatter reminded him that he was tired. So this was war. Well, they could have the damned war for all he cared. He was tired. He wished . . . And then he caught himself. A fellow couldn't do that. It wasn't decent. He was in it, no use wishing he was out. Then he saw he was straggling. Straggling was suicide. They were out in Richthofen's country. The Baron's men were devoted to stragglers. They ate 'em alive. He looked up. His intuition again.

His throat closed abruptly and his knees melted. An Albatross was coming down fast. His wing fabric was ruffling into lace and the wood of his camber ribs was splintering. He pulled up sharply and pressed his trigger.

Both guns vomited. He was firing wildly. The Albatross slipped under him. Oh, for a fast bus! His Camel would do 100. An S. E. would do 135. A Spad would do 140. And an Albatross would beat that. A butter-fly-winged Albatross. *Rat-tat-tat-tat-tat.* *Rat-tat-tat-tat-tat.* Sping! A shower of gasoline. His motor corked. He fell over in a dive. The Albatross followed him down. The Spandaus were rattling. He could hear them above the bite of the motor. A hundred red-hot needles hit him in the shoulder. He damned something warm back with his lips. Something warm and wet. The dirty, lousy swine! Fine stuff! What the hell? He was done . . . he was falling. The Spandaus rattled *fortissimo.* A drum-like roar, blackness swept, swirled over him. . . .

A high-ceilinged room. The penetrating smell of anesthetics. A face that bent over and shut out the depth of the room. An enormous face by contrast. He slowly made it out. He moved his body and winced. Bandaged. The face grinned. It spoke.

"Never," said a high, irritating voice, "break formation. How did I hit everything but your head?" The face came closer. The *Pour le Merite* swung out on its ribbon. "Byfield, my name is. You're my personal prisoner . . ."

Jerry tried to laugh. Instead he fainted. . .

That had been eleven years ago. The vision passed and its present significance came upon him so suddenly he went into a *renversement* that almost popped his neck. Byfield! The German Ace! Crouch! By God! There was dirty work somewhere. His first vague hunch, even so soon, assumed the form of reality. There could be no doubt that he was on a trail that would lead somewhere.

Out of the mists loomed the Amicable Building, perennial landmark sertinel of the Brazos, gaunt and lonely for want of companionship. Bearing to the left, he came over the field and settled down. He was trembling as if he had been out on his first patrol.

Byfield!

A luxurious cabin plane idled down and disgorged two men. One was Casey. The other was Crouch, *né* Byfield. It was all Jerry could do to keep his hands off the man's throat.

"You must have been in a hurry," said the high voice.

That voice! There was no doubt of it now. Von Byfield. Every step of the way now was fraught with danger. He half hoped Crouch wouldn't see it in his face.

"I was," he said finally.

"Well, there's a lot to do. We'll brush up and visit the newspapers."

They brushed, breakfasted, visited. Crouch planted all his ideas. But that was simple. He had them talking about it already. There were a dozen pilots coming in from New Mexico and Arizona to take part in the circus. A dozen men who, Jerry knew full well, were bums. And then he thought it was funny that he should be walking beside this man in such a placid way . . . the man who called himself Crouch, who had shot him out of control and then followed him down. He had prayed to meet him a hundred times—and now he had. And he was helpless. Funny.

That afternoon the pilots dropped in. That afternoon they were not an impressive collection. Just as Jerry thought, they were tramps. He thought they were a tough-looking bunch of eggs to be pilots. Had it come to the point where there was as much evil in the air as on the ground? God forbid. The air was the last outpost of chivalry. Of romance. It was dead as hell e v e r y w h e r e else. And it wouldn't be long—

But his big shock came in the afternoon.

E discovered a portion of the hangar falsely constructed. From the outside it seemed all right, but from the inside it seemed shorter than it should be. He opened a door and stepped into semi-darkness. A ghostly form confronted him. And another.

There is nothing quite so ghostly as to come across an airplane in a poorly lit hangar. Even if you are expecting it, you are half startled. There is something weird about it, even if you are an airman. It strikes at the roots.

Jerry recovered from his shock and opened the door wide.

The light revealed two planes. Two planes so lovely, so trim that his breath came in a swift intake of admiration. Two tiny planes that seemed unreal. Watch fob types. He moved closer. And stopped.

He saw they weren't so lovely. They were grim. Trench mortars looked like that. They looked like playthings —until they belched. Then they were hideous. On the cowling of each of the planes was mounted a machinegun, its squat muzzle merging almost indistinguishably into the background.

He was amazed. He hadn't, in his wildest fancies, anticipated anything like this. He hadn't seen a plane like this since he had left the Polish front. Not even then. Those things were hayracks compared to this. Before him stood two of the highest products of a scientific civilization.

"Good looking, eh?"

The voice cracked through the hangar like a sputtering electric wire that has found a ground. For a moment Jerry was disconcerted. Only for a moment.

"I'd give a month's salary to fly one of them!" he breathed.

"Yes?" It was evident Crouch didn't know whether to be angered or amused. He decided on the latter course. "Maybe you will. They're patented. I'm trying to sell them to the government. I wouldn't like for *anybody* to know I had them."

Jerry caught the faintest hint of a threat in the words. Of course, it was a lie. It wasn't even a good lie. He knew that, and he knew that Crouch knew he knew. Crouch must have thought he was several different kinds of a prize fool to swallow that one. But he was just as anxious to repair the damage as his employer.

"Not a word. You can trust me."

When they went out, Crouch locked the door with a padlock. Jerry looked back over his shoulder and decided the compartment was well hidden. And he decided something else. To dally with this thing was to play with T. N. T. Crouch and his gang were dangerous. One man couldn't stand in their way. They had too much to protect.

But what had the air circus to do with it? Jerry felt that everybody knew more than he did. The flyers knotted into little clans and got their heads together. He stumbled around stupidly. It made him, for the first time since he had won his wings, terribly self-conscious.

He stopped Casey later in the day. "Say, I guess I stumbled on to a little family secret this morning."

"Yeah?"

"Yeah. I saw two of the sweetest little battle wagons—"

"Easy, feller." Casey turned on him and glowered. "Don't go around popping off your face. They're inventions. The old man's a nut. He's afraid somebody might steal his plans."

Jerry gestured disdainfully. "Don't make me laugh. I wasn't born yesterday. How come I don't rate some of the secrets."

"Listen, you! If there are any secrets, the old man'll let you in on them. In the meantime, keep your trap shut—*tight!*"

For the second time that day, Jerry was tempted to crown somebody. But

that would have spoiled everything. He had been acting; he could continue.

"Now, now; ain't I one of the outfit? You pulled me away from a good job —for why? I don't even know what I'm supposed to do."

Casey melted somewhat. Maybe the kid was right. Maybe he ought to rate a few secrets.

"Well," he said, "I can't tell you nothing but this: if there hadn't been something big doing, the old man wouldn't have wanted you. He's a pretty good student of human nature— and he figured you'd been in a jam somewhere and wasn't too particular what you did as long as it was in an airplane. There's something about an airman that's written all over his face. He's like a schoolboy in love. He doesn't know it's there, and even if he did he couldn't do anything about it. You sit tight."

Jerry made up his mind to sit.

THE air circus came off as scheduled. Good advertisement. It packed the field and roads for miles around. The spectacle of fifteen pilots in the air doing all manner of stunts was appealing anywhere—especially in Waco. They hadn't seen anything like it since the training days of the war.

Crouch's business acumen was sound. The trade rolled in. There were innumerable hops. Everybody wanted to fly. The young men visioned themselves not as Foncks and Guynemers and Bishops and Lukes, for they belonged to another age. It was Lindbergh now. The old people grinned as they came in contact with the onrushing age. Jerry caught a passenger to Austin one morning. He had gone on a rush call. He had an hour to wait.

He visited the capitol and found the Adjutant-General in another rage. This was getting to be the best thing the Adjutant-General did.

"What's the big idea?" he bellowed. "We're wasting time. I've had to fight with myself to keep my hands off.

From your reports, we've got enough on those fellows to get a conviction now."

"From my reports—yes," Frost replied. "But my reports wouldn't convict them because I haven't got one single fact. It's pure hunch. But I'm going to nail them to the cross, and it won't be long. This is the toughest, nerviest outfit I've ever run across in my life. They'd stick up the National City Bank in New York with a little encouragement. But something's in the wind. I need help."

"Take anybody you want."

"It isn't that kind of help. Listen."

For five minutes he talked, all the while the Adjutant-General nodded and drummed on his desk top. Hardly had Frost left the office when the state official reached for the telephone and placed a call for the commandant at Kelly Field, the army base.

And thus, that night, one of the new A-3 battle planes, carrying six thousand rounds of ammunition and mounting six machine-guns, dropped out of the darkness at Withers Field and was quickly rushed into the hangar of the Mid-West Air Transport Company and covered with a tarpaulin.

Given that impetus, Jerry felt more confident. Nothing was likely to happen at Waco. If anything broke, it would be at Jamestown. And something was going to break—soon.

Riding his hunch, Jerry was sure Crouch and his gang had wrecked the air-mail plane a year before. They had held up the Rio Grande express. God knows what else they had done. Jerry felt it had been plenty.

He had fitted himself up a bunk in one corner of the hangar on a collapsible cot that was hidden away each morning. He didn't want to jeopardize the confidence Crouch might have in him.

A few nights later, as he lay there and stared into the darkness, and made up his mind to force the play within the next twenty-four hours, he heard the low drone of a motor. He rolled over and strained his ears. It was faint, then louder, then faint again. Then he heard another sound—a drone. There was enough noise to make him think it was a bombing raid.

Jerry looked at his watch. Four o'clock. Of course, it would be an hour like that. Something was up. Something was going to happen. He slipped into his pants and boots, knocked down his cot and shoved it under a fuselage and strapped on his guns. He went to the far corner of the corrugated hangar. There was an opening there wide enough for him to see. If there was anything to see. Right now it was black night.

Louder and louder the drones came. They were directly overhead now. Jerry wondered how Crouch expected to get away with anything like this. It amounted to pure suicide. And then it dawned that perhaps this was the very reason they had held that air circus. Adjacent residents might not be so curious if they heard motors at night. Or could Crouch have been that much of a psychologist?

Staring through the aperture, Jerry was momentarily blinded by a flash of light as the field was illuminated by two great searchlights. The motors throbbed, clawed furiously as they lost traction, and then whistled as the ships landed.

One was a cabin monoplane. The other was a tiny battle plane.

Then the lights went out. The entire operation consumed not more than two minutes.

Presently there were footsteps. Shuffling footsteps . . . and low voices. Out of the low conversation his ears picked strange words. Chinese!

Then: "Keep those Chinks quiet!"

Under cover of night, Crouch was running in Chinese.

Frost lay there for ten minutes, thinking. Crouch seemed to have his hand in everything. He heard echoes of automobiles on the highway, the grind of gears coming loud and clear through the stillness; then two men walked back. The office door opened, and a faint glow appeared through the cracks.

He got up and moved closer. He recognized the voices of Crouch and Casey.

"God, I'm glad that's over." This was Casey. "Two more trips and then we're Europe bound."

"Thompson's waiting in Mexico City."

"You wasn't sap enough to give him the dough, was you?"

Crouch laughed shortly. "Certainly not! Nobody knows where that money is—nobody but I."

"What do you mean?" Casey asked.

"Well, I moved it."

"You mean you moved our dough from that train job?" He was incredulous.

"Yes. Remember seeing some guys working on those old asphalt tennis courts behind our hangar at Withers Field?"

"Sure."

"Well, you thought they were repairing them, didn't you? So did everybody else. But they were just putting the asphalt over a little hiding place I'd previously fixed up."

"My God!" Casey ejaculated. "Suppose we wanna get away quick?"

"That's all right. We can smash that stuff in five minutes. And it was the safest place—believe me."

"Maybe it was wise. By the way, this wild man we got off the Mid-West ain't so certain everything's on the level. He cornered me and asked a lotta questions. I told him if there was anything to say, you'd say it. Might not be wise to stall him. He looks pretty sharp."

"I don't intend to. I'm going to talk to him today and he'll run in the next batch of Chinese. I figure he's got the nerve to help us pull a sweet one down South pretty soon."

"Course, you know what you're doing. But I don't see the point in hiring him. Never did."

"Perhaps there wasn't. But I collect good pilots just like other men collect stamps and books. I like to have them around. But you don't need to worry about this guy. He's been in a lot of jams before. You can look at him and tell that."

"I dunno—"

"Help me get that Moth in." They moved out on the field.

Captain Jerry Frost came alive. He had them nailed. His suspicions were confirmed. They had done the train job. And unless he missed his guess, those bonds from the air-mail plane were in that cache Crouch spoke of. He moved up in the dark until the two men got into the hangar with their plane. Then he started off on a dog-trot down the road.

At dawn the law forces of the sovereign State of Texas swung into action. They had long been waiting for this moment. The great, ponderous, clumsy law, with its thousands of tentacles, got going. The tide itself was not more relentless. It struck here sometimes, there sometimes, in a circle sometimes—but eventually it straightened out and began to roll. It was inevitable.

The Adjutant-General sat at his desk and manipulated the controls. He was the puppeteer.

Shortly after sunrise, two state planes were in the air. There were six men in each besides the pilot. Six tight-lipped, grim men, who would shoot their way into hell and back again to get their men.

The Rangers were moving up.

In the hangar at Waco, the telephone jangled. Casey answered it.

"Yeah, Casey . . . all right, Tommy . . . What's that? I can't hear you . . . wait a minute." He handed the receiver to Crouch. "The goof is excited. Get an earful."

Crouch took the instrument. "Hello, Tommy . . . Yes . . ." a long wait. Casey moved closer. Something had happened. One look at Crouch's face told him that. Finally: "Who told you? . . . hell!" He slammed the receiver on the hook.

"We're fools!" He spat the words out. "One of the Mid-West fellows told Tommy this morning that this guy Femrite is a Texas Ranger. Come on!"

"Where?"

"That's the trouble with you damned Americans," Crouch cried. "You lose your head in a tight place. We're going to get that money. Maybe we can make it. He's waited this long without tipping his hand, maybe he'll wait a little longer."

"But what about the others?"

"This is no time to think of them. We can be in Mexico in five hours. Come on!"

They moved quickly to the hangar door, swung it open. They wheeled their tiny, speedy planes out into the starting line. They swung each other's props, the motors barked into life, and dust and pebbles swept into the backwash and puttered against the side of the hangars.

Crouch was first off. Casey followed. Tails whipped up and wheels bounced lightly on the uneven ground. They zoomed into the air in broad climbing turns. Casey saw Crouch was loading his guns.

They didn't know it then, but they were to be disappointed. Jerry already was at Withers Field, had been there when Ranger reinforcements arrived. And, of course, a perverse fate decreed they would start at the wrong end of the tennis court.

To see a half dozen apparently intelligent men digging into an asphalt tennis court in the early morning is not a sight calculated to be passed without stopping for a moment. Mechanics stopped, workmen stopped. There was a great textile mill near the field, and a crowd begets a larger crowd.

Jerry was trying to direct the traffic and the Rangers at the same time. Three young men in handcuffs, late of the No. 6 hangar, looked on in undisguised amusement.

Then a shout. Somebody had the pouch. Jerry grabbed it and with a single movement, slit the side. A hand-ful of currency was extracted. Torn currency.

"That's it!" he said. "That's it! Take those men and this pouch into the office. Those other fellows are coming here sooner or later. We'll make a reception out of it."

The news swept about the airport like wildfire. The textile mill was all agog. For the first time in many of their lives, they were sitting in the middle of a big event. "The train robbers have been found!" The doorman at the textile mill told the switchboard operator, and the switchboard operator told the secretary. The secretary thought the police ought to know so he telephoned them.

Eagle-eyed news hawks caught the message the moment the desk sergeant finished his yawn and copied it. They flashed their papers. Editors stirred their stumps, called circulation managers, engravers, operators and pressmen. Reporters on the city staff got going, the rewrite man lighted a fresh cigarette off the butt of an old one and rammed copy paper in his mill. He pulled the telephone close. And muttered: "I hope to Gawd this is as big as it looks!"

The word got about Jamestown. Sirens shrieked through the traffic carrying enough police to take Mont Sec. In thirty minutes, the highways leading to Withers Field were choked. Some of them knew what was going to happen, but most of them didn't. This was the Great American Public.

SPEEDING north for their plunder before seeking safety, neither Crouch nor Casey were aware of the plans being made for their welcome. Crouch, being of higher mentality, probably thought he had pushed his luck too far, but that was all.

He couldn't see Withers Field, he couldn't see Captain Jerry Frost beside the A-3 single seater, positively the finest thing in battle planes. If Crouch's ships were lovely, there was no superlative for this. Jerry stood there, his eyes glued on the southern heavens, his propeller swinging idly.

He seemed just a little ridiculous to himself. He couldn't, for example, grasp that this was 1929. Imagine such a thing with so large a gallery? It was like an *opera bouffe*. Still, he tingled. He almost, once, half admitted he liked it.

From out of the distance came a drone. Two planes were seen; they roared onward, still unaware of what awaited them. One dipped downward, the other, which was higher, began a long glide.

The cordon of police started forward.

"Wait a while," Jerry shouted. "Those ships have got guns on 'em! Take your time!"

But the police disregarded the command. They, too, had waited long. And neither were they self-conscious before the crowd.

Casey was in the first ship, and no sooner had his wheels touched the ground than he realized all was lost. He shot the throttle to his ship and the smoke belched from the exhaust. A policeman fired. The bullet whistled through the fuselage.

Then Casey either tried to zoom, or he lost his head. He later claimed he didn't know his finger was on the trigger. His guns barked through the propeller and two policemen pitched forward, twitched and lay still. A second later a shot got Casey and his plane dived into the ground.

Crouch had seen and heeded. He had gone into a climb—and he was going South.

Jerry throbbed and pinched. It was the old feeling. Something in him seemed to say, had always said: "Enjoy this for it may be your last one." Not fear—and yet it might have been.

He swung his arm out for the chocks to be pulled. His motor whined and then caught with a roar. Something throbbed in his hands and feet and played along his nerves like tiny electrical impulses. He was talking to himself, and there was something terrible in it—prayer and hatred intermingled.

He opened his throttle and his propeller disappeared in a thin circle of light. Like a living thing his ship bounded forward. For a while he bounced along and then he went straight up like an elevator. He climbed 500 feet before it began to stall, then drifted his stick forward and presently flattened out at 140. His bus never even felt it. Tight. Solid. Maneuverable.

He warmed his guns with a burst of twenty. He rather hoped he wouldn't have to fight. Still, never could tell. Everything was different in the air. Once before, he had been in the same air with Crouch. He had remembered. Maybe there would be a fight after all.

He climbed to 7500 and buckled on his straps. He had done that before, too. But this was something like. No straining the eyes to the right and to the left and above looking for black specks. No wondering if that was an L.V.G. two seater—a decoy—with a half dozen Albatrosses lurking above. His man was just in front. Only one.

He crawled up on Crouch's tail and motioned for him to land. Crouch climbed to the left and got into fighting position. Jerry motioned again. His answer was a burst that raked through the A-3 ailerons.

"O.K." Jerry bellowed. "Here we go!"

He half rolled to get on top, so did the other. Jerry touched the trigger and pulled up, dived again. Crouch Immelmanned and straightened out on Jerry's tail and another burst ripped through the fins. Jerry kicked it off into a slip and leveled out. Crouch was diving away. He was going to run for it. No doubt of that.

Jerry pushed his stick forward until the rush of air gagged him. The rattle of his guns came through the chatter of the motor. Crouch went into another Immelmann and Jerry dived by him. The German was a flyer. But he was not matching skill with the kid he had knocked down that day at Toul. This was another fellow.

Jerry pulled up and went into a climb. He banked sharply and started higher and higher. That was Crouch's mistake. His ship couldn't climb with the A-3. Jerry was so close now he could see the wheels on the other's undercarriage spinning.

Well, there he was. He had him. The trim white belly of Crouch's ship glinted along the tip of his guns. There he was. There was von Byfield, the great ace. *The* von Byfield. The one who had followed him down. He could still hear those Spandaus clacking as they raked his body in a steel flail.

Jerry touched his trigger. He could see holes tearing in the linen. He kept his guns open. There was a fan of flame. He noticed his altimeter. 14000. Too high. And yet . . . He stalled and whipped out in a spin.

Crouch's ship hung momentarily like a leaf undecided whether to fall this way or that. Then it dipped its nose and wabbled. The glide became a dive, the dive went into a lazy, aimless spin, wings flopping, to the floor. The plane flattened, whipped out upside down, stalled, snapped out again in a final effort, and then again went downward in that grotesque way. Over and over. Over and over. Jerry watched it, fascinated. It was only a dot now, flashing in the sun as it keeled over. It was coming closer to the floor—closer, closer.

Then suddenly a tiny sheet of flame lashed out, a puff of dust. That was all.

Jerry sideslipped down, landed and taxied slowly in. He climbed out stiff-legged. He looked down and saw his pants were slightly torn. There was a gash in his leather coat. He looked into his cockpit. The floor boards were splintered. He looked up. The center section was riddled. The linen on his fins was ribboned.

Far down the field a group of police and civilians were rushing to the wrecked plane.

"Cigarette?"

Somebody gave him one.

"Match?"

Somebody else struck it. Frost thought those fingers were familiar. Long . . . white . . . He looked into the face. The Adjutant-General. He had his arms extended.

"Hurt, Jerry?"

"Nope. Tired." Quite matter of fact. The curious crowded around. The Adjutant-General very plainly was ill-at-ease. It had stirred him tremendously. He wanted to say something nice, but he couldn't. Men are like that. Especially men who are suddenly overcome with pride. They try to say flowery things, but the words clog up in their throats. They think them right down to the tip of their tongue, and then strange words come out.

It was like that now. The Adjutant-General said: "Well, take a rest. California Florida. Any place."

"Nope, Galveston."

"Galveston?"

"Yep, Galveston. Unfinished business."

The Adjutant-General nodded. He didn't understand; he didn't want to understand. Captain Frost had come through. That was the code of the Rangers. It had been that way when the Conostagas squeaked their way through the Indian country, and it was that way in the day of science and aviation. When all else fails, when there is a knotty problem, when there's dirty work—the Rangers. Yesterday and today and tomorrow, to the ends of the earth—get him!

You'll meet up again with Captain Jerry Frost, and Hell's Stepsons, IN OCTOBER BLACK MASK.

Hanging Friday

By ERLE STANLEY GARDNER

Bob Larkin goes the limit for a friend.

PRESSURE on my right arm, above the elbow t u r n e d me around. My glance swept from the hand to the face of the Border Immigration Inspector.

His eyes were curiously unemotional, steady, gray, slightly hostile.

"Come with me, and don't act rough about it."

I went.

We entered the low, substantial building of the department and the office door banged behind us.

"Now I'll hear from you, Bob Larkin. You've been a disturbing influence on the Border for the past month. You're leaving, and you're not coming back."

I locked eyes with him.

"I'm staying. I've *got* to stay."

His eyes didn't deviate by a hair.

"You're leaving."

I leaned forward.

"Listen. I'm coming clean with you. I'm a friend of Frank Mayo."

He shook his head impatiently.

"Don't know him, and it wouldn't matter if you was a friend of President Hoover. You're leaving."

"Frank Mayo," I explained, "is in the death cell at San Quentin. I'm not trying to work a pull. I'm explaining."

His eyes narrowed.

"The fellow that was convicted of murdering his sweetheart?"

"The same. He didn't do it. I know something about him and about the affair. But the jury said he did it. The Supreme Court took a guess at it and guessed wrong. He's to be hanged on Friday, the thirteenth. This is Thursday, the twelfth. I think I know who did it. I can't tell you the details, but it was someone in Big Jim Broke's gang. Big Jim's been holding it over some of the crowd.

"I struck the trail, located a fat guy named Butterfield who was said to have some letters I wanted. I missed out; a friend re-located Butterfield, got him where he'd talk, and somebody silenced him with a knife."

His eyes were a bit wider now.

"Was the somebody who helped you a woman?"

I hesitated for a moment then nodded again. If he knew so much he might know more.

He sighed.

"Vera Rayon," he said. "Only a few of us know she's in the service. Society kid, too. Lots of money. But she's in the game because dope wrecked her family. Think Jim Broke was mixed up in it. He's the smuggling king in these parts. I'd heard something of the fellow that helped Vera on the last couple of jobs. You're that Larkin, eh?"

I nodded.

His eyes dropped to my battered cane, surveyed it with curiosity.

"How come you can do so much damage with that?"

"Years on the stage as a juggler," I told him. His question, and the way he asked it, told me that I had won.

I got to my feet. He did the same.

"They'll be laying for you over there," he said with a jerk of his finger.

"They are, and they have been," I said.

"Remember me to Miss Rayon when you see her."

I jerked my head toward the north.

"She dusted out until things quieted down. That last mix-up with Butterfield and Jim Broke almost got her."

His smile came back to me afterward. It was filled with more meaning than amusement. I didn't notice it so much at the time.

"Working on anything definite?"

I shrugged my shoulders. "Only using myself as live bait, hoping somebody'll set a trap. The gang's crawled in a hole and pulled the hole in after 'em."

I moved toward the door. The sun was dipping below the western horizon. Frank Mayo had less than twenty-four hours to live. In spite of myself, my mind went through its old treadmill of thought—Friday, the day society plays its last grim jokes on criminals, starting them on their last journey on an unlucky day. The death uniform, the collarless shirt, the bleak breakfast, a veritable repast of food for a stomach that will soon cease to function. Steps echoing down the corridor. A shuffling procession of grim men. The reading of a death warrant, the march down the corridor, the door that swings open, thirteen steps, chipped and scarred by unwilling feet that have gone before, a flutter of hurrying hands, straps, the rope, a black cap. . . .

I shuddered, sighed, and inhaled the fresh air.

About me clustered buildings. The Border city sprawled in the gathering dusk. On one side of the Line it's listed as Cantu. On the other side it's Los Algodones. On the maps it's either Andrade, or nothing. Pay your money and take your choice.

The muddy Colorado flowed to the east, forming the jog in the Border where Arizona dips down a few miles south of California. It's nothing but a jog on the maps, but in real life it's the toughest, wildest stretch of river a smuggler could desire.

Yuma was seven miles away. It looked like my best bet. Somewhere about, Big Jim Broke and his gang were laying low. And I was willing to stake my life they had the information that would save Frank Mayo. One of the gang had committed that murder. Could I prove it? Two months' effort had been in vain. Would the last few hours change things?

I looked across to the Border city.

A man and two women emerged from the cantina and dance hall. The women were wobbly. The man was a blunt shouldered, squat individual who walked as straight as a flying crow.

He came closer, singled me out as a target for his booming voice.

"Hello, Buddy. Goin' to town?"

"I haven't a car," I said, glancing wistfully at the line of parked cars.

"'S what I thought, Buddy. You can ride with me. Big-Hearted Charlie, that's me. Give you a lift an' a chicken. Nothin' selfish about Charles W., old Big-Hearted Charlie, himself."

It was the break I'd been looking for. This man was the kind who might be hooked up with Big Jim Broke's gang. It was an even break that he was; and I had to get in touch with that gang before eighteen hours had passed.

Big Jim had an organization that stretched from Juarez to Tia Juana. He dealt in drugs, liquor, women and murder. Bartenders, dance-hall girls, thugs, Border officers and scum were on his pay roll. And he had marked me for death.

I climbed in the car, a Packard. One of the women lurched in beside me. From the door of his office peered the Immigration man.

As I looked, he tilted back his head, raised his rigid forefinger, as though it had been a knife, and drew it across his throat from ear to ear.

Then he turned and stalked back to his office.

His simple gesture seemed to tell me that I had guessed right.

If I had, this was a trap, and that suited me, too, for it would bring me in touch with the men I sought.

"Say, kiddo, you goin' to buy me a li'l dinner if we take you into Yuma?"

It was the voice of the woman next to me. She was gazing at me with an expression that was intended to be amorous. And she was trying her best to sober up. Her mouth was unsmiling. But her eyes held a look of dazed stupor. She was reciting her lines like a drunken vaudeville actor.

I nodded.

"Sure, sister, sure."

She flopped against my shoulder.

"That lets me out," she said, and went to sleep.

The man in the front seat drove the car slowly over the dirt road. From time to time he looked back by the mirror over the windshield. Every time he did so he caught a glimpse of me holding the woman with my right arm, the left casually sliding my billiard cue cane back and forth across my crossed knees.

I'd heard of men being taken for a ride where paid women flung restraining arms about them while killers reached for guns. There wasn't going to be any of that in this party, for two reasons. And only one of 'em was the fact that the woman next to me had passed out.

The driver didn't seem to be in any hurry to get across the river. His forehead wore a frown that dropped his eyebrows half an inch. Once he tried to whisper something to his companion, but she was too jingled to get it.

We rolled up to a restaurant.

"Sally said you was throwin' a dinner, and wanted us in on it."

That was a patent lie. Sally had gone blotto after being crude about it. He'd have been a mind reader if he'd got anything from her.

"That's the sketch," I said. "But the girl seems to be catching up on sleep."

"Go on in. Get a table. I'll bring the girls in," he rumbled in that deep voice of his.

I smiled and walked into the restaurant, turned, and glued my eye to the door. Whatever the game was, it didn't seem to be running smoothly. That bothered me as much as it did the fellow with the innocent eyes. My best move was to play into the hands of the gang until I saw who held the cards and what they were. Right now this chap was my only point of contact. I was on a cold trail.

He crawled into the back of the car.

Sally was snoring her troubles to the night world.

He took a cigarette case from his pocket, ripped open a cigarette and took out a pinch of tobacco. Then he pulled up Sally's left eyelid and dropped a few grains of tobacco under the lid, right into the open eye.

Then he did the same thing with the right eye and crawled out, standing by the open door, waiting for Sally to wake up.

I'll say this for the boy, he was thorough.

It took a second for the moisture of the eyeball to start the tobacco smarting. Then the eye naturally watered. The more water, the more action. Sally woke up. She woke up telling the world.

I'd seen enough. I picked a table, and I picked it where I wanted it. There was a rear exit not far from it, and I managed to stroll out and look the country over while Sally was recovering her feminine composure.

It was nearly five minutes before they came in.

Sally's eyes were still playing fountains. Tears streamed down her cheeks. The eyes were as red as a spanked baby. The other girl was scared sober.

"My name's Creeger. You know Sally. The other moll is Edith. Sit down an' throw some coffee into 'em. If they talk sense, all right. If they don't, we throw 'em out on their ears before they've stuck us for a supper. Personally, I ain't got no use for a stewed fluzee."

And the whole restaurant knew that he had no use for a stewed fluzee. He'd have made a good radio announcer, that bird, only they wouldn't have needed a microphone. Just turn him loose on the roof and every receiving set within a mile would have tuned him in.

A waiter bustled up.

"Four hot coffees, double dose for the broads. Come back in ten minutes for an order. You'll get two dinners, may-

be four. An' this guy is stuck for the check. What's your name, bo?"

"Bob Larkin."

"All right, Bob. You an' me's goin' to get along. Rush up that coffee, waiter. And make it black. Don't stand there gawking. I'm back from Algodones an' I'm hungry. Two quarts of Bacardi always gives me an appetite."

The waiter scuttled for the kitchen and soon returned.

Creeger looked at Edith.

"Drink your coffee, kid."

"You go to hell!"

He yawned.

"Tell the waiter to write your dinner check on a sheet of asbestos then, funny-face."

I thought for a moment she would throw the scalding coffee into his face. But she didn't. And it wasn't anything about him that held her back. Something whipped her into line, but it wasn't Creeger.

"Drink the coffee, Sally."

Sally's reply was even less conventional than Edith's.

Creeger stuck his face across the table. Of a sudden the innocent expressionlessness of his eyes melted under the glitter of white hot rage.

"Say-y-y-y, lis'n, you cheap flop. You put me up a proposition you didn't think I had guts enough to pull. So you thought you'd get me pickled first. Well, there ain't enough booze in Algodones. I'm here, ready to carry out my end. You two skirts have got pie-eyed. You've ranked the job right at the start. I'm giving you one more chance. Big-hearted, that's me. Do I get any thanks for it? To hell with you and your proposition and . . ."

He broke off. Edith had flung her bare arm around his neck, was pressing incardined kisses on his snarling lips. The caresses throttled the blast of noise that was giving me an earfull.

Edith whispered something to him, turned, handed Sally the coffee cup.

"For God's sake, drink!"

And Sally drank her coffee like a good

little girl, but her eyes were blazing.

The waiter returned.

"Four dinners. The other guy gets the check. Make it snappy."

The waiter nodded. The nod became a bow, the bow a bend. He scraped, bowed again, and was gone.

Creeger seemed to get lots of service. There was the whisper of shuffling feet behind me. I flung an arm over the back of the chair so I could get my head twisted. My right hand toyed with the water carafe.

He was a little, dehydrated whisper of a man. He wasn't old and he wasn't young. He had as much personality as a bit of dry blotting paper. His hands rubbed together in a vain attempt to work up a little temperature by friction. He looked as cold as a dead oyster.

And he was scared. His eyes had the look of a rabbit just one jump ahead of the dogs.

"You'll pardon the intrusion, gentlemen and ladies, ladies and gentlemen, that is, but could you tell me whether it is possible for me to get across the Line at this time. I am quite anxious to reach Algodones, but I understand the Border closes at six. Therefore, I made no attempt to cross the Line because my watch showed six fifteen.

"But you people apparently have arrived from there, just arrived. Therefore, I deduce that you must have left after six. Ergo, if the Border was open at that time my information must have been incorrect, at least to the extent of . . ."

It was Sally that interrupted.

"Aw fer Pete's sake!" she said.

I looked over at Creeger. I gathered the newcomer was due to receive a lot of information regarding itineraries he hadn't asked for.

Creeger snarled his lips, glittered his eyes, sucked in a deep breath—and held it.

I was watching his face as the expression changed.

A look of puzzled wonder speedily became one of utter joy. He arose, crossed the space around the end of the table in three strides and extended his hand.

"Not at all, not a'tall, not 'tall. Mighty glad to be of service. The Border closes at six, but that's Sonora time. There's an hour's time differential between there and here. Makes it seven Yuma time. Too late for you to get across now. But I'm going across in the morning myself. Be glad to show you the road.

"Sit down and join us at dinner. You seem to be all alone. I'm buying the crowd a little dinner, an' I'd be glad to have you along. It's all on me."

The little man quit rubbing his hands long enough to extend a timid paw.

"Mr. Souther," he said.

"Creeger, Charlie Creeger, an' mighty glad to meet yuh, Souther."

"But I can't join you. That is, I must respectfully decline the invitation. My own meal is already ordered at another table. In fact it is partially consumed. Only my very great desire to cross the . . . er . . . that is to see Los Algodones, caused me to leave my food.

"I thank you for the invitation, sir, very much indeed. I had heard of Western hospitality, but . . ."

Creeger interrupted.

"All right then, I'll join you. The broads are pie-eyed, anyway."

And he pushed the little man before him, over to the corner table at which a single dinner appeared, half eaten.

"Say, waiter, transfer me over to this table. It's the same dinner the guy with the broads is payin' for. I'm eatin' over here."

The remarks of the girl on my left would have made an excellent preface for a prayer, but they didn't end up right, and the tone was wrong.

Sally slumped her head on her arm and went to sleep.

Personally, I saw my chance for a direct contact with those I sought go glimmering.

I smiled at Edith.

"Nice quiet boy friend you've got."

"He ain't nice. He ain't quiet. He ain't a boy, an' he ain't a friend," she spat. And then she proceeded to enlarge on just what he was. I gathered his mother had been liberal minded, and that the hereditary taint had been further emphasized by unfortunate habits on the part of the son.

Midway in the tirade she arose, crossed to the other table and curled a seductive arm about his neck.

"Aw, honey," she crooned, and whispered something.

The man did not look up, He flung his voice over his shoulder in a snarl of impatience.

"What t'ell do I care. I promised the guy I'd do the job an' you were goin' to help. You try to get me ginned up to keep my nerve goin' and get pie-eyed yourself. You two broads gum the game and then want me to hold the sack. To hell with both of you. Go tell your boss I'm sick of bein' tied to apron strings. When I do a job I do it right. Now beat it!"

He snapped her arm from his shoulder.

She came back to the table. Every eye in the room was on her and on me. A fat individual with greasy lips came oozing over toward me.

"I'm sorry, but the management reserves the right to refuse service. I think you'd better get another place to eat."

"Suits me!" snapped Edith, and she threw the words in his face with a tongue as bitter as any I'd heard for a long while.

I arose. It suited me.

"And the other young lady . . ." suggested the manager, suavely.

"Throw her out yourself," said Edith, and strode toward the door.

As I gained the night I heard a booming voice remonstrating from the lighted interior of the restaurant.

"Stop that guy. He's payin' for my dinner. . . ."

I took Edith's arm.

She whirled on me like a tigress.

"Get t'ell away from me!"

That, also, suited me. I crossed the street, apparently in a huff. Then I doubled back and followed her. She was too mad to bother about looking behind her. It was as easy a job of tailing as I'd ever tackled, and I'm not particularly expert.

She went two blocks and strode into the lighted entrance of one of the town's better hotels. She was as sober as a cake of ice.

I let her get into the elevator before I approached the desk, registered under the first name I could think of. It was Charlie Creeger. Ten seconds afterward I could think of a thousand other names, a thousand reasons why I shouldn't have used the name of Creeger. But, at the time, the words Charlie Creeger flowed from my pen as naturally as gravy dripping to a clean vest.

"Five three eight," drawled the clerk. "Front. . . . Show Mr. Creeger to five three eight."

We went up. While the boy messed around with curtains and lights to make sure of a tip I doubled back to the elevator.

"Which room did the blonde hit?" I asked.

He started to look virtuous, but when he saw the figure on the bill that crinkled his palm, he became an encyclopedia of information.

"Three aught nine. Thanks, thanks very much. She comes in once in a while. Think she works across the Line at Algodones, one of the entertainers. Don't know her myself, but if you was to go over there tomorrow. . . ."

I was already half way back to my room.

Half a dollar got rid of the bell boy that had shown me up.

That left me free to take a look at three aught nine.

It was a door, just like any other door. There was a light over the transom, silence within. Not so much as the rustle of slippered feet on a carpet, no hum of voices, not even the creak of a chair or the sound of breathing.

I walked down to the office.

"Fifth floor's too high up. Hot near the roof. What else have you got?"

The clerk fingered his charts, offered me something on the second. That didn't suit. He had a room on the fourth. I didn't want that. A room on the third floor was at the other end of the corridor from 309. I kicked on the price. Finally he offered me 303, twin beds and a bath. The price was higher. I decided to take a look at it.

It was two doors down from 309. Another half dollar sent the bell boy away satisfied. I waited with an eye glued to a crack in the door.

Two hours passed and nothing happened. The transom in 309 still showed a golden oblong. The room remained silent as a grave.

I got up from my chair, stretched cramped legs and gave it up as a bad job. I walked down to the telegraph office, inquired for messages under my own name, and was handed a yellow envelope.

I ripped it open, expecting another indefinite report from the detective I had hired to trace a certain hat that had been left me as a single tangible clue to the murder of Sid Butterfield, the man who might have talked.

The telegram was brief and to the point.

Hat traced Stop *Sold transient who gave initials only* Stop *Had G. F. Y. stamped in band* Stop *Description indefinite* Stop *Canvass of local hotels discloses a George F. Yardley registered at the time in one of the cheaper hotels* Stop *Address given on register as San Francisco* Stop *San Francisco directory discloses no such individual.*

The telegram was signed by the operative who had been charging me eight dollars a day and expenses. It had taken him ten days to unearth the information. It was worth it.

I walked back to my hotel.

"Got a George F. Yardley registered

here?" I asked the clerk, casually.

"Yeah. Steady in 309. Want me to ring 'm?"

I shook my head.

"I may want to meet him later. Not right now. How's your memory?"

He looked at me sharply.

"Very good."

I slipped him a five.

"Now how is it?"

"Rotten."

I took the elevator to the third floor. There was a light in 309. From behind the transom came a booming voice Once heard it could never be forgotten. Creeger was addressing conversation to someone.

"You can go to hell!' rolled over the transom opening and was followed by silence. I gathered Creeger was running true to form.

I slipped down to my room, opened the door with the clumsy key and entered. I didn't bother to switch on the light. I wanted to hear more of what was going on.

I settled myself with an ear to the crack in the door. It was hot and it was dark. Sounds traveled very well indeed. I felt I was getting warm on the scent. Yardley was due for a visit. Perhaps he'd talk. If he wouldn't, I'd most certainly find out whether he had any documents. Yardley was on the American side of the line. That gave me a chance.

But I didn't want to butt in on Creeger. In the first place two to one meant a nasty scrap with hotel people running in to see what the commotion was all about. In the second place, Creeger might give me some information.

I settled down in the chair, felt a vague uneasiness, heard a rustle of motion in the darkness behind me, tried to get my feet parked in under me, sensed the hissing of some object through the air, saw ten million comets all trying to crowd into the same orbit at once, and went out like a snuffed candle.

THERE was a vague sense of steel biting into my wrist with cold embrace. My eyes ached with a sudden light, and then I heard cuss words, plenty of 'em. They were in a woman's voice.

I tried to sleep. I was weary of everything, particularly of cussing women. A faint aroma of cosmetics stung my sense of smell. There was the intoxicating nearness of a woman, a bare arm under my neck, soft, warm lips pressed against mine, and then I was swallowed in a gulf of nauseating darkness.

Dimly I knew that I was being quite ill. My stomach looped the loop and went into a tail spin. Then I remembered nothing more for quite a spell. After that, something cooling was pressed against my forehead. My aching eyes were massaged with cool fingertips.

A soft voice breathed in my ear.

"Dearest!"

I opened my eyes.

Vera Rayon was bending over me. She straightened.

"Of all the damned fools!" she said.

I tried to get up. My right wrist was handcuffed to the head of the iron bed. She slipped a key from her stocking and snapped the handcuffs open. I pulled the wet towel from my aching head and tried to make my eyes see one object instead of two.

"What did you hit me with?" I asked.

"Everything I had," she snapped, "and it served you right!"

My head was groggy. There was the memory of a kiss as well as a blow, of terms of endearment and profanity.

"What served me right?"

"Getting tapped to sleep."

"What have I done now?"

"Registered under the name of Charlie Creeger, you poor sap!"

I sighed. I'd thought of ten reasons why that name hadn't been so hot. This was the eleventh.

"I'm looking for him," she went on. "If I can catch him on this side of the Line I can shake him down for some information I want. So far he's kept on the other side. I heard he was over here, looked as the register, saw he'd been in 538, then transferred to 303. The bell boy tipped me off he looked like a crook. I slipped in here with a pass key and waited.

"When you came in and started listening at the door I was sure of my ground. I tapped you with a sap, turned on the light after I'd handcuffed you and found out we'd both pulled a boner. How's the head?"

"Thick," I groaned.

She laughed, a little worried, nervous laugh.

"Come on, we'll go get Creeger," I said.

She watched me with wide eyes while I swayed to the door, flung it open and pointed dramatically down the hall.

"Well?" she asked, following the direction of my finger.

I turned back and slammed the door.

309 was dark as a pocket. The transom showed as an oblong of pitch blackness. There wasn't a sound in the corridor save for the snoring of someone who had an inside room across from the elevator.

I sank into a chair. Vera took another, elevated her neat ankles to the bed and lit a cigarette.

"Shoot," she said.

I patted my head, felt of the bump, tried a cigarette, didn't like the taste, and flung it to one side.

"Where's the towels?"

"You were sick. I played nursemaid."

I felt of my head again, groaned.

"Oh, forget it. I've been batted harder. Go on and shoot. You're lucky I didn't push your face down in your collar."

That was like Vera Rayon, hardboiled on the surface, a fast worker, grim and determined. I thought of the surreptitious kiss, the terms of endearment and twisted a smile.

"Shoot."

"Well, there ain't much to shoot on. We finished up the last job with Butterfield murdered, Big Jim Broke on our trail with a gang of killers, and a lone clue."

"A clue?" she asked, her forehead puckered.

"Yep. A hat with the initials G. F. Y. I hired a detective to trace that hat. He found it was sold to a transient who might have been George F. Yardley. I inquired for that name here. It was registered in 309. Creeger I'd met earlier in the evening. He'd evidently been hired to take me for a ride. His name popped into my mind when I registered. When I came in he was in 309. The room's dark now.

"I thought you were going to dust out until things blew over? I left you on a train headed north out of Yuma, the midnight express, tickets to Portland, Oregon. How come you're back here?"

She smiled at me, sweetly.

"I left you on the same train, Bob. You promised you were going to leave the Border until things quieted down. How come you're back?"

"Had to. Frank Mayo's to be hanged Friday the thirteenth, for a crime he didn't commit. My work's here. I ditched the train when it slowed for a crossing."

She nodded. "My work's here, too. I only seemed to run away to decoy you off the track. I went to San Bernardino and took a plane back."

We gazed at each other for a few moments.

The girl was class. She was slim, fast on her feet, red haired, laughing eyed. And she had more cold nerve than a steel trap in action. High class society breeding and background, a horror of dope and a hatred of those who waxed rich and powerful from smuggling it in, she'd joined the Secret Service. They gave her a free hand on the Border. She crowded the limit. Why she wasn't killed long before was a mystery. Shrewd thinking, devilish daring, cold nerve and sheer tenacity had seen her through.

I wanted Big Jim Broke's gang because they knew something of the inside of the murder of Velma Banco. My friend had been convicted of that crime, and the conviction had been affirmed on appeal. She wanted Big Jim because he was the real smuggling king of the Border. Naturally our paths had crossed. I'd come clean with her. She knew why I was there and what I wanted. And now things had come to a showdown.

She kicked her feet down off the bed, straightened her stockings, grinned.

"Well, what are we standing here for? Let's go take a look at 309. Maybe our man's there, maybe Yardley's there. I got handcuffs. You've got a cane. I've got a gun. What more do we want?"

"A cigarette," I said.

She did the honors. I took a couple of puffs, then tossed the rest of the smoke away.

"Ready."

"The head?"

"Bigger and better."

"Let's go."

We went.

A gentle knock accomplished nothing. There was the sound of metal against the plate of the lock as she tried a skeleton key.

"Watch your fingerprints," she whispered.

I caught the flutter of lace as she pressed a handkerchief about her hand and turned the knob. The door swung inward. A little light from the hall illuminated the interior.

A bed, covered with a spread, an extra blanket at the foot, a suitcase, open, half emptied. There was a couple of empty ginger ale bottles, a bowl that had once contained ice and was now half filled with warm water.

The girl closed the door, snapped the bolt on the inside and produced a compact flashlight. Its beam swept the room in searching scrutiny. An ash tray showed a litter of cigarette ends, the stub of a black cigar.

Vera poked a finger into the mess, extracted two of the white paper ends. Her nail rested upon little blotches of red.

I nodded. No need for words. Some woman had been in here, smoking. Her lip stick had stained the white paper. I thought of Edith, the blonde.

A card lay on a little tray. It was such a tray as a bell boy might have used in bringing up the card. It had, perhaps, been set down while the boy was sent on another errand, then forgotten.

I glanced at the tray. Vera sent the beam of the flashlight shooting my way. The letters on the card snapped into jet black on dazzling white.

"CHARLES W. CREEGER."

I grinned at her. Her answering smile was rather tight lipped.

The beam of the flashlight swept the suitcase, flickered over the dresser, and paused at a door. Evidently it opened on the bath. Taking a cue from her, I thrust a handkerchief over my hand and turned the knob.

Then I stepped back, gave a grunt that was more than an exclamation of surprise.

The tiled floor of the bathroom that should have reflected the light in white smoothness showed huddled shadows, red stains, a grotesque something that was a human foot, twisted at such an angle that it told its own story.

Once it had been a pretty foot. The silken ankle above it had swept in a smooth rhythm of graceful curve. Now it was stiffly awkward, as expressionless as marble.

A stylish skirt, torn half off, disclosed the rolled tops of the stockings. An arm had been flung up as though to ward off a blow. The bust caught the light, shadowed what had been the face. But not even shadow could cover the evidences of a violence that must have

been viciously excessive for even the fell purpose in which it had been employed.

I looked at Vera. She snapped off the flashlight. For a second we stood there, in the presence of death, in a strange room where we had no right to be.

The flashlight snapped on again. The beam played pitilessly about. The hand that held it was as steady as the bracket of an automobile spotlight.

There was a long strip of paper, stained in red. Part was torn off. A picture had adorned the upper half. It was not entirely legible. Apparently the double column spread had been cut carefully from a newspaper. Then, for some reason, it had been torn across the bottom, torn carelessly.

I bent forward. Something about the soggy picture seemed familiar.

"Cashier Embezzles Hundred Thousand," I read.

Then I recognized the picture. It was that of the thin man with the rubbing hands, the man who had been so profuse with his language in the café, the man who had been so anxious to get across the Border at the earliest hour possible. At the time I had attributed that anxiety to a desire to be free of prohibition's restraint. Now I suddenly sensed another motive.

I glanced at the date line. The clipping was two weeks old.

Vera sensed that I knew something, that the clipping told me more than it did her.

"I think," I said, "that we'd better get out of here and notify the authorities."

"The song ain't so bad. The chorus is rotten."

"Meaning?" I asked.

"Meaning that half of the idea is jake. We get out of here. But we don't notify the authorities."

"No?"

"No. Not with you registered under the name of Charles Creeger; not with a bell boy who'll remember that Creeger came up to the room just before the corpse was discovered; not with you being mixed up in the whole mess the way you are. You know the girl?"

I nodded.

"And the picture of the absconding cashier?"

"A man that joined the party tonight."

"Yeah. Well, we dust, and we keep our discovery to ourselves."

"Where do we go?"

"Across the Border. That's where they'll have gone."

"Border's closed."

"Don't be silly."

We got out of the room, out of the hotel. The streets of Yuma were stagnant. A moccasined Indian from the reservation, tall, magnificent, bronzed, stalked his stately way in utter silence. His beady eyes were held rigidly ahead.

A bunch of high school kids, shrieking their paen of youth to the star-filled skies, flivvered past.

We walked the echoing pavements in silence. Two blocks and a slight pressure on my arm indicated a light roadster. I climbed in. The girl fitted a key to the ignition lock, pressed on the starter and backed away from the curb.

"Who was the picture of?"

"Fellow who gave his name as Souther. He got to talking to Creeger. Creeger seemed to recognize him. He left us flat to chase around with the windbag."

Vera nodded, slowly, thoughtfully.

"Put two and two together," I summed up for her, although it hurt my head to do it. "Creeger is tough. He was hired to take me for a ride. Two of the girls were to keep him in line, act as witnesses for him afterward, and serve as a lure to keep me occupied. They were instructed to liquor Creeger, but Creeger's tough. He's got a copper lined stomach.

"I watched him so closely he didn't have a chance to pull any rough stuff. At the restaurant he was disgusted with the whole plan. He saw Souther, tumbled to him from a picture and decided the embezzler must have his loot either on him or readily accessible.

"So Creeger started rushing Souther. The girl, Edith, went to Yardley and made a report. Yardley is Big Jim Broke's right hand bower. He started making things difficult for Creeger. Creeger went to the room to remonstrate. Yardley threw a gun on him and went through him, using the girl to make the search. She pulled the clipping about Souther from Creeger's pocket. That set off the fireworks.

"Creeger grabbed for Yardley. The girl threw her arms about him. A lucky punch accounted for Yardley. Creeger vented his rage on her, then beat it. Yardley came to consciousness and took up the pursuit."

I grinned.

"That's as good a guess as anything."

"No," said Vera, "that's more than a guess. I'm betting you're right."

"And Creeger?"

"Creeger doesn't care for a murder more or less. He's with Souther, and the cashier has a hundred thousand and wants to get across the Border the worst way. You can figure that out for yourself."

"Haven't we extradition with Mexico?"

"On paper. But the country south of the Border offers a safe refuge when one can spend money."

I thought over several angles of that phase of the situation.

"Yardley and Creeger will fight to the last ditch?"

"More likely they'll patch up their differences and divide the hundred thousand."

"Think Creeger'll kill Souther?"

"Perhaps, perhaps not. But he'll get the money. You can see how smooth he is. He clips the account from the paper knowing there's a chance the absconder will head for the Border. When he shows up Creeger drops the game he's on and goes after the big money."

The car was whining smoothly over pavement, headed toward the south.

"And we're crossing the river?"

"We're going to sit in at the finish. This is either going to be the end of a fight or the beginning of a defeat. We've got one punch left. That's got to get us a knockout."

I settled back on the cushions. Her reasoning was logical. I'd let the cards run for a while, see what was dealt and then make my bets.

The night was warm, velvety. The stars shone with unwinking brilliance. I didn't know where we were going other than that we were crossing the Border. How we were going to do it I hadn't the faintest idea.

The car swung down a side road, between two irrigation ditches. The springs swayed, the wheels rattled. Headlights showed cotton on one side, alfalfa on the other. The cotton sent up dead, rustling stalks with balls of white tufting the tops. Weird shadows danced over the road.

The smell of dampness dispelled the desert dryness of the night air. A clump of willows showed in the headlights. The girl leaned forward, snapped the light switch. Instantly thick blackness enveloped us. She stopped the car, but made no move to get out. After an interval she eased in the clutch. The car crept forward. My straining eyes could barely make out a winding ribbon of gray that might have been a road. Willows stretched in dark clumps. The stars shown between.

The car eased its way over the road. The girl had the eyes of a cat. After the first scattered bunches of willows gave way to thick growth of river bottom brush I couldn't see even a hint of road. The girl drove steadily but slowly.

The car came to an abrupt stop. The motor was shut off. I could hear the lapping of water against a muddy bank, the little sucking noises made by drifting whirlpools.

"This way," she said, and opened the door.

It was dark there in the river bottom.

The brush absorbed the light of the stars as a sponge soaks up water. I was able to get a glimpse of the girl as she strode swiftly and surely through the darkness. I followed.

Five minutes and I couldn't have found my way back to the car on a bet. The girl stepped as softly as a cat, as sure of herself as a deer.

Abruptly she stopped. A pocket flashlight sent a single point of light glimmering skyward. Then she sighed and sat down.

"Wait, don't smoke, and don't talk."

I waited, sliding my fingers along my billiard cue cane, getting the heft of it, more than half creepy.

Abruptly I smelled a pipe. After a bit there was the sound of a paddle scraping along a bit of wood. A black bulk loomed upon the surface of the river.

The girl got to her feet.

"I'm going over first. There's only room for one at a time. They'll come back after you. If there's danger I'll show a red light. If you see that red light don't come. Wait. This flash light's got three bulbs, white, green and red. If you see red it's a sign of danger. Green means you're among friends."

She turned to the boatmen, addressed them in low Spanish.

"Let me go first," I said.

She grunted a single sharp negative.

"You don't know the country, don't know what you may run into, and I can get out of it if a Border patrol should pick me up. You'd be shot."

I wanted to argue, but the boat swirled out into the darkness and melted from sight.

Minutes passed. I wanted a smoke, but was afraid of the end of a cigarette. I wished I'd brought a pipe. I gripped my cane the tighter. Little night noises became suddenly ominous, significant. The darkness seemed teeming with menace.

And, as I peered cautiously about me, listening with every nerve strained, there sounded the splash of a paddle and the dark outline of a boat appeared.

"*Señor*," muttered a cautious voice. I advanced.

"You are ready?"

"We are ready. Enter."

There were two of them, one in the bow and one in the stern. I climbed in between them. The craft shot out away from the bank. On one side was the United States. On the other was Mexico. It was as tough a spot as could be found on the map.

I peered at the two boatmen, getting them outlined against the star-studded sky. One of them was chewing an unlit cigar. I turned to the other. He also chewed a cigar. I thought of the pipe I had smelled when the boat first came across.

We seemed to be getting rather farther downstream than the girl had gone. Was it possible there had been two boats? One laying in ambush, filled with enemies? Then they had started for me while the friendly boat was coming back, and . . .

Abruptly a red light shone from the far bank. It was, as I had surmised, much farther upstream. For a second it flashed its red warning, and then it whirled up in the air and went out.

I heard the rustle of stealthy motion behind me. The man in front laid down his paddle.

I acted promptly, without so much as a second of hesitation. My hand was gripping the side of the boat. I threw my entire weight over upon it. The boat lurched. The man behind me stumbled, cursed, a knife clattered on the side of the boat and then rushing water swept over the side.

The red, muddy water swirled about. The boat rolled over. On both sides of me was a great splashing, a cursing in the Spanish tongue.

I dived, swam directly under one of the floundering bodies, came up, trod water silently until I could get my bearings, and then struck out steadily for the far shore.

The current swept me downstream. My clothes impeded me, but the water was warm, and I managed to keep my faithful cane with me, thrust through the back of my belt.

Seconds lengthened into minutes. The swirling, whispering, lapping current seemed an interminable waste of waters, but, at length I was where my knees struck a clay bank. I scrambled up, sank to my ankles in silt, and then floundered over sand and gravel. Brush stretched forth rough branches and scratched my face.

I wanted to sit down, but I remembered that red light, the crazy way it had acted, and I bent my steps up the river, keeping to the brush as much as possible, straining my eyes to see some trail or opening between the clumps of thick growth.

I came to a sand bar. That made easier walking.

Abruptly the darkness was split by a flash of fire. The spiteful crack of a rifle shattered the silence. For a moment, while the echoes chased about, the water was still, then, as the noise died away the ripples took up their everlasting lapping against the bank. The whirlpools whispered a soughing song of their own.

In midstream sounded hoarse curses. There was the sound of blows. Another shot crashed the night air. Something fell with a splash. Then, again, all was silence save for the nerve racking babbling of the water.

I turned away from the bank.

Either the two boats had encountered each other, conceding that my two had been able to right the boat and climb in, or else the friendly boat had run upon a hostile swimmer. But I had bigger fish to fry. Certain it was that the girl had been betrayed in some manner; and I had been tricked.

I went more slowly now, searching the bank of the stream, yet keeping as far from it as possible. Finally I detected the faintest possible trace of pipe smoke. I tried to run down the odor.

It became more intangible, dissolved upon the night air.

There was the sound of a horse snorting a warning. Plunging hoofs crashed the brush toward me. I flung myself in the shelter of a bit of prickly growth and waited.

The horse went snorting and charging through the darkness. A voice sent forth a challenge in Spanish. There was no answer. The river kept up its gurgling of mysterious waters sweeping past, unseen in the darkness.

Again there was a stretch of sand reflecting the starlight. It seemed churned up with struggling feet. I leaned over, studied the soft surface, found that it was literally pitted with footprints.

Something glinted. It was the buckle of a shoe. I picked it up. The circle, set with brilliants, had been torn from the shoe of Vera Rayon. I slipped it in my pocket and turned away from the river bank. She would not be near the river, not now.

The horseman was dashing back and forth. There were no further noises of struggle. A flashlight, used by the mounted man, began to sweep the river, the brush. It was time for me to be going.

Reluctantly I moved away, following the general direction of the footprints churned in the soft sand.

The night had been warm, but my swim, the touch of my wet clothes, gradually started my blood to chilling. I walked more rapidly, came to a road. It was ankle deep in dust, uneven, rutted, but it gave me a sense of security, and I followed it.

A building showed at the side of the road. After an interval there was another. Then my eyes caught the flicker of lights ahead. Los Algodones, free of the tourist incubus, was going about its furtive night life.

And there were those in Los Algodones who remembered. They would have cheerfully slid a knife along my throat or plunged the cold steel into my heart.

I had to work under cover, and I had to work fast. As Vera Rayon had said, we had one punch left. And that punch must be a knockout.

I slid down the side street, avoiding the main thoroughfare upon which the resorts fronted. There were but a few of them, and watchful eyes patrolled their entrances.

The back was as the back of such places always is, stinking to heaven of mixed smells, each one assailing the nostrils with the disagreeable effect of a blow.

I waited, listening.

There was the tinkle of a musical instrument, the wailing notes of a *señorita's* voice, the soft guttural of a Mexican, using words that were too indistinct to be individually audible, coming to the ear only as a blended cadence of mellow conversation.

I sighed. It seemed an impossible task, delivering that one punch.

I moved up closer. I would begin with them one at a time, search the town.

". . . Found this rabbit an' he's my meat!"

There could be no other throat that emitted such a volume of snarling sound. Charles W. Creeger, big hearted Charlie; and he was probably fighting for the possession of his prize.

The words came from a building that showed as a dark blotch on the landscape, blotting out stars with a blob of shadow, unbroken by any glimmer of light.

I walked boldly toward it. There was no time for any great amount of finesse. Vera Rayon had given the danger signal and disappeared. Yardley had sneaked out of his room in the hotel. Souther was supposed to be carrying something over a hundred thousand dollars. Creeger was hot on the trail, half hostile toward everybody, inclined to throw over Big Jim Broke. Such a combination, thrown together south of the Border does not long remain static.

I stumbled over a pile of rubbish, slipped along a fence, tried a door and found it locked. A window was a black square of fixed glass, shuttered and barred. I worked around the corner, knowing that the chances of discovery were greater, yet realizing that the situation within was coming to a showdown.

Then it was that the darkness gave forth a husky sound of dry menace, as ominous as the slithering of a rattlesnake's belly across dried leaves.

I could feel my spine tingle with emotion.

That sound was the voice of Big Jim Broke himself.

I could not make out all the words. Those that I heard were crisp and to the point. But the point was that Big Jim had emerged from his underground concealment, was directing the final scenes of what was destined to become a grim tragedy of the Border.

And I gripped my billiard cue cane as I walked boldly to the front door of the place, and shoved it open.

Now or never, and I needed to pack a knockout in the one last wallop I could deliver.

They did not notice me at first, and then, when they did, so engrossed were they with what was going forward that they did not recognize me.

There were others in the place, a scattering of black mustached smugglers, a *señorita* or two; but the group was sitting in a little booth, the curtain thrown back.

Big Jim was standing, his bull neck swelling with emotion, his hands gripping the edge of the table. Souther was at the corner, his meek face twisting from one to the other, turning on his thin neck as a toasting marshmallow turns on a limber stick.

Creeger's voice again.

"I'm playing a lone hand and you can all go to hell!"

"You're on my side of the Line now. And I've a personal matter to settle with you."

Big Jim's voice was packed with husky menace.

"Gentlemen, gentlemen, I'm sure I do not understand what this is about. Your language seems most inappropriate. Perhaps I had better . . ."

George F. Yardley, thin, sardonic, reached out one of his long hands and placed it on the little man's shoulder.

"You better stay right here . . ."

His hand was flirting with the slim throat.

"You better . . ."

There was the flash of motion. I caught the glitter of light on metal. Flame spurted. There was a boom of throbbing sound that reverberated from wall to wall.

The whole top of Yardley's head seemed to disappear.

For a moment I was as dazed as anyone in the place. Only by degrees did intelligence soak back into my dome. Even then it took the scream of a *señorita* to give me full consciousness of what had happened.

The little man was out in the center of the floor.

One shoulder was higher than the other, pathetic reminder of days and days spent at a desk, posting entries, making marks on paper. His thin neck twisted around inside his collar with inches of room to spare. His meek eyes were as apologetic as ever.

"You forget that I have something to say about what is to be done!"

And his method of reminding them was by thrusting the automatic at them in little ominous jabs.

That automatic evidently shot soft nosed bullets. What was left of Yardley's features testified to the calibre of the gun, the accuracy of its aim, and the character of the bullet.

The *señorita* who had done the screaming was bending over Yardley, shouting her grief to the ceiling of the dive. She begged him to speak to her, called down curses upon his murderer, demanded vengeance, hugged the mutilated form to her breast.

Big Jim Broke, always prudent, stepped slightly to one side, gave Creeger an opportunity to get into action. And Creeger, hardboiled as ever, grasped that opportunity.

It looked like my chance as well.

Either Yardley or Big Jim had certain things in their possession . . .

I twisted my eyes.

Big Jim was watching me with cold, snake-like eyes. For the first time since I entered he had turned his vision on me, and it needed but one look at those eyes to tell the story. Big Jim wanted me even more than he wanted the hundred thousand dollars that was almost within his grasp.

I correctly interpreted the sudden rigidity of the elbow.

Then Big Jim exploded into the cat-like action of which only a fat man is capable.

I hurled a water glass at the lone light that illuminated the ceiling and dived forward.

The glass crashed into the light and the room was plunged in churning darkness, and that darkness was filled with the sounds of motion.

I caught the limp form of the man who had been Yardley, Big Jim's right hand man. I swear there was not a second which had elapsed between the time the light tinkled out and the time my hands eagerly quested his clothes.

Swift as I was, I was too late.

His pockets were wrong side out. His coat had been flung back, the shirt ripped open. My eager hands found nothing.

The beam of a flashlight stabbed the darkness.

"Get him, men."

The words were in Spanish, and the dry, husky voice was unmistakable.

A revolver spat viciously.

I made for a curtained passageway.

Behind me roared the heavy boom of Souther's automatic. Creeger's bellowing voice sounded as the challenge of a charging bull.

The flashlight swung, settled on me.

I dived behind the curtain. Another shot. A bullet spattered mud from the 'dobe wall.

The flashlight went out. I sensed a passage ahead, a sure guide for bullets, a deadly trap. I twisted back under the curtain. Rushing forms spilled over me. There was a chorus of cursing and running steps in the street.

A small calibre automatic vomited a stream of lead.

Creeger's voice rose in a triumphant shout, and then someone switched on another light.

Souther was twitching on the floor.

Creeger, half way to him, looked up, saw me and snarled.

Big Jim Broke, his gun still in his hand, regarded me with baleful eyes and raised the pistol.

At the curtained passageway a struggling mass of humanity, men and women alike were engaging in a free-for-all.

Big Jim's gun hand steadied. The end of my cane jarred his wrist. Behind me, Creeger flung up his automatic. A single backward sweep of the cane caught his jaw. He toppled, staggered, and my cane, piloted with every ounce of speed I could muster, caught Big Jim Broke on the jaw, right on the button. And it wasn't any disconcerting tap. It was a knockout, delivered with every bit of force I could manage.

At that moment someone shot out the second light.

Darkness once more. Cries at the door, a sudden desire for flight twisting the emotional minds of the Mexican henchmen. The knowledge that a stream of something warm was trickling down my arm.

There had been a hand truck back of the bar. Two cases of whiskey were on it, brought in from the back for the evening's trade. I ripped the faded curtain from a booth, spilled the whiskey from the truck, wrapped the curtain around Big Jim, and piled him aboard.

I could hear Creeger regaining consciousness. His vocabulary was un-

impaired by the solid tap on his jaw.
"If I could find . . ." he bellowed.

I thought I might accommodate him.
Picking the sound of the voice, I lashed
out with my cane, and missed. There
was no time for pleasantries. I wheeled
my truck toward the passageway.

The street door radiated light from
twin automobile lamps. There was the
rattling of a cheap motor, cries in Spanish. I paid no attention. Trundling
Big Jim as though he had been a sack
of meal, I went toward the rear.

I could feel the steady trickle of blood
on my arm. As soon as possible I must
tie that up. But right now I had other
things to consider.

I turned down the alley. The small
wheels didn't work so well in the dust.
I stumbled, caught myself, managed to
gain the street. There were cars here.
I picked the nearest. As to what I
intended to do I hadn't the least idea.
There was a lassitude gripping my
mind. I knew that I had stirred up a
hornet's nest, that I must get away, that
Big Jim mustn't escape me this
time.

Shots sounded behind me. Shots
that couldn't have been intended for
me. Creeger, probably, battling the
whole of Mexico for the loot of an
absconding cashier. Hardboiled was too
mild a term for Charles W. Creeger,
professional gunman and killer, imported for the purpose of bumping me
off, but staying to fight the whole
gang.

I got Big Jim into the rear of the
car. It seemed an interminable and impossible task. I climbed in the front
seat, groped for the ignition switch.

As I bent over, darkness seemed to
well up on either side like rushing
waters. There was a sudden nausea, a
gripping weakness. I remembered that
hole in my shoulder. I must bandage
it. I couldn't fail now. I straightened,
felt the darkness rush upon me, smother
me with close embrace.

The bottom dropped out of everything. I seemed to be sinking gently
through limitless realms of darkness.

SPANISH voices tinkled in my ears.
There was the smell of a pipe.
Something swirled and babbled. I
thought of the water, of that swim, of
the everlasting persistence of the lapping
fingers of water swirling past clay
banks.

The thought occurred to me that
water always ran. Long after men
ceased to live, water ran. Water was
endless, always running, immortal. Yet
it ran from the mountain to the ocean.
Life was like that. The individual
made his journey from the brook to the
river, the river to the sea, and that was
the end. Yet the stream always ran,
on and on.

I tried to sit up. My hands touched
something cold. There was no sensation of motion. My fingertips touched
cold stone. Was it a vault?

Horror of premature burial snapped
me out of it. I opened my eyes. Bril-
liant stars swam about in a floating con-
stellation, finally narrowed into a single star, a reddish incandescent that
glittered faintly down from a distance,
grew brighter, and suddenly fixed itself
in a concrete wall.

Iron bars grilled the space below that.
There was a sickening sweet smell about
me. Jail disinfectant. Once smelled it is
never forgotten. Gone was the freshness
of the night air. About me was the dank
aroma of huddled bodies, sleeping,
emanating unclean smells to the night
air.

Fingers touched my forehead. I
clutched frantically for my cane. It
was gone.

The voice of a woman.

"Hey, for the love o' Mike, bring
back that flask!"

I sensed the smell of whiskey, felt
a cold bottle-neck between my lips.
Fiery liquid choked me. I swallowed,
felt more liquid, gulped deeply, gasped,
coughed, and raised my eyes.

Vera Rayon was grinning down at

me with mixed relief and triumph. "Where. . . ."

"Jail at Yuma," she said, and smiled. Somewhere along the line she'd accumulated a peach of a black eye.

She sent exploring fingertips around the edge of the optic as she noticed the direction of my gaze. Her face was yellow, a peculiar color. At first I couldn't get the connection. Then I noticed that her hair was no longer red, but black.

"I was the gushing *señorita* who frisked Yardley," she grinned. "My boat went across all right. But it was an accident. They had a fake boat rigged up to trap me. You got the second boat. I flashed a danger signal, and then things got hot. But I'd worked a disguise and that saw me through. They took me for a native girl and dashed off hunting the real me.

"I percolated into the *cantina*. I figured you could take care of yourself with my danger signal to help you. But I sure didn't figure you'd come on across and start a roughhouse.

"Gosh, but you lost a lot of blood. I bandaged you up the best I could. You'll have to keep quiet for a while."

That brought me to a sense of the present. I tried to sit up, failed, slumped back, fighting for breath.

"Tomorrow . . . hanging Friday at San Quentin. . . . Got to save Frank Mayo. . . . Big Jim. . . ."

She pressed a light hand over my lips.

"Hush, the doctor said you weren't to talk. Big Jim's caught dead to rights.

Yardley had letters on him, letters that had been taken from Butterfield. They told the story. Big Jim Broke was mixed up in the crime. Yardley had the letters and held them over Broke. Creeger was imported to get you, but the job got bungled. Then he went off on the trail of Souther. Yardley followed, demanded a split. It was a sweet mix-up.

"But you were trundling Big Jim toward the river. I spelled you at the wheel. We loaded him like a sack of meal. He didn't come to until fifteen minutes ago. He's safe in jail, and we've got the deadwood on him. That means a lot to the Border service.

"The United States Secret Service is wiring the Governor of California. Your friend'll be pardoned. Tomorrow is hanging Friday all right, but Mayo won't hang. Big Jim will be the one to get measured for a suit of prison gray with a black cap thrown in for good measure."

In my ears was a steady monotone of husking sound.

Big Jim Broke, cornered at last, was talking, and I knew there'd be a court reporter to take down what he had to say.

A clock boomed the hour of midnight.

With my job finished, Vera's kiss on my lips, Big Jim Broke brought to the end of his career, it looked like the end of a perfect day.

I drifted off to sleep. Hanging Friday! And it wasn't such a bad day, after all.

STRAIGHT FROM THE SHOULDER, by Erle Stanley Gardner

A red-hot yarn of ED JENKINS, the PHANTOM CROOK,

IN OCTOBER BLACK MASK

New Guns For Old

By FREDERICK NEBEL

Richmond City tries to reform.

POLICE Captain Steve MacBride was on leave. He had it coming to him. As one of the main factors in the scouring of Richmond City's corrupt municipal government, he was due some little respite from the shield and the gun. With the passing of a self-seeking Mayor and a Police Commissioner who had played with him, the city was in a position to recuperate from a long siege of political disease. It all depended, however, on how the convalescent municipality was nursed back to normalcy.

It was spring, merging into summer. MacBride had passed two weeks of his long-promised vacation at his bungalow out in Grove Manor. He had puttered around in his garden, painted the white picket fence and the screens that enclosed the latticed veranda. He planned to spend the last two weeks in the mountains with his wife. They had a car, and it was their intention to drive up and camp out, and call it a kind of second honeymoon. For MacBride was only forty—lean, clean-clipped, with the spark of youth still in his blood.

He was busy packing on the day before their impending departure, when a boy rode up on a bicycle and handed him a telegram. He carried it up to the veranda, sat down and tore it open. The message was brief and to the point:

Report at Headquarters tomorrow morning.   *Collins.*

Collins was the Police Commissioner.

"Hell," muttered MacBride, and went into the house.

He showed the message to his wife

61

She read it slowly, and then looked at him.

"What does it mean, Steve?"

"That I'm to report, Anne."

"I know, but—"

He cracked fist into palm. "Something rotten in the wind, else Collins wouldn't have taken the trouble to wire me."

"Oh, I hope our little trip won't fall through!"

"Looks as if it might."

"Oh, Steve!"

He patted her on the shoulder. "What I get for ever having taken up the shield. If they call me back, I'll raise hell."

When he walked into Collins' office next morning, he suspected the worst. Collins sat behind his desk wearing a strained and somewhat worried look. Inspector O'Keefe was there. Captain Hamlin, Detective-Sergeant Brunner, Detectives Morina and Stein.

"Sit down, MacBride," said Collins. "The Mayor will be here any moment."

"What's up?" asked MacBride.

"Let the Mayor tell you." Collins smoked his cigar and stared at the desk.

Mayor Burkhart came in ten minutes later. He was a large, well-groomed man, who held his head well back and looked at the world through rimless spectacles. His gaze was direct and piercing, his lips wide, thin and determined. He put aside his hat and stick, clasped his hands behind his back and stood silhouetted against the window.

"Men," he said, "I've had you come here this morning for a purpose. As you know, I'm a reform Mayor. I demand reform, and my psychology is that of taking the offensive. Also, to strike quickly and brook no opposition."

He paused, flexed his lips against his teeth, gave each man a brief, penetrating glance.

He proceeded, "I have studied your methods and do not approve of them. I do not approve of half-way measures. Since Richmond City experienced one of the worst crime waves on record, it seems to me to be a case in point that your methods were not altogether efficacious."

The men, outstanding arms of the law, listened in silence.

The Mayor's voice was sharp, incisive. He bared his teeth over certain emphatic words, delivered them neatly clipped, his chin raised.

He said, "Remember the horrible gang wars, the blood-shed, the insidious corruption, against which the department fought like men in the dark—"

"Pardon, Mr. Mayor," interjected Collins. "I was not Commissioner. The men who took their jobs seriously were hampered by a crooked Mayor and Commissioner."

"But lax police methods permitted such conditions to gather impetus. Reform can only be acquired through stringent methods. You must take the bull by the horns. Now listen to me." His eyes flashed about the room. "I intend to rip out the root of crime. Within the next twenty-four hours I want every speakeasy in Richmond City closed. I want every night-club raided. There are at least a dozen barber shops in this city where liquor can be purchased. I want them raided, too, and their business licenses revoked. There are a dozen more delicatessen stores selling liquor. I want those establishments raided and their business licenses also revoked. Understand! Every night-club, every restaurant, every back-alley speakeasy, every barber shop and every delicatessen store. Within twenty-four hours." His teeth snapped shut.

The men looked at one another. MacBride looked at Collins, saw the Commissioner's lips tighten.

MacBride stood up. "Mr. Mayor, I still have two weeks' leave coming—"

"That will have to be postponed. Your record in the recent clean-up is outstanding. You will affect plain-clothes and attend to the closing of the night-clubs. Any place where ginger ale is sold, you can be sure that liquor is sold also."

"It can't be done," said MacBride.

He was known for a holy terror among the criminals. He was also known for a captain who had loose ideas about authority.

"It can," said the Mayor.

"Too sudden," insisted MacBride. "Try to close all these places in twenty-four hours and there will be hell to pay. The crime wave has died down. Why stir it again? I've handled crime for twenty years. I know there are some things we've got to tolerate. A certain amount of liquor traffic is one of them. If we crash the places that we know exist, places will open whose existence we'll never know about, and they'll breed crime. Crime doesn't breed in a place that is known to the police. It's the other places."

The Mayor rocked on his feet and thinned down his lips. "MacBride, do you presume to tell me my business?"

"Not at all. I'm airing my own business—which has to do with a sensible handling of crime. And—this is not presumption—I think I know crime a little better than you do. I've handled it in the raw."

"Tut, tut!" said the Mayor. "Please be quiet until I have finished. There are other places to be closed."

Collins creaked in his chair.

The Mayor went on, "These Jewish pawnbrokers and jewelers. These so-called fences. You know many of them —you men?"

Heads nodded somewhat reluctantly.

"So!" clipped Burkhart. "Another medium for crime. Jewels, silks, merchandise, furs are stolen. The criminals dispose of them through the fence. If there were no fences, there would be no market. Is that not logic?"

"No," said MacBride.

Collins flung him a worried look. The other men shifted. They all knew Mac-Bride—knew what a tough egg he was, a man who held opinions of his own and stood by them; a man who often injured his own chances with the powers-that-be by saying just what he thought,

regardless of circumstances or cost.

"No?" asked the Mayor, restraining his annoyance.

"No," reiterated MacBride vigorously. "I know every fence in Richmond City. Some of them are my friends. It was through a fence that I nailed Red Hennessy, the guy that killed Barbour three years ago in a stick-up. A fence is an unofficial intelligence department for the police. Look it up and see how many men have been trailed through them."

"But if there were *no* fences—"

"If," said MacBride, "there were no fences in Richmond City, there would still be fences in New York, Chicago, every other city in the United States. By doing away with the fence here we would severe what contact we have with the underworld. And the underworld can't be snuffed out in a day. It's an institution, the same as the police department."

Burkhart knocked the ash from his cigar. His voice lowered. "MacBride, I know what sort of man you are. You take things in your own hands a lot. You're stubborn. Well, maybe I'm stubborn too. You have your orders. That goes for all of you men. Close up every place that sells liquor. Bar the doors of every known fence. Tighten the bolts on these doors of crime, and watch the grand exodus of criminals from Richmond City. Remember!" He raised a forefinger. "Within twenty-four hours."

He picked up his hat and stick, strode to the door, pulled it open.

"Gentlemen, I bid you good-day."

II

 HE news clicked through Police Headquarters. It fell like a bomb-shell in every police station. Precinct captains, who had gritted their teeth under the lash of the late régime, gritted their teeth again. From extreme

measures used by a corrupt administration, they found themselves in the hands of an extreme reformist, a man fired by ambition, a man who believed he could thwart destiny itself.

Even as they had been bound by orders before, so they were bound by orders again. Though many of them believed that reform had to be coaxed, not driven, they were of necessity forced to drive. They were all cogs in the tremendous wheel of municipal government, and each cog had to move with the wheel. Strictest secrecy was demanded by the Mayor. Each precinct captain was told of the plans that day by a sealed letter from the Mayor. Each captain was warned to say nothing until the appointed hour. After eight o'clock that night he was ordered to be prepared for any emergency call.

At four that afternoon the men detailed to close the delicatessen stores known to sell liquor, started out, the idea being that in such establishments more gin is bought between the hours of four and six than at any other time —the cocktail time. At seven the men detailed to close the barber shops, left Headquarters. At the same time, a detective-sergeant and two plainclothesmen, were dispatched to handle the known fences.

At eight MacBride was eating in a small restaurant, a block from Headquarters. Kennedy, of the City *Free Press*, wandered in, spotted him and came over.

"What the hell, Mac?"

MacBride went on eating, said, "Well, what the hell?"

Kennedy sat down. "I mean, you being around here. Thought you were going to the mountains."

"So did I."

"Well?"

"Changed my mind."

Kennedy grinned. "Or did somebody change your mind for you?"

"Go to hell," said MacBride, casually.

Kennedy chuckled. "Poor old Mac."

"On your way, Kennedy. This is one of the times when you get on my nerves."

"Something's up, Mac."

"My temper, if you don't breeze."

"Now, Mac—"

"Kennedy—" MacBride put down his fork and sat back. "Kennedy, there are times when I like you. There are times when I don't. I've got a touch of liver tonight. Now get the hell out of here."

Kennedy shrugged. He rose, a lazy-eyed, whimsical young man. "All right, Mac." He put on his hat, lit a cigarette, grinned. "Poor old Mac. They can't even do without you in peace, eh?"

MacBride ignored him. Kennedy sighed, turned and wandered out. MacBride stared after him. They were old friends, these two. Too bad he had met Kennedy then, mused MacBride. Kennedy was no fool. He suspected that something was in the wind.

At ten MacBride blew into Headquarters and went straight to the office that had been given him. Moriarity and Cohen, the two detectives allotted him, were playing poker dice. They had been attached to the Second Precinct during the reign of crime and had been MacBride's best men.

"Any news?" asked MacBride.

Cohen said, "Brunner busted into ten barber shops and nailed them up. He just phoned in. O'Keefe got eight delicatessen stores. Hamlin is still working the fences. Cripes, this is my idea of a burlesque show. But it ain't even funny."

"Keep your ideas to yourself, Ike," recommended MacBride.

He still was loyal to his shield.

"But, cripes, Cap," said Cohen, "you know yourself it's a lunatic's idea."

"Never mind, Ike," said MacBride. "We've got a job to do. We'll close every damned joint in this town. That's our orders."

"And see what happens," chimed in Moriarity. "It can't be done, Cap."

"We'll close 'em all," said MacBride. "It can be done."

"But what will it start? I'll tell you what it'll start—"

"That's another matter, so don't worry about it. The first place on the list is The Palm Club—at eleven-thirty. Incidentally, the guy that owns it, George Clark, is a good friend of mine. He runs the cleanest place in town."

"Good old George," nodded Cohen. "He gave three thousand berries to the City Poor House."

At eleven MacBride and his two aides walked out of Police Headquarters and climbed into a taxi. At eleven-thirty sharp they walked into The Palm Club, in the heart of the theatrical district.

An after theatre crowd was already there. The orchestra was playing. Huge imitation palms and colored lanterns lent a tropical atmosphere. A fountain sparkled in the center of the parquet dance-floor. It was a high-class rendezvous, a place that had never given the police a bit of trouble.

MacBride, hands thrust into his pocket, met the headwaiter and nodded.

"Where's George?" he said.

"Busy now, Captain. What can I do for you?"

"Get George."

"But—"

"Get George."

Puzzled, the headwaiter moved off. A few minutes later George Clark appeared. He was a large, well-poised man, with a benign smile. He thrust out his hand.

"Well, well, Mac!"

"Hello, George," said MacBride, and shook. "We're in a hurry. Now don't get sore. You've just got to close up. You know and I know that there's a highball on every table. Padlock, George."

Clark looked incredulous. "For God's sake, Mac, you don't mean—"

"That's just what I mean, George. No fuss. Do it quietly. I won't hang around. I'll depend on you to be shut tight in fifteen minutes.

"Orders, George." MacBride turned

B.M.—Sept.—5

to Moriarity and Cohen. "Come on, boys."

They walked out and left Clark like a man in a trance.

A block farther on they entered The Three Aces, run by Billy Kildane. Kildane met them at the door, and MacBride said:

"Hello, Billy. Just dropped in to tell you that I'm staging a padlock act."

"A—what!"

"Lock and key. Chase out the boys and girls and lock up tight."

"But, Mac, look at the crowd!"

"I know, that's tough. I'm merely relaying orders. So long, Billy."

MacBride and his men went out. Inside of an hour they closed seven of the most famous supper clubs in the theatrical district. Everything went along smoothly. There were no arguments. MacBride carried out orders with a minimum of words.

At twelve-thirty he led the way into The Jungle, a colored night-club run by Max Lebowitz. A bizarre, garish place, with a howling orchestra and dark-skinned entertainers tap-dancing and moaning blue melodies. Lebowitz bobbed on the scene grinning and rubbing his hands together.

"Max," said MacBride, "you've got fifteen minutes to chase out the crowd and close up—tight."

"How's this?"

"Padlock."

"Come now, Mac—honest?"

"Honest. Stop the band, clear the place and lock it up. Orders."

Max frowned. "Hell d' you suppose I can chase all these people out? What's the meaning of this, anyhow?"

"Now don't let's go into detail, Max. Be nice. I'm trying to be. You've got to close down."

"Ah, that's a lot of nonsense, Mac. What the hell kind of a game you trying to hand me?"

MacBride sighed. "If you want me to close it up personally, I'll do it."

"But I don't see—"

"Never mind what you see, Max.

You heard me. Now don't hand me an argument. Close up."

Max snarled, "I thought you were my friend, Mac. This is a fine thing—"

"Ike," broke in MacBride, "go down and stop that band."

"No—no," urged Lebowitz. "I'll do it. I'll close up. All right, Mac, I won't forget this. It's a lousy trick."

"Good night, Max," said MacBride, and started out. "Come on, boys."

As they went down the scale in night life, they found each succeeding place more difficult to close. They had to close The Parrot themselves, had to drive the crowd into the street. And when they left it darkened and with barred doors, Cohen wagged his head.

"There will be hell to pay, Cap," he said.

"Number twelve is The Blue Moon," said MacBride.

The Blue Moon was in the heart of Bohemia, a cellar club, low-ceiled, fantastically decorated, patronized by a mixed crowd. Lew Gates ran it.

"Well, Mac, what the hell are you doing down this way?" asked Gates.

"Poking around, Lew. Do you think you can close this place quietly in fifteen minutes?"

"No."

"Well, close it."

Gates peered keenly. "What's that?"

"Ask the gang to go home, Lew, and lock up."

"I don't get you, Mac."

"Now, Lew, of course you do. You're closed for business."

"Who said so?"

"I did."

They regarded each other steadily. Then Lew shrugged. "That's a lot of crap, Mac. I ain't heard anything about it."

"You just heard me."

"You're kidding."

"I'm in earnest, Lew. Close up."

Gates turned away. "Ah, be yourself Mac. You ain't that kind of guy."

MacBride caught him by the arm.

"Look here, Lew. Use your head. I mean what I say."

Gates pivoted sharply. "I'm damned if I'll close!"

"Want me to close it for you?"

"Try"—Gates pointed to the crowd —"try to clean that bunch out."

MacBride turned to Moriarity and Cohen. "Let's start."

He strode across the dance-floor and stopped at the orchestra stall. The leader was on the point of swinging into a new number.

"Wait a minute," said MacBride. "The music's over."

The leader lowered his hand. "Huh?"

"Pack up. You've got ten minutes." He left them and returned to the center of the floor; raised his voice—"Ladies and gentlemen, you will have to leave. This place is being closed by the police. You've got ten minutes."

A low murmur of surprise rose, followed by a rumble of disapproval. A few rose.

A man shouted, "Hold your seats. This is funny."

"It will be funnier," said MacBride, "if I take you by the neck."

"Yeah?"

MacBride flung over his shoulder, "Moriarity, collar that wiseacre."

"Yup," clipped Moriarity, and made a bee-line for the man.

The man rose, a little more than three sheets in the wind. He made a pass at Moriarity, but Moriarity grinned. ducked, and catching hold of him, dragged him across the floor. His companion, a flamboyant woman with blonde hair, began shouting:

"I call this a nerve, I call this a damned shame. I and Ken weren't harming no one. I ain't going to let no man make no fool out of Ken." With a grand gesture she swept plates and glasses from the table, stood up, glared, and jammed her arms akimbo.

"Madame," said MacBride, "sit down and shut up."

She stamped her foot. "That for you!"

Lew Gates appeared on the floor. "Hey, you, what the hell you mean by busting that stuff?"

"Well, Lew, these guys—"

"Aw, pipe down!" snapped Gates. "Park your hips, Katie, and sign off." He turned to MacBride. "All right, Mac, I'll close, but that's what I call a rotten deal."

"Think hard, Lew. We've always been friends," said MacBride.

"And this ends it."

"Have it your own way, Lew. Be sure you're closed in ten minutes."

He turned and walked off the floor. Moriarity had deposited the girl's companion in the cloak room. He joined MacBride on the way out and Cohen followed. In the street, they breathed with relief.

"That's all for tonight," said Mac-Bride.

"Thank God," said Cohen. "The beginning of the end. I see another reign of terror, Mac, and I don't mean maybe. If all these guys hadn't been friends of yours, there'd been some trouble—and some gun work on the side."

Moriarity nodded. "Yeah. But I've got a hunch, Cap, that you've lost some of those friends."

MacBride walked on in silence. He had carried out the Mayor's orders. He had done a neat, bloodless job—bloodless because those men knew him. Some had argued, but that was natural. He had expected worse.

And by the time he reached home he had definitely put thoughts of a vacation out of his mind. For the ear of his mind heard the distant rumble of another conflict with the shield and the gun.

THE press howled. The *Times-Courier*, a colorless sheet, patted the Mayor on the back. It said that Providence had sent him to Richmond City, that within six months the city would be the cleanest in the East. The writer waxed elo-

quent, used every complimentary adjective he could call to mind, wound up by calling the Mayor a high-minded patriot.

The *Free Press* was more subtle. It said, in part, "We were surprised, but not pleasantly. We approve of reform, as every sensible citizen should, but the ways of reform are manifold. We recommend, however, a gradual pressure. Richmond City has been ill with crime. It was recovering. In our opinion it has suddenly been ruptured, and we believe a rupture rarely heals completely."

The *News-Examiner*, a frankly blatant sheet, laughed out loud and wanted to know what peculiar disease of the mind had fallen upon the Mayor.

The *Post-Express* was hopeful but refused to commit itself one way or the other. It leaned tentatively toward the Mayor. The writer seemed chameleonic.

TWO days later MacBride sat in his office at Headquarters. The day before he had closed fifteen speakeasies, and he had made more enemies. This, perhaps, was due to the fact that he refused to take each man aside, tell him that it was the Mayor's orders and that personally he, MacBride, had other ideas. Of course, personally he had other ideas. But he was loyal to his badge and in some measure loyal to his Mayor. Wherefore he held his tongue and closed one place after another with brevity and dispatch. Many claimed that he had become self-seeking, that he was looking for promotion under the new régime. This was a blow to MacBride's pride, but he swallowed it, albeit hard.

He also had a premonition of disaster. It was undefined, but it persisted in his policeman's mind. He did not venture to predict in what manner the whip of crime would crack over Richmond City. But privately he held that it would crack.

Kennedy said, "Burkhart may even

be murdered. His ideals don't jibe with logic. He thinks he's hard-boiled. His methods are centuries old. Time has passed him by."

"We'll see," muttered MacBride.

"What are your own opinions, Mac?"

"They don't matter."

"But they do."

"And no matter what they are, they're not for publication."

Kennedy chuckled. "Good old, loyal old Mac. Bet it hurts, though. Well, well, hell is simmering. Every club bolted, every speakeasy barred, twelve barber shops run by Wops out of business, ten delicatessen stores shut tight, every fence in town closed. Air-tight, you say? My eye, Mac, my eye! It's like a balloon blown up to the bursting point. Somebody'll prick it. Watch it bust. Reform is predicated on intelligent administration. Reform can be brought about by tightening the screws bit by bit, but you can't suddenly walk into the ring, haul off and kick prevailing conditions out into the cold. New York, Boston—even Boston!— and Philadelphia, are pulling a tremendous horse laugh. And so are some of us right here. I am. So are you."

MacBride scoffed. "You think you know more than you do, Kennedy. Go out and cool off."

Kennedy leaned forward, tapped the desk. "I know this, Mac. I know that under the skin you agree with me. But I know, too, that you've got a queer sense of loyalty, and that you'll carry out a command even if you break your neck doing it. And you'll never chirp. Oh, I know you, Mac."

"You know hell, Kennedy." Mac-Bride stood up, jammed his hands into his pockets and paced the floor. He stopped short, spun, stood spread legged. "I've closed those places and they'll stay closed so long as I have anything to do with it."

"Sure. You're on orders. You've got to back up the Mayor, whether you like it or not. Listen, there are other guys in the Department giving free voice to what they think. Why the hell do you have to go around close-mouthed? You're a fool, Mac—a poor fool!"

Days swung by. Night life was at a stand-still. Petitions reached the Mayor day after day, imploring a sensible compromise. Some of these petitions were signed by men prominent in business and professional circles. But the Mayor was adamant. And by way of reply he closed five lunch-wagons suspected of traffic in liquor. He made his own laws.

Possessed suddenly of an idea that a certain dairy company was surreptitiously moving liquor in their trucks, he sent out a special squad of plainclothesmen had all the company's trucks stopped and searched and also their dairies. No liquor was found, but the milk trucks missed fast night trains, much milk went bad and a lot of money was lost. The company protested vigorously, but the Mayor was undaunted. Law suits were instituted against the city. Municipal spies were sent out and many private residences were searched. A little liquor was found, but it did not compensate for the hard feeling that was thereby aroused.

And MacBride, faithful to his badge, continued to carry out orders. One of the closed speakeasies had dared to open, and on express orders of the Mayor, MacBride was sent to close it. He went, alone, walked into the place and found six men drinking whiskey. Tony Morilla, the owner, stood stock-still, a cigarette between his lips. He was a hard case, but he had always called MacBride friend and during the last crime wave he had kept his hands clean and aided the police in the apprehension of a coked gunman.

"You know why I'm here, Tony," said MacBride.

"I got an idea, Mac."

"I told you to stay closed."

"I know."

"And here you're open."

They faced each other, silently. In Morilla's eyes smoldered dark fire. The cigarette was motionless between his lips.

MacBride jerked his shoulder. "Clean these men out."

Morilla turned to the men. "You'll have to go boys. Pay me some other time."

Muttering, the men went out.

"Now, Tony, you'll have to come along."

Morilla shrugged. "That a clean break, Mac?"

"No. Quietly, now, Tony."

Morilla's lips tightened. "All right."

An hour later Morilla was behind bars.

Next morning MacBride was called into the Mayor's office. Burkhart looked expansive. He grinned broadly and shook MacBride's hand with keen warmth.

"MacBride you're doing wonderful work," he said. "You haven't fallen down on a single job. You've done everything with a neatness I admire. Have a cigar."

MacBride took a cigar and lighted up. After the first puff he said "I've merely carried out orders."

"Merely!"

"And look here, Mr. Mayor. Take a tip from me: you're headed for a fall. This business can't go on."

"But, MacBride, look how successful we've been!"

"I'll give you one reason why. I know all those men I've jumped on. They gave in because they knew me, and now many of them are bitter against me. It was so sudden—no warning, no compromise—"

"Which is why we've been successful."

"Look farther. We're not successful, and I don't approve of your methods. You're paving the way for another reign of terror. You're making Richmond City fertile ground for criminal exploitation. Please take a little advice from a man who knows his business. I know mine. I've given twenty years of my life to it, and if I say it myself I've got a damned good reputation."

"Which is why I like you, MacBride," smiled the Mayor. "At first we had a little argument. I know how you feel. It's hard on you, telling old friends that they must close shop, but if you have the interest of the city and the Department at heart, you'll forget that. I need you, MacBride. You're the best man I have. Carry on and inside of a year I'll put you in plainclothes for good and"—his voice lowered, and his smile spread—"I'll make you an inspector!"

"It doesn't stir me. Put me back in uniform right now and plant me in my old Second Precinct. I'm a precinct man, Mr. Mayor. I could very well use an inspector's pay, but not at that price. And don't think I've carried on as I have through any thought of promotion."

"I know, MacBride. You're a modest man."

"No. I'm not modest—"

The Mayor chuckled. "MacBride, if I had more men like you—But no matter. Think things over. You are now attached to my personal staff."

"What!"

"My personal staff, MacBride. Now pardon me. I have another engagement in a few minutes. Good luck."

MacBride left, boiling. *Personal staff!* He had not anticipated this, did not want it. It meant that now he was closer to the Mayor than before, and that the Mayor would rely on his honesty to a greater degree. The news spread through the Department.

Captain Hamlin met MacBride next day and almost sneered. "I guess you're the Mayor's right hand man, Mac. And you were the guy who talked so big at that first meeting."

"Pipe down, Hamlin."

"I guess we all know how you stand now."

"Easy, Hamlin."

"Easy hell, Mac. What are you doing, getting ambitious too? Is there an inspector's job around the corner?"

MacBride's windy blue eyes cut Hamlin sharply. "You close your jaw, Hamlin, or I'll close it for you."

"Hurts, eh?"

MacBride's fist doubled. "Another crack out of you and I'll cave in your nose!"

Hamlin stared hard, but after a moment his eyes wavered. He forced a weak laugh, turned and moved off. MacBride continued on his way, banged into his office and brooded over his pipe.

He was the only man of that group who was elevated to the Mayor's personal staff, and the sudden coolness with which they treated him was clearly apparent. It hurt MacBride to have them think that he was cheek and jowl with Burkhart. They were fools, and perhaps they were a little envious too. But he believed that they despised him more than anything else. Hence he became more or less a lone wolf.

Kennedy, who was more discerning, chuckled and said, "Poor old Mac."

And MacBride barked, "Damn you, shut up!" But secretly he regretted the outburst, for Kennedy and he, though always bickering, understood each other perfectly. And Moriarity and Cohen showed no change toward him. They were good men, and they had on more occasions than one gone through gunsmoke and flame with the hard captain, and they knew his worth, his honesty, his rough courage.

At the end of six weeks the Mayor was still holding his own. He was always on the lookout for loopholes in what he termed his air-tight campaign. He closed two famous restaurants and another barber shop and he circulated a large amount of spies throughout the city. He ignored complaints, and presently finding time heavy on his hands, he passed an ordinance that made all restaurants and dancing casinos close at midnight sharp. Then he closed a popular burlesque house and banned presentation of three plays which he considered slightly off color. The *Post-*

Express screamed at this, because two of the plays had had successful runs in Boston.

MacBride came in late one morning and the clerk said, "Kennedy dropped by. He wants you to meet him for lunch at the Brown Coffee Pot."

The Brown Coffee Pot was only four blocks away, and at noon MacBride walked in. Kennedy was waiting for him and led the way to a table in the rear. The reporter was grinning. He rubbed his hands gingerly. He chuckled.

"Well, spill it," said MacBride.

"I knew it," said Kennedy. "I knew it."

"Knew what?"

"That it would happen."

MacBride leaned on his elbows. "Come on, Kennedy."

Kennedy laid down his cigarette. "Chick McTurk is in town."

"He's in Chicago."

"He's in Richmond City."

MacBride sat back. His eyes narrowed. "I gave McTurk his walking papers three years ago."

"But he's back again. And he's worth dough. I saw him hurrying through the railroad station. With him was Jazz Millio."

"Another rat!"

"Sure. And why do you suppose they're here? Why would Chick leave a normal racket in Chicago to come to Richmond City? Because there are good pickings here. The place is ripe for a guy like Chick. And ten to one all his gunmen are pouring into town, too. There's liquor here—gallons of it lying idle—and Chick is going to do a bit of hi-jacking. He always was a nervy hijacker, and at this time Richmond City certainly is meat for him."

"I told him never to show his face here again. I warned him, Kennedy. He's a damned trouble-maker, and that Millio would kill a guy for two cents."

Kennedy quickened his voice. "Look here, Mac. Lie low. Don't make a move. Burkhart has come to the end of his tether. He brought this on. Nobody else. It's not your fault—no one's but the Mayor's."

MacBride's eyes were narrowed. "I told McTurk not to come back. It's my game, too. He raised hell here three years ago. I could have sent him up, framed him, but I gave him a break. He promised never to come back. If he thinks he can kick me in the slats this way, he's dumb."

"Think, Mac. It's a glorious opportunity to show how futile the Mayor is, to show that his ideas of reform are rotten. It will crush him. For cripes' sake, stay out of it and show the guy up. Don't be a fool all your days, Mac."

MacBride flattened his lips. Kennedy was hard, but he was also in some measure right. Yet his plan soured in MacBride's mind.

"Kennedy, it's not square. I know Chick is here. I'd be a lousy bum to pretend ignorance and let hell bust loose."

"Nonsense, Mac! For the love o' God—"

MacBride shook his head. "No, Kennedy. I'm going to land on McTurk like a ton of brick."

IV

acBRIDE returned to Police Headquarters. There was something keenly purposeful about him. A new snap was in his movements. It was simple: he had something to do, something definite, something tangible against which to release his accrued vigor.

He breezed into his office and found Moriarity and Cohen waiting for him. Both were sound asleep, their feet on the desk. MacBride heaved the feet off.

"Snap out of it, boys."

They yawned awake.

"Quick!" clipped MacBride. "Wake up. Peel your ears and listen to this. Chick McTurk and a dago named Jazz Millio are in town. I want McTurk."

"Where is he?" asked Cohen.

"That's what we've got to find out. Kennedy saw him coming through the railroad station this morning. McTurk's here for a purpose. I'm going to railroad that baby out of town, and if he yaps I'll frame him."

Moriarity asked, "What did the Mayor say about it?"

"He doesn't know. And he's not going to know. He'll ball up the works. All this is between you and me, and don't breathe a word to anybody. If we let McTurk get a head start on us, he'll pitch the city into a new gang war, mark my words. He's a hi-jacker and he's here for big money. I'll give you copies of his handwriting. Fan the hotels. I'll do the same."

Moriarity and Cohen went out. MacBride started a fresh cigar and followed a few minutes later. On the way out he ran into Hamlin, and Hamlin said:

"You and your two little boy scouts seem to be doing a lot of running around."

"If you a did little more, Hamlin, you wouldn't be so fat," clipped MacBride.

He did not stop, but continued on, leaving Hamlin with a dark scowl. He visited six hotels that afternoon, and returned to Headquarters unsuccessful. Moriarity and Cohen came in a little later and shook their heads.

"We've got to find him," said MacBride, "at any cost. And we've got to find him in a hurry. Look everywhere. Pay a stoolie, I don't care what. If you find a guy you think knows something, make him talk—frame him—anything. We've got to nail McTurk before he starts the ball rolling."

"Right," said Cohen.

"Right," said Moriarity.

And they left with a business like air.

MacBride sat thinking, looking back, recalling incidents relative to his old case against Chick McTurk. It was a bit hazy. After a while he went out to the Bureau of Criminal Identification and began running through the files.

While he was doing this, Hamlin wandered in.

"Oh, you here, Mac?"

"See me, don't you?"

Hamlin chuckled. "What the hell are you and those two gumshoes up to?"

"Just a little diversion, Hamlin.'"

"Secret work for the Mayor, eh?"

"Hell, no!"

"I'd like to believe it."

"I'm not asking you to, Hamlin, and I don't care."

Hamlin sighed. "Tell me, Mac. What kind of work do you have to do to get on the personal staff?"

"Nothing."

"And to slip into a soft inspector's job?"

MacBride looked up from a metal file box. "Are you trying to crack wise, Hamlin?"

Hamlin laughed softly. "You're not kidding anybody, Mac."

MacBride started to say something, but shrugged, snorted. "Go 'way, Hamlin. You're a nuisance." He proceeded to ignore the man and continued looking through the files. Presently he drew out a card and read it. His lips tightened. He slipped the card back into place and replaced the file box.

Then he strode out, passing Hamlin as if the man did not exist. He went to his office, picked up his hat and left Headquarters. A block farther on he hailed a taxi and giving an address, jumped in.

He alighted before a small apartment house in a street that was otherwise flanked by old brownstones. He entered the lobby and instead of going to the desk, approached the elevator man.

"Miss Kelsey's apartment."

"You'll have to telephone up first," said the man.

"No I don't." McBride flashed his shield. "Up we go."

He entered the elevator and it slid up to the third floor, then stopped.

"Number thirty-two, chief," said the man.

"Thanks," nodded MacBride, and proceeded down the corridor.

He pressed the electric button at 32. He listened, received no answer. He pressed it again. Presently a woman's voice—"Who is it?"

"Telegram."

"Slip it under the door."

"It's collect."

There was a pause. Then the door opened on a crack. MacBride jammed his foot in the opening and then shoved. He muscled into a small ante-chamber.

"Hello, Clara," he grinned.

"What the hell do you want, MacBride?" The woman, a henna haired beauty, glared at him. "Is this nice, busting in this way?"

"No." MacBride strolled past her and into the salon. He looked around. "You alone, Clara?"

"Of course I'm alone," she snapped.

MacBride sighed and sat down. "Oh, I just thought Chick might be around."

"Chick! He ain't in town."

"No?"

"No."

"Hell, I thought he was. See you're dressed for dinner."

"What about it? Can't a girl dress for dinner? I'm going out. I'm in a hurry too, MacBride."

"I'm not. Sit down and take life easy. You look nervous, Clara."

She put her hands on her hips. "Say, I'll tell the world you got one hell of a nerve! You get out, MacBride!"

"Now, Clara, be a nice girl. I'm in no hurry. I was looking up old records and saw that you testified once in Chick's favor, four years ago. I just dropped around to say hello."

"Well, you've said it. Now get."

MacBride chuckled and settled back more comfortably into the chair. Clara raved on. She paced the floor. She stamped. She heaped abuse upon MacBride's head, but he answered with nothing more than an occasional chuckle.

Suddenly the telephone rang. She stopped short and caught her breath.

MacBride was on his feet. He muttered, "Don't answer it!"

Her eyes blazed. "A frame-up!"

"Don't answer it!"

"Damn you!" She turned and dived for the telephone.

MacBride caught her by the wrist, spun her from her feet, dropped her into a chair.

"You heard me, Clara!"

She panted hoarsely, her cheeks flaming, her lips quivering with inarticulate abuse.

The bell rang insistently. Clara stared at the instrument. MacBride watched her. He stood spread-legged, calm, determined. Silence. And then another series of rings.

Clara sprang to her feet, tense and desperate.

"Damn you, MacBride, let me at it!"

"Sit down."

"I won't! You're a dirty louse, that's what you are! You're a snake! I—I'd like to brain you."

"Shut up."

"I won't—"

He caught her again, clapped his hand over her mouth, held her firmly. "Now listen to me, sister. I've got work to do. Close your jaw."

She struggled, kicked, clawed. MacBride tightened his grip, stifled her curses.

A bell rang. It was the door bell.

Clara stiffened.

Still holding her, MacBride pulled his gun with his free hand and dragged her to the door. He turned the bolt. The door clicked open and he stepped back.

"Come right in, Chick," he said.

Chick McTurk gasped. He was a tall man, dark-skinned, black-eyed. He wore evening clothes. His fists clenched.

"In quick, Chick!" snapped MacBride. "Keep your hands clear or I'll drill you."

Chick came in, and MacBride kicked the door shut. Then he flung Clara away and covered both of them.

"Raise 'em, Chick" MacBride frisked

him and drew forth a small automatic. "Now sit down—both of you."

Chick dropped into a chair, sighed. "Well, MacBride, what the hell's the meaning of this?"

"I told you once, Chick, not to show your mug in Richmond City again."

"Well, I've shown it."

"And you're going to do an about face and fade away—you and that greaseball playmate of yours—Millio."

McTurk sneered. "Trying to run the town again, eh?"

"On my own, Chick. I guess I've just about nipped you in the bud. We won't talk here." Manacles clinked in his hand. "You and I will leave quietly, Chick. Get up."

McTurk got up. MacBride clicked one of the bracelets on his own wrist, the other on McTurk's. McTurk turned to Clara.

"Sit tight, Baby. This ain't going to last long. Mac's got a screw loose again."

"He's a big bum," said Clara.

"Better look for another meal ticket, sister," recommended MacBride.

He took McTurk out. He hailed a taxi and they climbed in. The street lights were just going on.

"You pulled a fast one, MacBride."

"I told you not to come back, Chick."

"Headquarters will seem like old times."

"But," said MacBride, "we're not going to Headquarters."

"I don't get you."

"Be patient."

Fifteen minutes later the taxi drew up in a dark, deserted street. MacBride hauled Chick out and they entered a dark hallway. He knocked on a door. A face appeared in the gloom.

MacBride said, "Charley, give me a room. I'll take the key here. You don't have to go up."

"Sure, Mac." A moment later the face reappeared. "Number twenty."

"Thanks."

MacBride took Chick up two flights of stairs to room twenty and opened the door. He found the light-switch and turned it. They were in a small, bare room, that contained nothing more than a chair, a bed and a washstand. MacBride removed the manacles from his wrist.

"What does this mean, Mac?"

"Your room for a while."

McTurk frowned. "You've got no right to pull this!"

"I'm taking the right," said Mac-Bride.

He manacled Chick to the bed post. McTurk snarled, "I'd like to know what the hell you're up to!"

"You'll find out, later. I'll see you get food and water."

McTurk cursed him as he went out. MacBride locked the door, went down the stairs and out into the street. A few blocks farther on he caught a cruising taxi.

When he walked into his office at Headquarters Moriarity and Cohen were there. They shook their heads.

Cohen said, "Not a trace, Cap."

" 'S all right," said MacBride. "I've got him."

They looked at him, grinned.

"Good old Mac," said Moriarity.

But MacBride was not smiling. He looked thoughtful.

"But it's only the beginning," he replied.

He sank into a chair, an abstracted look in his eyes.

"Ike," he said, "go over and hang around in front of Number 12 Murdock Street. Clara Kelsey lives there. You and Moriarity work shifts. Watch the place. Watch her. We want Millio."

"Okey, Cap."

"And, Ike. If you get him, take him to Charley's place. I've got McTurk bottled in room twenty. Take Millio there and then ring me." He added, "We've got to jump this game while it's hot."

Cohen left. MacBride and Moriarity went out for a bite to eat in the Brown Coffee Pot. Hamlin was there and he came over to join them.

"You guys sure seem to be working overtime," he said.

"What makes you think so?" asked MacBride.

"Hell, you're never in Headquarters. Let's in on it, Mac. What's up?"

MacBride grinned. "Remember, Hamlin, I'm on the personal staff."

"Mayor's little poodle dog, eh?"

"Sure," chuckled MacBride. "What's the matter, you sore?"

"Kind of, Mac. But we all are—when a guy plays poodle dog to his boss. Here's hoping you get that promotion."

"Here's hoping I paste you on the jaw some day."

Hamlin moved off, and MacBride said to Moriarity, "That guy's just dumb enough to get in my way. If he balls up my parade, I'll put him in the city hospital. You relieve Ike at midnight."

"Yeah."

They went back to Headquarters and to pass the time away, played two-handed pinochle. At eleven the phone rang and Moriarity grabbed it. He listened and then shoved it across the desk.

"Ike, Cap."

MacBride clamped the receiver to his ear. "Shoot, Ike. . . Eh, what's that . . . *Good!* Be right over."

He slammed down the receiver, said, "Ike's got Millio."

"Cripes" grinned Moriarity. "Where's my hat?" He leaped up.

MacBride had his and was already on the way out. Moriarity bounded after him and they caught a taxi in the street below.

"What luck!" chuckled Moriarity.

"But it's only the beginning. It all depends on—"

"On what?"

"On tomorrow."

A little later they walked into Charley's place and went up the dark staircase two steps at a time. MacBride had his key out. He poked it in the key-hole, but Cohen opened the door and grinned. MacBride pushed in, and Moriarity closed the door.

Millio was sitting on a chair. There was a black-and-blue welt on his face and dark murder in his eyes. He was small, dapper, deadly-looking.

"Tried to get wise," explained Cohen. "Tried to pull his smoke and I slammed him."

"Yeah, you lousy Jew!" snarled Millio.

"Pipe down you spaghetti-bending pup," clipped Cohen.

"I'll pipe down hell—"

MacBride barked, "You'll pipe down. —D' you frisk him, Ike?"

"No."

MacBride stepped forward and went through Millio's pockets. He produced a wallet, letters, various papers, threw them on the wash-stand. Then he examined them. Finally he opened one sheet of paper, scanned it, tightened his lips.

"Look at this, boys!"

Cohen and Moriarity looked. They saw a typewritten list of addresses:

46 Jockey St., Cellar, 30 Cases Scotch
20 River Road, 2nd Floor, 40 Cases Scotch
6 Bell Street, Cellar, 50 Cases Gin
38 Western Road, Barn, 150 Cases Gin
92 Farmingville Tpke., Barn, 200 Cases Scotch
88 Old Stone Road, Cellar, 210 Cases Gin
11 Princess Street, 3rd Floor, 90 Cases Rye
75 Starlight Blvd., House, 400 Cases Scotch
9 MacAllister Alley, Cellar, 350 Barrels Wine
25 Rock Street, Cellar, 380 Barrels Wine

"Cripes!" muttered Moriarity.

MacBride said, "Eleven hundred and seventy cases of booze, and seven hundred and thirty barrels of ink. What a haul—if they get it." He turned to Millio. "Where'd you get this list, wop?"

"Try and find out."

MacBride folded the sheet of paper and tucked it away in his pocket. "You'll warm your slats here for a while, Millio, same as your boy friend."

He manacled Millio to the other end of the bed. Then he left with Moriarity and Cohen. And as they walked down the street, Cohen said:

"But how the hell did he get that list?"

"I don't know," said MacBride.

"What next?" asked Moriarity.

"I have an appointment with the Mayor—tomorrow."

V

T ten o'clock next morning MacBride walked into the Mayor's office. Burkhart sat behind his desk smoking a Corona and looking pleased with himself.

"Well, MacBride, I guess my campaign is working out smoothly, eh? City is quiet as a tomb. Have a seat."

MacBride sat down. "Don't you believe it," he said.

"What's the matter?"

"Richmond City is primed for another gang war."

"Oh, nonsense!"

MacBride shook his head. "I know. I've been poking around, and I'm in a position to forestall it."

The Mayor leaned forward. "Why haven't I known about this before?"

"It wasn't necessary. I'm going to dicker with you, Mr. Mayor."

"Dicker with me! How dare you propose such a thing? Remember, you are in the employ of the city, bound by duty to have its interest at heart."

"Just that. I have its interest at heart, and that's why I'm here to dicker."

"I detest that word. I refuse to dicker."

"Call it compromise."

"I refuse to compromise." Burkhart's

lips thinned against his teeth, and his chin went up. "I am serving the people."

"So am I, and dammit, you've got to listen to me. I don't give a rap if you are the Mayor. I'm here to strike a bargain. You don't know, evidently, that at present there's a gang in Richmond City—from Chicago. A gang of hi-jackers headed by two notorious gunmen. This gang is here to take advantage of the conditions that prevail. They're here to raid.

"I ask you to open every place that you've closed, because there are places open now, I'm sure—places we know nothing about. The barbers' union is rising against you, because you've put barbers out of work. That milk company will beat you in the damage suit. The league of restaurant owners is fighting the midnight closing order, and they have the citizens behind them. Lift the ban and I'll meet you half-way. I'll nip this gang war in the bud. I'll railroad the leaders out of Richmond City."

"But first you must get the leaders."

"I have got them!"

"I heard nothing about it."

"I have them in a hide-out of my own—two of them—the leaders."

Burkhart stood up. His eyes narrowed. "And you told me nothing about it. This is treason, MacBride! I won't have it! I shan't bargain with you. You are self-seeking!"

"God Almighty!" exploded McBride.

"You worked on your own. You excluded me, when I made you an attaché on my personal staff and promised you the position of inspector."

"I didn't ask for the personal staff— didn't want it! And I don't want an inspector's job. I'll refuse it if you offer it to me."

"Don't worry, I shan't offer it to you!" clipped the Mayor. "What's more, I demand the information that you possess regarding this new gang."

MacBride was on his feet, too. "At my price!"

"There is no such thing as price!"

"There is! I have the city's interest at heart. Put me back in my old precinct when it's over. I don't want any return. I've given my life to this job, and I hold the whip-hand. If you fall down on me, the city will be thrown into a reign of blood and you'll be the laughing-stock of the country. You are now—"

"Careful, MacBride!"

"Careful hell! I was never known to be careful and I'm not starting now. Open these places. Lift the ban. Stop making a fool of yourself, and I'll stop this impending trouble!"

Burkhart wiped his lips. He had paled. "I demand that you place your two prisoners in the hands of the Commissioner so that I may deal with them according to law."

"This gang is big, I tell you. Chuck those guys in jail and their gang will bust loose on general principles."

"We have a police department, MacBride."

"Yes, and if this war breaks we'll have a large funeral list and many non-combatants will be killed. I'm trying to prevent blood-shed. Can't you see?"

He was trying hard to put over his point. Sincerity was in his eyes, in his voice, in every gesture. Sweat gleamed on his face. He was a man fighting alone, fighting against the will of a mad zealot.

Burkhart stood motionless. The light, flashing on his spectacles, hid his eyes.

"MacBride, I am a man for the law as it is written. Produce those two men and let the responsibility rest on my shoulders."

MacBride groaned. His fists knotted. He shook them. "Will you go in the streets and fight this gang? Will you pack a gun and meet cars armed with machine-guns and bombs? No. The cops do it, and when they're dead they get medals and nice funerals and flowers and they're called heroes. Bah! I'll bargain with you. You've got to meet my terms if you call yourself a sane man. You can't go on running this town like a maniac! I refuse to produce those men until you meet me half-way."

"And I refuse," said the Mayor. "I'll strip you of your shield. I'll throw you in jail."

"You try it. Throw me in jail, and within two days Richmond City will be a bloody field!"

"We'll see." The Mayor smoothed down his coat. "I'll call my sergeant in and have him put you behind bars."

"Call him in!" snapped MacBride. "You can't buffalo me!"

The Mayor leaned forward to press a button. MacBride jumped and caught his hand. "Let that go!" he snapped.

"Let go of my hand!" gritted the Mayor.

MacBride looked up, muttered, flung the Mayor away. He pivoted and jumped for the door, flung it open and dashed out. In a minute he was in the street. At the next corner he jumped into a taxi, dropped to the seat, breathless. The blood was pounding in his temples, and anger boiled in his heart. The cab rolled on. MacBride drew forth the typewritten list he had taken from Millio. He studied it. His lips pursed and he muttered an oath.

The car ground to a stop and Mac-Bride leaped out, paid the fare and entered Charley's place. He raced up the stairs, the key already in his hands. But as he bumped against the door it swung open and he almost fell in. Then he stopped short.

McTurk and Millio were gone. The revelation staggered him. He cursed bitterly. There would be no way possible for him to prove to the Mayor that, by way of vengeance, he had not let these men go. Even now, no doubt, the Mayor had issued an order to apprehend him.

He hurried downstairs and burst in upon Charley.

"Who went in that room, Charley?"

"Huh? Nobody, so far as I know."

MacBride crashed fist into palm. "Those birds got away!"

He left Charley standing open-mouthed, and rocked out into the street. He strode along in a daze. The world seemed to be crashing down about him. He stopped in at a small lunch-room and ordered coffee. He tried to formulate some plan. That gang war would break now—no doubt about it—and the Mayor would be in a position to send him up for ten years.

Desperate—he had a wife and a daughter out in Grove Manor—he swung out of the lunch-room. He was more the lone-wolf than ever. He looked at the list of addresses again. He was near 46 Jockey Street, and hurried to that address. It was a three-story building, and when he rang the bell a man opened the door. MacBride pushed his way in.

"I want to talk with you," he said. "Now don't get scared. You've got some Scotch downstairs. Get in touch with your boss and tell him to remove it. There are a lot of hi-jackers in town and this place is booked for a raid."

"How do you know?"

"Never mind. Do what I tell you, and then clear out. I don't care where you put it, but get it out of this cellar."

"Cripes."

MacBride left and walked around to 20 River Road. He delivered a similar message there and then hurried on to the next address. There was no time to waste. He had to hurry. At five o'clock he walked in on George Clark, owner of The Palm Club.

"Listen, George," he said. "You've got two hundred cases on Farmingville Turnpike, haven't you?"

Clark was suspicious. "You on the prod again, Mac?"

"No. Take a tip. Chick McTurk and his hi-jackers are in town. Your hide-out is known. Shift that stuff, George. Do it quick, and leave nobody out there after you've moved."

"Is this straight goods, Mac?"

"Have I ever framed you, George?"

"No."

"Then snap on it. I'm trying my

damnedest to prevent a gang war."

He left Clark and hastened to the next address. In all cases he was brief and to the point, and since many of the men knew him, they did not doubt his word. By ten o'clock he had covered all the addresses. It was the only thing he could have done, and he thanked his stars that those men believed in him sufficiently to count his word as gold.

And then he proceeded to disappear into the dark heart of the city. He called his wife from a telephone booth and said that he would not be home, and that if she should not hear from him in a couple of days, not to worry. She pressed him for details, but he reassured her that everything was all right and then hung up.

He slept that night in a Greek boarding house near the river. He stayed in all of next day, and went out when night had fallen. He bought a newspaper and was relieved to find that nothing unusual had happened. Another night passed, and another day, and still MacBride trod the ways of a hunted man.

He was on his way back to the Greek rooming-house that night when a taxi skidded to a stop and a man jumped out. MacBride whirled, ready to fight, when he recognized Kennedy. Kennedy gripped his hand.

"Mac!"

"Well, Kennedy?"

"What the hell happened?"

"How should I know?"

"Headquarters is looking for you. Hamlin has been detailed to run you down—"

"That rat!"

"But what happened? Why should you be hunted?"

"You'll find out soon enough, Kennedy."

"There's something queer somewhere. Some house-breaking went on last night. A place on Jockey Street, one on River Road, a farmhouse out on Starlight Boulevard. Are you mixed up in that?"

MacBride grinned. "Of course, not."

"Give me a break, Mac. Tell me."

"I've told you."

"I mean, the truth. Look here, Mac. I wised you that Chick was in town. I told no one else."

MacBride gripped Kennedy's shoulder. "Kennedy, we're old timers. I've never put one over on you yet. When there was news to tell, I gave you first crack at it. But there were times when I held news back till the last. This is one of those times."

"Hell, Mac, if you weren't so damned honest you'd get somewhere. You always insist on fighting a crowd—"

MacBride chuckled. "Forget it, you news-hound. Omit the bouquets. I'm running along. G'-night."

He grabbed Kennedy's hand, shook it and strode off. He knew that Kennedy would say nothing in regard to their having met. He turned into the next block, walking rapidly, his heels re-echoing in the deserted street. It was a strange sensation to be hunted, after having hunted men for twenty years.

Another day swung by, and when MacBride went forth into another night he was satisfied to know that the papers carried no startling headlines. He even glowed a trifle, for it was obvious that his plan had worked, and there was some little reward in knowing that he had succeeded even while being hunted. He had remained loyal to the tradition which he had built around himself. He had defied the highest city authority for an ideal of his own, and thus far that ideal was not in vain.

He ate at a lunch-room near the docks, sitting back in the corner, watching the door. It was raining, and the rain hammered against the windows. Men rocked in, their rubber coats swishing, gleaming wet. Plates banged. A big nickel percolator whistled. The cash register jangled.

His meal finished, MacBride put on his hat, turned up his coat collar and went out. A man stepped in front of him.

"All right, MacBride. I've been waiting."

Drops of rain trickled from the turned-down brim of Hamlin's hat. A street light played on his wet chin. His hands were in his slicker pockets, and one pocket bulged.

"Took you long enough to find me," said MacBride.

Hamlin smirked. "No matter. I've got you. You're in for it, Mac."

"Makes you feel big, pinching me—doesn't it?"

"Not at all. Duty."

"Personal vanity, Hamlin. You don't know the meaning of duty."

"Let's get along."

Hamlin flagged a taxi and they climbed in. MacBride leaned back in the seat and puffed on his cigar. The red end glowed with each inhalation, revealing his grim, sardonic mouth; flickered in his eyes. The taxi rolled off, its tires swishing on the wet pavement.

"You may get ten years," said Hamlin.

"Don't let it worry you."

"It's not."

"Then shut up."

They rode on in silence. The taxi turned into a dark side street, narrow and deserted, walled in by black faced houses. It cruised leisurely. Suddenly another car thundered alongside, cut sharply in front. With an oath the taxi driver tugged on his wheel, jammed his brakes and screeched to a stop halfway across the sidewalk.

"What the hell!" clipped MacBride.

Hamlin shoved his hand into his pocket.

Even as he did so the door of the cab was yanked open, and a voice snapped, "Easy, you guys!"

A gun glinted.

Other men piled out of the touring car—four of them—and closed in around the taxi. Hat-brims were flapped down low over their eyes.

One said, "Out, you—lively!"

Hamlin started to say, Cripes, Mac—"

But MacBride climbed out. The sit-uation possessed some measure of irony. Hamlin fumbled out of the taxi and someone ripped his hand from his coat pocket. Hamlin half-spun, in anger.

"I got your gun, Hamlin," said the man.

Three men gripped MacBride, and a fourth took his gun also. MacBride grinned his hard, tight grin.

"What's the joke?" he said.

"D' you see a joke?" The voice was harsh, brittle.

"Millio," drawled MacBride, and added, "Yeah, you." And then he chuckled.

"You'll laugh the other way any minute," grated Millio.

"Lay off," came another voice. "Snap on it, guys!"

"Oh, you Chick," said MacBride. "All here, eh? All you nice little boy scouts."

A cigarette end glowed under McTurk's nose.

The men rough-housed MacBride and Hamlin into the touring car. Millio paused with his foot on the running-board and looked back.

He mused aloud, "That taxi guy. . . ."

McTurk said, "Well?"

Millio reached into the car, drew out a long-barreled pistol to which was attached a silencer.

"Hey, you!" barked MacBride.

Hamlin sat quite still, pale, breath bated.

Crash!

It was not the gun that made that noise. It was the wind-shield on the taxi. The driver fell sideways.

"Didn't have to bust the glass," observed McTurk.

Millio chuckled and climbed into the touring car.

MacBride was straining at the three men that held him. "You—lousy—pups!"

The roar of the exhaust, the crashing of gears, drowned his protest. The car slewed back into the street and hissed on through the rain. The curtains were closed. Millio and McTurk and the chauffeur sat in front. MacBride and Hamlin and the others were jammed in the rear.

"Tough on you, Hamlin," said MacBride.

Hamlin had been so cocky when he collared MacBride. He was not so now. His lips seemed to have been sealed. He sat in stony silence, like a man petrified.

The car sped on. MacBride could not tell what course they were following because of the curtains. He was mystified. Why did they want him now? He supposed that eventually they woud kill him. But something else first. If it were just a matter of killing, they could have done that in the street. But why drag in Hamlin?

Smoother going, with fewer stops, indicated that they were well out of traffic. But soon there were many turns, much shifting of gears. Then presently the car rolled to a stop. Millio jumped out and pulled open the rear door. MacBride and Hamlin were jostled out into a narrow, deserted street in the darker depths of the city.

They were rushed across the sidewalk and into a black hallway. One of the men snapped on a pocket-flash. The others followed in and the door was closed. The man with the light moved toward a staircase and went up backwards, throwing the light down upon the others.

At the first landing he waited. McTurk took a key from his pocket and opened a door, reached in and pressed a light button. Light flooded the room. MacBride and Hamlin were pushed in.

McTurk said, "Come in, Millio. You other guys wait in the other room, and don't get tight."

Millio entered, closed the door, bolted it. He covered MacBride and Hamlin while McTurk took off his hat and slicker.

"All right, Jazz," he said, fingering his gun gingerly.

Millio shrugged out of his wet clothes and lit a cigarette.

"You guys park," clipped McTurk.

Hamlin and MacBride sat down. Millio took another chair and sat with his gun lying across his knee. McTurk remained on his feet, spread-legged, a drawn and deadly gray look on his face. Millio hummed to himself.

"Can it!" muttered McTurk.

Millio shrugged and puffed his cigarette in silence.

Hamlin sat quite rigid, his arms straight, his hands braced on his knees. He stared at the floor with an abstracted look. Neither fear nor thought nor challenge shone in those eyes. He seemed dazed. His face looked like an inaminate mask of dough.

MacBride looked quizzical. His eyes were narrowed, alert; thin chips of living steel. He was primed for anything; his brain tense but his body at ease.

"Somebody's got to come clean," said McTurk.

"What I say," supplemented Millio.

"Pipe down," recommended McTurk. "I'll say what's to be said."

Millio smiled and conceded the floor to his companion.

McTurk went on, "I want to know where that booze is. One of you palookas know."

"Not me," said MacBride. "And I'm sure Hamlin doesn't."

Hamlin pursed his lips.

McTurk clipped, "Come on, Hamlin!"

"I—don't—know."

"You don't know!" snarled McTurk.

"Ha!" chimed in Millio.

McTurk shot him a lacerating glance. Millio looked innocently at his cigarette.

"Of course he doesn't know," said MacBride.

McTurk's jaw squared. "Hamlin, don't you know?" His voice was barbed.

"No," murmured Hamlin.

"You slob!" McTurk's hand tightened on his gun, "I paid you two thousand bucks for a tip! And what kind of a tip did you give me? Tell me that!"

MacBride's scalp contracted. He looked at Hamlin. The man was wilting. His breath, long held, was pumping through lips that fluttered.

"Spill it, Hamlin!" barked McTurk. "Come across! You k n o w , you bum."

"No—no," choked Hamlin. "I don't." It seemed as if he wanted to look at MacBride, but fear, shame held his eyes to the floor.

Millio stood up, fingering his gun. He eyed McTurk, a twisted spectre of a smile drawing at his lips.

"Hamlin—" McTurk stepped forward. He stood before Hamlin, tight, murderous lines on his face, his body taut. "Hamlin, you double-crossed me! I paid you two thousand in cold cash for certain addresses. I went to those addresses and every joint was dry as a Baptist church. Now where the holy hell do you think you get off?"

Hamlin squirmed. He looked at the door. He seemed to be choking and gasping for air.

"I didn't—double-cross you," he muttered. "Something went—wrong."

MacBride's lips were flat against his teeth. Vertical lines were on his cheek, and muscle lumps bulged at either side of his jaw.

McTurk said, "You get the works, Hamlin." He spun on Millio. "Jazz, get the iron with the silencer."

Millio grinned. "Betcha, Chick!"

Hamlin's eyes bulged with fear. He held his throat.

MacBride clipped, "Hold on, Chick. Hamlin didn't double-cross you. Nobody did."

"What do you know about it?" snarled McTurk.

"Lots. You let Hamlin go and I'll tell you something. I'll tell you what happened to the booze."

"Let him go so he can come back with a gang of cops—"

"Chick," smiled MacBride, shaking his head, "you know he won't came back."

Hamlin bowed his head. In that

sentence MacBride had literally called him a coward.

"You mean it?" bit off McTurk.

"I'll tell you what happened to the booze," nodded MacBride.

McTurk backed up. "Hamlin, beat it, and forget you ever came here." As a final derisive gesture he returned Hamlin's gun.

Hamlin heaved up. He swayed, stared at MacBride, his mouth working. He extended his hand.

"Mac—"

MacBride smiled at the hand. "Hang it up, Hamlin. Breeze."

Hamlin sagged out, groaning.

MacBride chuckled. "Well, Chick, I'll tell you what happened to it. It was removed. Know why? Because I went around and tipped off all the addresses that they might be raided."

"Yeah? Go on. Where is it now?"

"Dunno," shrugged MacBride.

"What!"

"I told you what happened to it, didn't I?" droned MacBride.

McTurk's lip curled. "So that's your trick, eh? Clever guy, eh? Well, you bum, *you'll* get the works! Millio, go out and get the smoke. We can't afford any noise."

Millio needed no urging. The door banged behind him.

MacBride stood up. His jaw was squared. "You're a fool, Chick. You'll hang for this."

"Stay back," snapped McTurk.

MacBride grinned and moved closer. "There's a cop on beat somewhere near, eh? That's why you're afraid of noise."

"Stay back!"

Unexpectedly MacBride dived for him, a quick, elastic leap. McTurk dodged, holding his fire.

"By cripes, I'll blow—"

MacBride grabbed his arm, twisted it.

"Shoot, Chick!" he snapped.

He rushed McTurk across the room. They stopped at the window. MacBride caught a fleeting glimpse of two patrolmen talking beneath a street light. He crashed the window.

"Damn you!" snarled McTurk.

In desperation he fired. The bullet tore through MacBride's coat. There was a sharp sting in his side. He plastered McTurk against the wall, sank a fist in his face. The gun went off again, as MacBride ripped it from Mc-Turk's hand.

McTurk broke loose, lunged for the door.

"Stop, Chick!" barked MacBride.

The door whipped open and Millio broke in. His breath hissed. His gun belched. The bullet grazed McTurk and slammed into the wall. MacBride crouched. His gun burst into flame and Millio bent over. He fell forward. McTurk tried to grasp the gun as it fell. He got it as it hit the floor.

"Chick—don't!" called MacBride.

McTurk fell and twisted as he fell. He fired twice, and the shots went wild. Somebody fired from the hall and put a hole in MacBride's hat. But the hat stayed on, and MacBride cut loose. One shot hit McTurk as he was rising. He fell down again, screaming, and Mac-Bride put another shot through the doorway.

Somewhere a whistle blew.

MacBride shot out the light.

Feet pounded in the hallway. Blood was soaking MacBride's shirt. He felt dizzy. Pain ripped from his side up to his shoulder. The running feet sounded farther away. He groped for the door, reached down and felt the bodies of Millio and McTurk. In McTurk's pocket he found a flashlight. Somewhere in the farther regions of the house he heard doors banging. The gang was clearing out.

Below, nightsticks were banging on the front door. MacBride found the stairway. He dared to snap on his flash. He went down the steps, sagging. As he neared the bottom a face appeared in the white beam—a hand—a gun.

"It's me, Hamlin," said MacBride. "Careful."

Hamlin's face looked like a death mask.

"Me—MacBride, Hamlin. Open the hall door. Can't you hear the cops?—"

Bang!

MacBride fell against the banister. He cursed bitterly. Damn Hamlin! Another shot cracked. The bullet whistled by.

"Me, Hamlin! MacBride, you—"

Bang!

MacBride groaned, tumbled down the stairway. His flashlight fell from his hand, clattered down ahead of him. It stopped near the bottom, and it's beam again shone on the white, deadly face of Hamlin.

Hamlin fired at the light, smashed it.

MacBride, sliding down on his back, fired at the gun flash, the last shot in the gun.

Hamlin screamed.

MacBride fell to the bottom. He tried to stand up. He swayed, reeled, fell heavily—fell across Hamlin, who was lying on the floor, whimpering.

WHEN MacBride came to he was in a hospital bed, and the first thing he saw was his right arm swathed in bandages. Then he knew that his face was bandaged, and that his side was stiff. He felt like cursing.

"How are you, Mac?"

MacBride's eyes shifted. He saw Collins. Standing beside Collins was the Mayor. Burkhart looked haggard. On the other side of the bed was a doctor.

Burkhart leaned forward. "How do you feel, MacBride?"

"Lousy," said MacBride.

"You've been unconscious for twenty hours," said Collins.

"Hell, I must have missed a lot," muttered MacBride.

Burkhart said, "Your wife is in another room, sleeping. She practically collapsed, but is all right now, though the doctor suggests keeping her there. Your daughter is attending her."

Collins leaned over the bed, holding

a newspaper. "Can you read that, Mac?"
MacBride squinted.

Captain Stephen J. MacBride, attached to Police Headquarters, is again in the limelight. Last night he affected the capture, single-handed, of Chick McTurk, notorious hi-jacker, and Jazz Millio, Chicago gunman. He killed Millio and wounded McTurk. McTurk died five hours later in the City Hospital, leaving behind a confession which incriminates Captain Peter Hamlin, also attached to Headquarters.

According to the confession, Hamlin supplied McTurk with a list of addresses at which various quantities of liquor were stored. For this information McTurk paid Hamlin two thousand dollars.

The confession goes on to say that McTurk and Millio, who had been hidden in a rooming-house by Captain MacBride, were released secretly by Captain Hamlin who apparently had trailed MacBride there.

The confession continues with the assertion that when McTurk and his men raided the addresses given by Hamlin, no liquor was found and no opposition met with. McTurk, assuming that he had been double-crossed by Hamlin, sought vengeance. Quite by accident he saw Hamlin and MacBride enter a taxi on River Road. He and Millio, in a touring car with several other gangsters, followed and captured MacBride and Hamlin in Hector Street. McTurk declared that Millio shot the taxi driver with a silenced pistol, after which they took MacBride and Hamlin to a hide-out in Race Alley, intending to kill two birds with the proverbial single stone.

At this point the confession becomes jerky, due to McTurk's failing breath. He writes that Hamlin said the liquor had been at the addresses, but that something must have gone wrong subsequently. He then goes on to say that MacBride spoke up, declaring he knew what had happened

to it, and demanding Hamlin's release for such knowledge. McTurk let Hamlin go.

Further details must be got from MacBride and Hamlin, since McTurk died at that point in the confession. Both MacBride and Hamlin are recovering from gunshot wounds at the City Hospital.

There can be little doubt in the minds of disinterested, sane observers that this action of MacBride forestalled the inception of another of the bloody gang wars which were common in Richmond City not so long ago.

MacBride nodded and Collins stepped back.

Collins said, "What perplexes us, Mac, is why Hamlin was still in the building when McTurk claims to have released him. He was shot in the right hip. The cops found you and Hamlin lying together at the foot of the stairway. And about this liquor, too."

MacBride was staring abstractedly into space. "About the booze, I tipped off the owners that a raid was in the making. They simply removed it from those addresses. About Hamlin——" He paused. "Well, it looks pretty bad for Hamlin, doesn't it?"

"About ten years," nodded Collins.

"H'm," mused MacBride. "Well, I don't know why he was still in the house. I guess maybe he wanted to try getting me out. Too bad he was wounded. There was—some—mean shooting in the hallway."

Inwardly MacBride cursed himself for giving Hamlin such a clean break. He knew—oh, he knew!—that Hamlin had tried to kill him, to seal his lips. Well, anyhow, Hamlin had ten years of bars ahead of him. That would break him. Disgrace. . . .

The Mayor was saying, "MacBride, it has been a nightmare to me." He turned and asked Collins and the doctor to leave the room. When they had gone he went on, in a low voice, "I've been a fool, MacBride."

"You have," nodded MacBride.

"Yes, I have. And I need you more than ever, now. I want your advice on several things—particularly about revising—"

"Are you talking of compromise, Mr. Mayor?"

Burkhart bit his lip. "Yes, I am."

"Then here's my price. When I'm better, put me back in my old precinct—the Second."

"But, MacBride, an inspector's job—"

"Don't want it. I hate Headquarters. You're a good guy, Mr. Mayor, even though you've been a fool. We both stand for law and order, only you had a cock-eyed notion of what law and order means. I'm with you to the last ditch, if you'll meet me half-way."

"I'll meet you half-way."

"That's all I ask—that and my old job in the precinct."

Burkhart smiled. "MacBride, you're white. You're not bitter."

"The hell I'm not. When I get better I'm going to punch Hamlin's nose all over his face!"

Burkhart reached down and gripped MacBride's hand.

"When you do, Mac, let me know, so I can watch you."

The Pets

By HENRY WALLACE PHILLIPS

A common cause brings sworn enemies together.

ON QUINN, Wind-River Smith, and me were putting up hay at the lake beds. It was a God-forsaken, lonesome job, to say the best of it, and we took to collecting pets, to make it seem a little more like home.

Lon shot a hawk, breaking its wing. That was the first in the collection. He was a lovely pet. When you gave him a piece of meat he said "Cree," and clawed chunks out of you, but most of the time he sat in the corner with his chin on his chest, like a broken-down lawyer. We didn't get the affection we needed out of him. Well, then Wind-River found a bull-snake asleep and lugged him home, hanging over his shoulder. We sewed a flannel collar on the snake and picketed him out until he got used to the place. And around and around and around squirmed that snake until we near got sick at our stummicks watching him. All day long, turning and turning and turning and turning.

"Darn it," says I, "I like more variety." So that day, when I was cutting close to a timbered slew, out pops an old bob-cat and starts to open my shirt to see if I am her long-lost brother. By the time I got her strangled I had parted with most of my complexion. Served me right for being without a gun. The team run away as soon as I fell off the seat and I was booked to walk home. I heard a squeal from the bushes, and here comes a funny little cuss. I liked the look of him from the jump-off, even if his mother did claw delirious delight out of me. He balanced himself on his stubby legs and looked me square in the eye, and he spit and fought as

85

though he weighed a ton when I picked him up—never had any notion of running away. Well, that was Robert—long for Bob.

The style that cat spread on in the matter of growing was simply astonishing; he grew so's you could notice it overnight. At the end of two months he was that big he couldn't stand up under our sheet-iron cook-stove, and this was about the beginning of our family troubles. Tommy, the snake, was a good deal of a nuisance from the time he settled down. You'd have a horrible dream in the night—be way down under something or other, gasping for wind, and, waking up, find Tommy nicely coiled on your chest. Then you'd slap Tommy on the floor like a section of large rubber hose. But he bore no malice. Soon's you got asleep he'd be right back again. When the weather got cool he was always under foot. He'd roll beneath you and land you on your scalp-lock, or you'd ketch your toe on him and get a dirty drop. I don't think I ever laughed more in my life than one day when Lon came in with an armful of wood, tripped on Tommy, and come down with a clatter right where Judge Jenkins, the hawk, could reach him. The Judge fastened one claw in Billy's hair and scratched his whiskers with the other. Gee! The hair and feathers flew! Lon had a hot temper and he went for the hawk like it was a man. The first thing he laid his hand on was Tommy, so he used the poor snake for a club. Wind-River and me were so weak from laughing that we near lost two pets before we got strength to interfere.

But, as I was saying, the cold nights played Keno with our happy home. Neither Tommy nor Bob dared monkey with the Judge—he was the only thing on top of the earth the cat was afraid of. Bob used to be very anxious to sneak a hunk of meat from His Honor at times, yet, when the Judge stood on one foot, cocked his head sideways, snapped his bill and said "Cree," Robert reconsidered. On the other hand, Tommy and Bob were forever scrapping. Lively settos, I want to tell you. The snake butted with his head like a young streak of lightning. I've seen him knock the cat ten foot. And while a cat doesn't grow mouldy in the process of making a move, yet the snake is there about one seventeen - hundredth - millioneth part of a second sooner. And that's a good deal where those parties are concerned. Now, on cold nights, they both liked to get under the stove, where it was warm, and there wasn't room for more'n one. Hence, trouble; serious trouble. Bob hunted coyotes on moonlight nights. We threw scraps around the corner of the house to bait 'em, and Bob would watch there hour on end until one got within range. It was a dead coyote in ten seconds by the watch, if the jump landed. If it didn't Bob had learned there was no use wasting his young strength trying to ketch him. He used to sit still and gaze after them flying streaks of hair and bones as though he was thinking "I wisht somebody'd telegraph that son-of-a-gun for me."

Well, then he'd be chilly and reckon he'd climb under the stove. But Thomas 'ud be there.

"H-h-h-h-hhhh!" says Tom, in a whisper.

"Er-raow-pht!" says Robert. "Mmm-mmmmmm-errrrr-pht!" And so on for some time, the talk growing louder, then, with a yell that would stand up every hair on your head, Bob 'ud hop him. Over goes the cook-stove. Away rolls the hot coals on the floor. Down comes the stove-pipe and the frying-pans and the rest of the truck, whilst the old Judge in the corner hollered decisions, heart-broke because he was tied by the leg and couldn't get a claw into the dispute.

By the time we had 'em separated—Bob headed up in his barrel and Tom tied up in his sack—put the fire out, and fixed things generally, there wasn't a great deal left of that night's rest.

But children will be children. We swore awful still we wouldn't have missed their company for a fair-sized farm.

And now comes in the first little twist of the Big Bend Ranch, proper — all these things I'm telling you were the eggs. Here's where the critter pipped.

'Twas November, and such a November as you don't get outside of Old Dakota, a regular mint-julep of a month, with a dash of summer, a sprig of spring, a touch of fall, and sniff or two of winter to liven you up. If you'd formed a committee to furnish weather for a month, and they'd turned out a month like that, not even their best friends would have kicked. And here we'd been makin' hay, and makin' hay, the ranch people thanking Providence that prairie grass cures on the stem, while we cussed, for we were sick of the sight of hay. I got so the rattle of a mower give me hysterics. We were picked because we were steady and reliable, but one day, we bunched the job. Says I, "Here: we've cut grass for four solid months, includin' Sundays and legal holidays, although the Lord knows where they come in, for I haven't the least suspicion what day of the month it may be, but anyhow, let's knock off one round!"

So we did. I sat outside in the afternoon, while the other two boys and the rest of the family took a snooze. Here comes a man across the south flat a-horseback.

I watched him, much interested: first place, he was the first strange human animal we'd laid eye on for six weeks; next place, his style of riding attracted attention. I thought at the time he must have invented it, him being the kind of a man that hated horses, and wanted to keep as far away from them as possible, yet forced by circumstances to climb upon their backs.

His mount was a big American horse, full sixteen hand high, trotting in twenty-foot jumps. If I had anything against a person, just short of killing, I'd tie him on the back of a horse trotting like that. It's a great gait to sit out. Howsomever, this man didn't sit it out; what he wanted of a saddle beyond the stirrups was a mystery, for he never touched it. He stood up on his stirrups, bent forward like he was going to bite the horse in the ear, soon's the strain got unendurable.

Well, here he come, straight for us. I'd a mind to wake the other boys up, to let 'em see somthing new in the way of mishandling a horse, but they snored so peaceful I refrained.

"How-de-do?" says he.

I said I was worrying along, and sized him up, on the quiet. He was a queer pet. Not a bad set-up man, and rather good looking in the face. Light yellow hair, little yellow mustache, light blue eyes. And clean! Say, I never saw anybody that looked so aggravating clean in all my life. It seemed kind of wrong for him to be outdoors; all the prairie and the cabin and everything looked mussed up beside him.

As soon as he opened up, I noticed he had a little habit of speaking in streaks, that bothered me. I missed the sense of his remarks.

"Would you mind walking over that trail again?" I asked him. "I do most of my thinking at a foot-step and your ideas is over the hill and far away before I can recognize the cut of their scalp-lock."

"Haw!" says he and stared at me. I was just on the point of askin' him if red hair was a new thing to him, when all of a sudden he begun to laugh, "Haw-haw-haw!" says he; "not bad at all, ye know."

"Of course not," says I. "Why should it be?"

This got him going. I saw him figuring away to himself, and then I had to smile so you could hear it.

"Well," says I, better humored, "tell us it again—I caught the word sheep in the hurricane."

So we went over it, talking slow. I listened with one ear, for he had a white bulldog with him; a husky, bandy-legged brute with a black eye, and he was sniffing, dog fashion, around the door, while I blocked him out with my legs. Doggy was in a frame of mind, puzzling out bull-snake trail, and hawk trail, and bob-cat trail. He foresaw much that was entertaining the other side of the door, and wanted it power-ful.

"Here," says I, "call your dog. I can't pay attention to both of you."

"He won't hurt anything, you know," says the man.

"Well, we've got a cat in there that'll hurt *him*," I says. "You'd better whistle him off before old Bob wakes up and scatters him around the front yard."

Gee! That man sat up straight on his horse! Cat hurt that dog? Non-sense! Of course, he wouldn't let the dog hurt the cat, and as long as I was afraid—

I looked into that peaceful cabin. Lon was lying on his back, his fine manly nose vibrating with melody; Wind-River was cooing in a gentle, choked-to-death sort of fashion, on the second bunk; Tom was coiled in the corner, the size of half a barrel; the Judge slept on his perch; Robert reposed under the cook-stove with just a front paw stick-ing out. It was one of them restful scenes our friends the poets sing about. It did appear wicked to disturb it but—

"Will you risk your dog?" I asked that man very softly and politely.

"Certainly!" says he.

Says I, "His blood be on your shirt-front," and I moved my leg.

Well, sir, Lon landed on the grocery shelf. Wind-River grabbed his gun and sat up paralyzed. It really was a most surprising noise. I've had hard luck in my life, but all the things that ever hap-pened to me would seem like a recess to that bulldog. Our domestic difficulties was forgotten. "United We Stand," waved the motto of the lake-bed cabin. Jerusalem! That dog was snake-bit, and hawk-scratched and-bit-and-clawed,

and bob-cat-scratched-and-bit-and-clawed, till you couldn't see a cussed thing in that cabin but blur. And of all the hissing and squawking and screech-ing and yelling and snapping and roar-ing and growling you or any other man ever heard, that was the darnedest. I took a look at the visitor. He'd got off his horse and was standing in the door-way with his hands spread out. His face expressed nothing at all, very forci-ble. Meanwhile, things were boilin' for fair; cook-stove, frying-pans, stools, boxes, saddles, tin cans, bull-snakes, hawks, bob-cats, and bulldogs simply floated in the air.

"I wish you'd tell me what has busted loose, Red Saunders!" howls old Wind-River in an injured tone of voice; "and whether I shell shoot or shan't I?"

There came a second's lull. I see Judge Jenkins on the dog's back, his talents sunk to the hock, whilst he had hold of an ear with his bill, pullin' man-fully. Tommy had swallowed the dog's stumpy tail, and Bob was dragging hair out of the enemy like an Injun dressing hides.

A bulldog is like an Irishman; he's brave because he don't know any better, and you can't get any braver than that, but there's a limit, even to lunk-head-edness. It bored through that dog's thick skull that he had butted into a little bit the darnedest hardest streak of petrified luck that anything on legs could meet with.

"By-by," says he to himself. "Out doors will do for me!" And here he come! Neither the visitor nor me was expecting him. He knocked the feet out from under us and sat his master on top. We got up in time to see a winged bulldog, with a tail ten foot long, bound-ing merrily over the turf, searching his soul for sounds to tell how scairt he was, whilst a desperate bob-cat, spitting fire and brimstone, threw dirt fifty foot in the air trying to lay claws on him.

As they disappeared over the first rise I rolls me a cigarette and lights it slowly.

"Just by way of curiosity," says I; "how much will you take for your dog?"

"My Heavens!" says he, recovering the power of speech. "What kind of animal was that?"

"Come in," says I, "and take a drink —you need it."

So we gathered up the ruins and tidied things over, while the new man sipped his whiskey.

"My!" says he, of a sudden. "I must go after my poor dog."

I sort of warmed to him at that. "Dog's all right," says I. "He'll shake 'em loose and be home in no time. Now tell me about them sheep."

"Sheep?" says he, putting his hand to his head. "What was it about sheep?"

"Hello in the house!" sings out Lon. "The children's comin' home!"

We tumbled out. Sure enough, the warriors was returning. First come the Judge, tougher than rawhide, half walking and half flying, his wings spread out, "cree-ing" to himself about bull-dogs and their ways; next come Bobby, still sputtering and swearing, and behind ambled Thomas at a lively wriggle, a copious large smile upon his face.

"Ur-r-r-roup! Roup!" sounds from the top of the rise. The family halted and turned around, expectin' more pleasure, for there on the top of the hill stood the terrible scairt but still faithful bulldog calling for his master to come away from that place quick, before he got killed. But he had one eye open for safety, and when the family stopped, he ducked down behind the hill surprisin'.

"Well, I must be going," says the visitor. "My name's Sett — Algernon Alfred Sett—and I shall be over next week to talk to you about those sheep."

"Any time," says I. "We'll be here till we have to shovel snow to get at the hay, from the look of things."

"Well, I'm very anxious to have a good long talk with you about sheep," says he. "I've been informed that you had a long experience in that line in— er—Nevverdah—"

"Nevverdah?" says I. "Oh! — Nevada. I beg your pardon—I've got in the habit of pronouncing in that way. It wasn't Nevada, by the way, it was Texas, but that's only a matter of a Europe or so. Yes, I met a sheep or two in that country, I'm sorry to say."

"I—er—think of engaging in the business, dontcher know," says he, relaxing into his first method of speech; "and should like to consult you professionally."

"All right, sir!" says I. "I'm one of the easiest men to consult west of any place east. Can't you stay now and get the load off your mind?"

"Well—no," he says to me very confidentially. "You see that dog is a great pet of my wife's, and I'm also afraid she will be a little worried by my long absence, so—"

"I see, sir—I see," I answered him. "Well, come around again and we'll talk sheep."

"Thank you—thank you so much," says he, and pops up on his horse. Then again, without any warning, he broke into a haw-haw-haw! as he threw a glance at the family, what sat around eyeing him. "You were quite right about that cat, you know," says he. "Capital! Capital! But a little rough on the dog." And off he goes, bobbity-bob, bobbity-bob.

"Where'd you tag that critter, Red?" says Wind-River. "My mind's wander-in'."

"He comes down the draw much the graceful way he's going up it," says I. "From where, and why how, I dunno. But I kind of like him against my better instincts, Windy."

Windy spit thoughtfully at a fly fifteen foot away. "I shouldn't have time to hate him much myself," says he.

And there you are. That's how I met Brother Sett, and the Big Bend Ranch stuck her head out of the shell.

"He's Give the Works"

By LESTER REYNARD

The bad man hops off with the rescuer.

HE altimeter needle in the cockpit of Ted Bland's PT4 quivered at 3,000 feet, but the huge granite boulders jutting from the long ridge off beyond his left wing tip were hardly 200 feet away. He pulled back the stick and zoomed up for a quick look at the country beyond the ridge, then dropped down behind the rocky screen and carefully studied a map held on his leg by a rubber band. The map, given him six hours before by W. J. R., Immigration chief at San Dique, was a rough sketch of a valley, a stream and some ranch buildings.

The bumpy air around these rocky ridges buffeted and twisted the plane. Bland jerked his joy stick, kicked his rudder bar and swore. He couldn't get a chance to check closely on the pen marks.

"To hell with this," Bland muttered. "I think this is the place anyway."

He tore the map and rubber band loose and threw them out into the whipping propeller wash. He nosed the PT4 up, hurdled the ridge and slid down in a long power glide to the valley beyond.

A winding line of sycamores marked a stream and in one place widened into a grove, from which appeared brown-tiled roofs and weathered adobe walls of ranch buildings. Beyond the trees was a wide, flat field and in it Bland saw the wide loops of airplane tail skid tracks. At one side, half-hidden by the trees, he made out another plane, painted a dull olive.

But it was the house he watched most. He swabbed his goggles with a rag. An oil film blurred them. He swore, pushed his goggles up and leaned forward in the lee of the flared celluloid cowl.

A man came out of the ranch-house and stood a few paces from the door looking up.

"Heard me already—no chance to surprise 'em." Bland had a habit, born of long hours alone in the air, of talking to himself.

There was a sudden movement at the side of the house and Bland saw two other men, carrying rifles, running toward a small adobe outbuilding which stood near the edge of the field.

"Ah, my reception committee!" Bland chuckled.

But the PT4 was coming in fast and Bland gave all his attention to watching his landing spot. He shot over the buildings, caught the wind direction from a wisp of smoke curling from the tile chimney, zoomed up and around in a long turn and side-slipped down between two clumps of trees. He leveled off, touched his wheels and skid, lost his momentum and then taxied boldly up near the house alongside the other plane.

The man near the house did not move. Bland idled his motor a few moments while he unstrapped his parachute harness, then cut the switch and unkinked his lean six feet out of the cockpit. He unbuckled his helmet strap and walked stiffly toward the waiting man, careful to let his arms swing carelessly at his sides. Out of the tail of his eye he caught sight of two black rifle barrels resting on the window sill of the old adobe *tejadillo* into which the two other men had disappeared.

Bland estimated the man before him. *First* the eyes, black, deep-set, scowling; the face, well-featured, deeply-tanned, clean-shaven; dark glossy hair; the set of the head, thrust slightly forward; the clothing, riding breeches, expensive polished boots, a lavender silk shirt, and a .45 automatic hanging in a shoulder-holster.

"An Americano—onery cuss," said Bland, mentally. "But intelligent. Good looking, likes to dress snappy but still not a sap. Brains of the outfit. And that holster looks like the spring-clip type for a fast draw. I'll go easy."

"Hey pardner!" Bland spread a wide grin. "Just where the devil am I, anyway!"

"Mexico," the other man growled. "Castino ranch. Eighty miles southwest of Border City."

Bland let his jaw sag. "The hell I am!" Can you beat that? Huh!" He laughed genially. "Sure lost my bearings—saw your plane, so I came down. I'm headed for Crissy Field, 'Frisco—from Kelly back in Texas. This mountain country fools me." He grinned apologetically but the other did not thaw before Bland's smiles.

"Well, I hate to bother you," Bland went on. "But I'm going to offer to buy a meal. I'm that empty I could put a bulldog pup between two slices of bread—" Bland raised his hands to unfasten the collar of his coveralls. The other man flipped a hand to his shoulder and Bland gazed down the barrel of the .45.

"What the—" Bland extended his arms and waved them. "Put that thing down. No need to get excited about me. I'm just peeling off my flying rompers."

"I don't take chances—keep your hands up!" snapped the other man. "Oh, Sanch'—Castino—come on out here."

Bland heard footsteps hurrying through the sand behind him.

"You won't need to take off those flying togs anyway," continued the other. "You're leaving—pronto. You can wait another hour and eat back up in the U. S. A. Sanch'—frisk him for a gun. Castino, you stand off a little farther, not behind him, to the side of him—how many times I got to tell you boys to watch gun angles?"

Rough hands grasped Bland's cover-alls and peeled them down to his waist. The other man noted Bland's uniform, the shoulder bars and the silver wings.

"Army man, eh? Lieutenant—?" His voice rose inquiringly in polite interrogation.

"Bland, sir."

"Indeed a pleasure, Lieutenant Bland. Well, just call me Reno." His face relaxed into an ironic smile. "I'm leasing down here and running a few head of beef."

Sanchez found and drew Bland's .38 from its shoulder-holster. He gave it to Reno. Reno slipped it into his pocket.

"Anything more, Sanch'?"

Sanchez drew four extra clips, loaded, from Bland's hip pockets.

"Are you declaring war on Mexico, Lieutenant?" Reno put up his own gun. "All right then. Must apologize, Lieutenant, but this is the way it is. Climb back in your crate and on your way. Sanch' will help you get off—he can twist props and grab wings. Here, 'Stino, take the Lieutenant's gun. Unload it and give it back to him just before he takes off—watch him, though."

Reno turned and started for the house, then stopped short. Bland followed his gaze. In the doorway, leaning gracefully against the rough adobe, stood a girl.

Blood surged up in Reno's face. "Didn't I tell you to stay out of sight?"

She calmly looked down on him, put a cigarette to her lips, drew in smoke, blew it in Reno's direction and said: "Who cares?"

She looked at Bland, held his gaze a moment, gave him a slow smile.

Bland felt a thrill. He studied the girl while she turned back to Reno. He noted, first, the thin scar running from her cheek up under her hair that W. J. R., back in San Dique, had told him to look for.

"Gosh, she's a real beauty," thought Bland. "I like those black, half-sleepy eyes. She's seen a lot—knows a lot—wonderfully poised. Wish she was

mine." He noted her dainty, expensive dress, smooth stockings, her high-heeled shoes. "Wonder how she keeps herself so immaculate down on this Mex ranch. Sure is out of place—don't belong down here on this Border."

Reno started for the doorway. "Well, get back in there." He clenched his fists.

"Reno," she drawled, calmly. "You've been a fool again."

"How?"

"Didn't I hear you tell the Lieutenant to take his plane and go? Santa Claus sends you a nice, new government plane which has mysteriously disappeared on a long flight—and you without sense enough to keep it."

"Yeah?" Reno pulled a cigarette from his shirt pocket and lit it. "You're right, Fair One, for once. "We *can* use the plane—but we'll have to bump off the Lieutenant."

Bland felt a cold chill up and down his spine.

"No, no—not at all." The girl waved a hand impatiently. "You'd get in too much trouble. Use the plane till you've worn out the motor—keep the Lieutenant here a month. You'll have this job cleaned up and we'll be in Havana by then, won't we? A murder rap, though, is a tough thing to get around."

"Yes, but dead ones talk the least."

Reno stared at the girl, then stared at Bland. His brow wrinkled in thought. Finally he spoke. "And I have still another idea. I've changed my mind. Bland, this is Lola. Peel off the togs and come in."

Reno and Lola led Bland into a dim, cool room and seated him at a rough wooden table. Bland threw his flying clothes and helmet on a chair. Reno stepped across to another door and shouted orders for a steak—pronto. From the cook house just beyond came a shrill "Yah!" followed by a slamming about of pots and pans.

Reno turned back to Bland. "Well, Lieutenant, you may be with us longer than I thought. Make yourself at home." He crossed to the outside door, took a Stetson hat off a set of mounted deer horns and joined Sanchez and Castino outside. They moved off together toward an adobe building some distance from the house.

Lola rose and watched the three from a window. "They've gone into the stable," she announced.

"Good." Bland smiled. "How many people on the ranch?" His tone was casual.

"The three yonder and the Chinese cook. There are some more Chinese in the camp down by the willows but they don't count—just coolies who can't understand English."

"Just waiting for Reno to carry them over the Border to the U. S. A. in that plane out there. Have I called it?"

Lola merely smiled. She looked at Bland expectantly.

Bland looked about the room and listened carefully. The cook's straw sandals could be heard flapping about the kitchen.

"You couldn't possibly be mistaken," Bland insisted. "No one could be in the house here, listening, and you not know it?"

She shook her head impatiently. "Of course not." She gave him an expectant smile. "But I'm 'way ahead of you. Tell me, am I guessing you right?"

Bland left the table and put his lips close to the girl's ear. "W. J. R.—San Dique office—is worried about you. I told him I'd get you out if I could. Got a gun?"

"No. Reno took mine from me."

Bland shrugged his shoulders. "We need a gun to get the drop on Reno."

"Yes," she whispered. "Let me think it over. Meanwhile we'll just act natural. Careful—here comes the cook!"

A blank-faced Chinaman brought in dishes and presently Bland was enjoying a thick, juicy steak. Lola sat across the table from him, nervously smoking a cigarette.

"I'm afraid I overplayed when I talked him into keeping you and the plane," she said. "Whatever we do, we'd better do quick."

Bland waved a hand airily and smiled. "He hasn't shot me yet. Let's not worry about it."

Lola narrowed her eyes and gazed out the window. "You'd have to warm up your motor, wouldn't you?"

"Yes, no chance for a run for it."

"Did you come alone? Is there anybody else—any reenforcements. Will they look for you?" Her tone was hopeful.

"No, 'fraid not." Bland smiled ruefully. "This army business is all hokum. W. J. R. told me about you. I offered to drop in here, look the situation over, and if I got a lucky break I'd use it. W. J. R. borrowed an army plane—I borrowed a uniform from a buddy of mine. I thought maybe I could stick up the joint. But you see how Reno outguessed me. I'll admit the real reason I came here was W. J. R's. description of you. He thinks a lot of you—says you're a he-man's woman. What's more—"

"Be careful!" The girl raised one hand. "I see them coming back toward the house."

"Well anyway, if this is my finish and I never get another chance to tell you, you're more wonderful than W. J. R. said you were."

She smiled. "You aviators are all alike, aren't you." She shook her head wearily. "You're very nice—but why speak of love with the sink full of dirty dishes?"

Footsteps scuffed on the ground outside and Reno, Sanchez and Castino came into the house. Reno seated himself at the table. The other two sat in chairs back against the wall. Bland estimated them in a quick glance—Mexicans, ranch hands by their overalls and high-heeled boots; Sanchez, young, quick-eyed, the more intelligent, Bland decided; Castino heavy-jawed, sleepy-looking, a peon type.

"Well Lieutenant," Reno leaned forward. "I've found it's always good business to have everybody satisfied. I've decided to let opportunity rap on your door. How'd you like to make a thousand bucks a week?"

"It's too good to be honest." Bland smiled. "How'd I do it?"

"Ferrying chinks across the Line. You've guessed it already, probably."

Bland sat silent, considering. "Be fine, till I got caught."

Reno snorted. "Don't be silly. The Immigration Service can't touch you. How they going to catch a plane with the government flivvers? Barring a forced landing, there's nothing to it. Keep your motor in shape—you're a flyer—and you know yourself what the percentage of risk is."

"Where do you take the Chinamen, once you get 'em across?" Bland asked.

Reno looked at Lola and laughed. "Never mind the details, Son, but I've got an organization." He held out his hand. On one finger was a heavy gold ring with an elaborate dragon design curled around a flat jade setting. In the jade were engraved tiny Chinese characters. "See that ring? I'm even a tong member in Frisco's Chinatown."

"And if I don't agree?" Bland questioned.

A pained expression came over Reno's face. "Are you a damn' fool? There's hundreds of these hungry joy-hop pilots hanging around flying fields from here to Portland who'd give five years off the tail end of their lives to work with me—but I don't want 'em. They're a wild bunch—ain't got the flying hours either. But you look like a good man to me—I can judge 'em—level head—and I liked the way you set your crate down in this strange field. I need another plane and I can always use a good man."

Bland rose to his feet and paced the floor, his head bent. "Well, you see, Reno, I have a lot of things to think over." As Bland passed Sanchez, he noticed Sanchez' gun, a horn-handled .45 automatic, hanging down in its hip-holster beside Sanchez' chair. "My folks are what we call respectable peo-

ple. I'd have to be dead as far as they are concerned."

Bland paced closer to Sanchez. He shot a quick glance around. Sanchez was looking out the window. In his right hand he held a cigarette. Castino stared vacantly into space. Reno was watching Lola. Lola was watching Bland.

"Yeah," drawled Reno, in reply to Bland. "Better to let your folks think you're dead and it not be true than to have 'em know it for a positive fact—wouldn't it?"

Bland kept on pacing the floor, back and forth, past Sanchez. Sanchez flipped his cigarette butt out the window. He reached in his pocket and drew out a sack of tobacco and some papers.

Bland took a deep breath, walked past Sanchez, turned, took a step forward and dropped to one knee. His left arm and shoulder shoved against Sanchez' right arm. Bland's hand closed on the gun grip. Sanchez grabbed for the gun with his right hand but Bland's left hand caught Sanchez' wrist. Bland leaped to his feet and thumbed down the safety catch of the gun. Sanchez toppled over with his chair and sprawled on the floor.

Reno and Lola leaped to their feet. Castino sat still, blinking his eyes.

"All right," Bland snapped. "Elevate 'em and line up! Face the wall!" He gave Castino a boot with his foot. "Wait, Lola, you gather up the guns!"

Lola removed a .45 from Castino's holster and laid it on the table. She also found a knife with a keen, six-inch blade in a sheath in his boot. She took Reno's gun from his shoulder-holster and recovered Bland's .38 from Reno's pocket.

"You keep my gun," Bland ordered.

Reno half-turned and looked at Lola. His eyebrows lifted in surprise. "Well, Lola—why don't you plug him?"

"I don't want to, I'm going away with him." She smiled at Reno.

"Snap out of it, Reno," Bland growled. He backed over by the door. "Now you guys march out of here, single file—head for the plane and don't look back—pronto! Drop your hands if you want to."

Reno led the way. Sanchez and Castino followed. Bland picked up his helmet and goggles from the chair. The coveralls he gave to Lola. "They're big for you," he said, "but they'll protect you from the wind. Climb into 'em." He followed Reno, Sanchez and Castino, pulling on his helmet.

Halfway to the plane, Reno stopped and turned. He extended his hands from his sides, palms forward. "See here, Bland, you can't deny me an explanation of this. You can't take away the girl a man loves without giving him a chance to talk to her."

"Fair enough—but make it snappy." Bland halted a few paces from Reno, the gun held hip-high and pointed at Reno's stomach. "Lola, don't get too close to them."

Lola, the flying togs over her arm, stopped beside Bland.

"What's the idea, Lola," said Reno. "Think you're doing yourself a good turn?"

"Simply this, Reno. I have a chance to get away from you and back to the United States. I'm tired of being the same as a prisoner down here."

"Who's the Lieutenant—some other sweet daddy of yours?"

"I never saw him before."

Reno grinned ironically. "My compliments, Lieutenant. You're a fast worker." His face grew serious again. He scowled. "There's more to it than that, though, because I've been a damn fool over you—you've made a sucker out of me—you and I both know it. Didn't I take you out of that lousy Border City dance-hall? Didn't you have your own room here with a lock on the door? I took good care of you—I let you have your own way in everything. Damned if I'd do all that for any other woman—but you, well, I figured you were pretty high-grade. And you know I can give you the things women want when we get this racket cleaned up. I've been the kind of a sap that's the answer to a

dance-hall maiden's prayer—and you know it—yet here you take a run-out powder on me with this young squirt of a shavetail. There's more behind it—what is it?"

"There certainly is something more!" Lola snapped out the words. "Lieutenant, will your plane carry three people?"

"Why, sure. She's only a two-seater but she has plenty of power." Bland looked at her questioningly.

Lola looked at Reno. Her head lifted and her black eyes snapped in anger. "And that something more I want, Reno, is to get you on American soil just once where a Federal dick can see you. You want to know why?

"I guess you remember the Ferguson case well enough, back in Frisco? You ought to—you turned rat and were the district attorney's star witness. And in court, under oath, you swore you saw young Ferguson hold the gun in that mail truck stick-up—identified him for the D. A.—and you know as well as I do that he was nowhere near that spot at the time. You got him sent up, an innocent kid, just to give the D. A. and the cops and the newspapers a victim to satisfy themselves with. Well, Fergie happens to be my baby brother.

"No, I can't prove this in court—but you know it and I know it—and I know enough about you that if I can get you on American soil, the Immigration boys have plenty on you to keep you sitting in the big stone house quite a while. That's why I came to B. C. and was dancing in the Habana Cabaret. Then you— pft!—the rest was easy."

She stepped forward and leveled the .38 at Reno. "So just for that reason you can climb in that plane and come with us. I'm going to sit on your lap— you're always wanting me to, aren't you —in that front cockpit and hold this gun against your heart all the way. Now move—"

Reno's face flushed to a dark red. "I guess that's enough. In anger truth comes out." He waved a hand at Bland. "Boys, do your stuff. I'll handle her."

Reno and the two Mexicans started for Bland and the girl. Bland looked at their eyes. They showed no trace of fear. He sensed they felt superior to him and were not afraid.

"You fools—you think I'm bluffing?" Bland growled. He leveled his gun at Reno's middle and pull the trigger. A metalic click came from the gun. Bland seized the slide, pulled it back and forth. He aimed again at Reno and pulled the trigger. Another harmless click. The three came on.

Reno grinned. "No, you young sap—you're not bluffing anybody. You don't know what you are doing. Not a one of these guns is loaded. I just wanted to let Lola show her real hand."

A hot, red feeling surged through Bland. He shifted his grip and held the gun by the barrel end. "Get behind me, Lola," he muttered.

"Spread out—'Stino, get behind him." Reno stood back a little, giving orders. "Be careful. Grab his gun hand first. If he crowns you with that gun butt you'll have a long headache. Which ever one can get behind him first, rush him!"

The three circled warily. Bland gave his belt a hitch and crouched. "Come on, you yellow coyotes!" he snarled. Sanchez feinted a rush and stopped. Bland jumped for him, gun raised, then swerved and rushed at Reno. Reno flung up both hands and warded off the descending gun in Bland's hand. Sanchez, then Castino, closed in from behind and wrapped their arms around Bland. Reno sidestepped clear and dived for Lola. She poked at his face with her gun but he seized it and flung it on the ground. He bent, seized her knees and flung her heavily to the ground. He held one big hand on her face and pinioned her body with his knee. He looked back at Bland.

Bland saw Lola fall and cursed. He twisted, got Castino off balance. For a second Bland had his right arm free. He threw the heavy .45 with all his strength at Reno's head. Reno ducked,

threw up one arm and took a glancing blow from the spinning gun on his elbow. The gun flew on and buried itself in the dust.

Reno bellowed with pain and rage. His face went white. He caught sight of Bland's .38 lying beside Lola. He seized it and jumped to his feet. "Hold his arms, you two!" he roared.

Sanchez and Castino each wrapped themselves around one of Bland's arms. Reno leaped in and pounded vicious, chopping blows down on Bland's soft leather helmet. Lola screamed, covered her face with her hands. Bland's knees sagged, he hung limp. Sanchez and Castino looked at Reno in amazement.

Reno stepped back. His nostrils dilated and his chest heaved. The Mexicans let Bland fall, face down, into the sand. Reno wiped his damp hair out of his eyes. The color slowly came back into his pale, tense face.

Sanchez shoved one foot against Bland's limp body. "Ee's look like dead."

"Shut up—lemme think!" Reno paced back and forth. He looked at Bland, lying quiet, then at Lola. Lola got to her feet and knelt beside Bland.

"Get away from him, damn you!" Reno snapped. "I've got a notion to give you the same thing!"

Sanchez grasped Lola's arm. She slapped his hand away. She walked off a few paces. Her knees wabbled. She sat down. "Oh God—oh—" she murmured. Her face went white and she slumped limply to the ground.

"Let her alone—just a faint." Reno kept on pacing back and forth. He looked at the two planes. He strode over to Bland's plane, looked in the cockpit at the instrument board, at the parachute pack. He opened the fuselage locker behind the rear cockpit. He drew out a leather helmet and a pair of goggles. "The Looie's visit smells like a planned accident to me," he mused. He walked around to the front and studied the little brass plate on the motor crankcase which told the running temperature and the oil pressure.

Suddenly Reno turned and hurried to the house. He disappeared inside for a moment, then came out with a length of light rope looped in one hand. In the other he carried Castino's hunting knife in its sheath. He hurried back to the waiting group.

"Now remember, you two," he ordered pointing the knife at Castino and Sanchez. "You were over in Carrizo valley since this morning—get that —hunting stray cows. When you got back, Lola was gone—you don't know how or why." He looked at the house. The Chinese cook was staring out the window. "As for Ling Hai—well, we got to have a good cook. I won't bump him off just yet." He thrust the knife and its sheath into his hip pocket.

Lola sat up again. Reno picked up Bland's flying coveralls and crossed over to her. "Here, climb into this, Lola."

She looked up. "Why?"

"Put 'em on!"

"I won't!"

"Sanch', help me a minute." Reno held out the garment to Sanchez. He seized Lola. There was a brief struggle and Lola, kicking, was forced into the baggy flying togs. Reno knelt over her.

"Hold her hands, here, Sanch'." Reno tied Lola's wrists together with the rope. He seized her kicking feet. She tried to bite him. He cuffed her cheek. "Now Sanch', get up on the wing by the front cockpit of the lieutenant's crate."

Reno picked up the struggling girl and carried her to the plane. Sanchez, there ahead of him, helped to force her into the cockpit. Reno tied her hands with a short length of the rope to a tube of the steel fuselage frame. He took the spare helmet from the locker and pulled it over her head. He hung the goggles about her neck and fastened the safety belt around her middle.

"Now help me carry the stiff." Reno hurried back to where Bland lay. The three carried him over to the plane. Reno pulled the 'chute pack out and began to

snap it on. "Stick him in the cockpit. Set him right in the seat."

Sanchez and Castino, grunting, got Bland's long legs into the cockpit, then slid his limp body into the small metal seat. They turned and looked at Reno.

"W'at the hell you going to do, Reno?" queried Sanchez.

"Never you mind, Sanch'—get up there and let's see you twist that starter crank."

Reno walked over to his own plane and picked up a leather helmet and goggles from the pilot's seat.

Sanchez climbed up beside the motor of Bland's PT4 and engaged the starter crank. Reno climbed into the rear cockpit and planted himself in Bland's lap. "Now Sanch', you take the car to Border City. Get in before daylight. Park it up in that alley by Moraga's place. Savvy? All right—twist 'er tail!"

Reno flipped the switch. Sanchez tugged at the crank. The propeller turned slowly, the motor ticked over, popped and sputtered into life. Reno gently nursed the throttle forward and kept his eyes on the thermometer. Finally the motor settled into a steady roar and Reno nodded at Sanchez. Sanchez seized a wing tip. Reno opened the throttle and threw an air blast against the rudder. The plane rolled, swung around and Reno taxied slowly up the field to the head of his runway. He swung around, roared down the field, lifted quickly into the air and circled into the north.

"W'at you think ee's do with 'em?" Castino ventured.

Sanchez shrugged his shoulders and made the sign of the cross.

"He's give 'em the works."

BLAND became aware of a roaring in his ears. It faded away, then beat in on his consciousness in waves of sound. His head throbbed. He felt cold air whipping past his face. Then a pang of fear shot through him. Instinct made him aware of danger. He lay quiet, striving to clear his head and get control of his mind, trying to realize what his senses were telling him. He opened his eyes. He was up in bright sunlight, flying—clear, sharp sunlight that meant flying high. The heavy, oppressive feeling was caused by a man's body, a man sitting on him.

Bland recognized the lavender shirt inches in front of his nose—Reno! And Reno wearing a parachute pack, Bland's own, by the initials inked on the web strap. Bland kept quiet, sizing up the situation.

Off to the left sunshine glittered on the distant Pacific. Below were rocky brush-covered hills with yellow, grassy valleys between, merging into tawny desert haze far off to the right. No roads, no houses in sight. Still over Mexico then.

Reno was fussing with the throttle, easing the power on and off. Bland wondered what he was up to. The plane's nose rose and fell gradually. Finally it held steady. Then Bland saw from the position of Reno's arms he was flying "hands off" the controls. The PT4 was a well-balanced job, Bland reflected. With her powerful nine cylinders and her adjustable fins she could be flown "hands off" for hours. Reno, then, had just solved the trick.

The weight lifted from Bland. Reno was cautiously trying to stand up. Bland took a deep breath. His head cleared. Reno placed one foot in the seat between Bland's knees. He rose, groped forward for a hand-hold on the center section struts and braced himself against the ripping propeller blast. He leaned forward, pressed down the flared windshield and reached into the front cockpit. Then Reno's hand came back, fumbled under the 'chute straps and found his hip pocket. He drew out the hunting knife in its sheath. He placed the sheath in his mouth and drew out the knife. Again he reached into the front cockpit. His hands were busy for a moment. He threw overside some short pieces of rope.

Then Bland saw a head bobbing about in the front cockpit. Small hands waved in a gesture of appeal. A white, scared face came into view—Lola—her lips moving but her voice lost in the motor's roar.

Reno dropped suddenly back into Bland's lap. He thrust the knife back in its sheath and the sheath back in his pocket.

Bland's hand was on the knife handle immediately. He wondered if Reno had a gun. Better go easy, until he was sure. He carefully drew out the knife. Reno did not notice. The plane had nosed up and Reno was busy with the controls.

Bland considered a quick jab of the knife between Reno's ribs. But a limp body in the cockpit with him might jam the controls. Too messy, anyway.

Bland cautiously lifted his left hand up and over to Reno's right shoulder. He gently lifted the slack of the right parachute risers, the double webbing straps by which a man hangs from the shrouds while floating earthward. With his other hand. Bland cautiously raised the knife. He slipped it under the risers close to his left hand. The blade was razor-keen. Short, quarter-inch sawing strokes bit through the webbing. Reno did not notice. Bland reached both arms over to Reno's left shoulder and the other risers. A few more sawing cuts and the knife was through. Bland grinned. "You won't get away now, you dirty devil!" He waited to see what Reno would do.

Reno was again fussing with the controls. This time he nosed the ship down in a power glide. He held the PT4 steady for a moment, then suddenly stood up and slid one leg out of the cockpit and got his foot in the fuselage step.

Bland thought fast. Grab Reno? Warn him his risers were cut? But he might have a gun. It was life against life—and there was Lola. Two lives against one. Bland let his head fall limply. The knife was out of sight in his hand down by his knee. "Go ahead, you dirty cur," he thought. "Get the surprise of your life when you pull that 'chute ring and see yourself leave that 'chute hanging on the corner of a cloud."

But Reno did not dive off. He scrambled forward on to the lower wing. Lola reached out desperate hands, trying to hold him. He shook her off, grinned ironically, blew her a kiss and turned away. Bland grinned. He had caught sight of Reno's holster and it was empty.

Reno edged himself along the rear wing spar, holding on to the bracing wires. The air stream whipped and tore at his clothes. The parachute pack bobbed awkwardly. The plane began to sag to the left into a spiral.

His plan was only too easily comprehensible—to put the plane in a spiral dive to crash in the hills miles from anywhere, then jump. The plane, if ever found, would be all crashed up, and cover his dirty work.

Bland reached for the controls, smacked on all his power and jerked his stick clear over to set his ailerons and level the ship up under Reno's weight. Reno froze motionless, half-turned to swing out from the crossed bracing wires. He looked at Lola, then at Bland. Bland grinned at him.

A scowl twisted Reno's face. He started back along the wing. He reached the fuselage, grasped the center section struts with his left hand and with his right raised a menacing fist at Lola. She pulled at his fingers, trying to loosen his grip on the strut. Reno smashed a blow to her chin and she fell back limp. Bland thought of several unprintable names.

Reno's lips parted in a snarl. His right hand went to his hip, fumbled a moment. A look of surprise widened his eyes. He drew out the empty leather sheath. He fumbled again at his pocket.

Bland held the knife up where Reno could see it and grinned at him.

Reno's face twisted into a grimace of insane rage. His lips mouthed curses. The wind stream whipped into his cheeks, ballooned them out. He bit his lips and blood flecks whipped out upon his cheek. Then his eyes narrowed. He looked overside and to the north.

The plane had about a mile of altitude. Bland had once more headed north. Just ahead and below lay a long stretch of dark green squares and rectangles, the irrigated fields around Border City. Beyond lay a long, white, thread-like line stretching across the country into the distant haze—the state highway. Reno knew the Border line lay roughly three miles south of it. Once more he started out along the wing. He reached the outer strut, rested a moment. His left arm hugged the strut, his right hand fumbled for the release ring at his side.

"Hell!" Bland exclaimed. "He hasn't noticed those risers flopping around loose yet!" Bland cut the gun. The engine idled and the only sound was the swish of air past taut wires.

"Hey—no 'chute—don't jump you damn fool!" Bland shook his head and pointed to the cut risers whipping out behind Reno.

Reno turned. He heard the shout but not the words. He thumbed his nose at Bland.

Bland grinned in anticipation. "You never did a pull-off before," he commented, "or you'd never hug a strut like that. It'd rake all the hide off your arm when the 'chute jerked you."

Reno took a deep breath and pulled the ring. The pilot 'chute flipped out, then the larger mass of the main 'chute, dragging its shrouds, flashed out of sight to the rear. Reno waited expectantly. The severed risers fluttered in the wind. Surprise, then apprehension, flashed across Reno's face. He twisted his head for a quick look. Far behind he saw the tangled white fabric writhing and twisting earthward. Reno's face paled to a dingy white. He wrapped both arms around the strut and hugged it to his bosom. He wrapped both legs around it. He shut his eyes. His knees slowly sagged until he was an inert.

curled-up ball at the foot of the strut. Then came heaving movements from his middle and Bland saw that he was violently ill.

Bland laughed loud and long. He eased the throttle on and set the plane's nose for the brown Municipal Field just ahead and beyond Border City.

A little later he throttled down again. "Hey, Reno!" he yelled. "Get in—off the end—that wing! How you think— I'm gonna land?"

Reno gave no sign of hearing.

"Damn you! Froze solid! Now I wish you had jumped!" Bland pushed on his power again. "Angels reach down and hold up that wing! Bet we nose over!"

The roofs of Border City rushed past below. Bland circled wide to leeward of the Field. He pushed his throttle on all the way, gave his stick the last inch of aileron pull and lifted Reno's wing high up. He side-slipped steeply for the field, sighting his landing spot down along the lower wing.

Slowly Reno's weight drew the other wing down. Bland cursed absent-mindedly. They swept down over a hangar roof, past the wind cone and over the field. Bland kicked his rudder bar and swung the PT4 around out of the side-slip. Reno's wing sagged down. The wings hung level for a moment. This was the moment Bland had hoped to touch his wheels and roll but the plane had too much speed.

The wheels hit. The plane bounded upward, hung poised a second. Bland cut the switch. Reno's wing dragged, hit the ground. The plane swung around, the wheels dished, twisted off the axles, and the bent landing gear skidded along in the sand. A big cloud

of dry desert dust arose and hid everything.

Men ran from the hangar toward the dust cloud.

When the breeze lifted the dust cloud away, Bland was standing over Reno, fists doubled. Reno was down on the ground, digging his fingers into the dirt, babbling incoherently. His staring eyes looked at the men but did not see them.

"Gone cuckoo," explained Bland to Billy Ryan, superintendent of the Border City Field. He thinks solid ground is about the finest thing in the world right now—don't blame him." He turned to the plane and helped out the white-faced and trembling Lola.

"Keep that guy here, will you, Billy, and loan us your car? Kerrig and Dawes of the Immigration will be right out. They want him bad. Come on, Lola, let's go phone old W. J. R. back at San Dique."

Lola clung to him. "This has been terrible. I thought sure Reno killed you, back there, when he beat you over the head with that gun."

Bland laughed and gingerly pulled off his helmet. "He raised a welt all right. I was out for sure for a while—feel that."

Bland held out the helmet. Lola's fingers explored.

"Feel those little spring-steel plates under the leather. They overlap. Same principle as a bullet-proof vest. Buddy of mine invented it. The idea is to save an aviator's brains—if any—in a crash. Guess we owe him a dinner when we get back to civilization. *We*—get that?"

Lola smiled up at Bland. He laughed and slipped his arm around her. "Come on—that's Billy Ryan's heap over there —that roadster,"

The Squeeze

By RAOUL WHITFIELD

A pack of killers and a lone hunter.

ACROSS the dirty-surfaced table Pete Ranning sat facing Gary Greer, his blue eyes narrowed and holding a worried expression. It would be midnight in twelve minutes. Outside the River Street speakeasy run by one "Touch" Dillon, the rain battered down against the cobbles of stone. A gusty wind drove it against the alley window panes of the squalid room at intervals. Ranning spoke again, in a low voice, despite the fact that they were alone in the room.

"They're out to grab you, Gary—you can't fight 'em *now*. That was a rotten piece of killer business—that bombing of the Parson's place. And with a South Side Field ship! The papers are spread-ing the stuff—the *News* has a column, pinning the job on you. You've got to get clear, Gary!"

Gary Greer shook his head slowly. The news had given him a jolt—a ship registered and hangared at his own airport, the South Side Field, had been used for the bombing of Parson Jennifer's River Street joint, hours ago. Jennifer had been killed—two humans on the street had been killed. And they had found Lamonte, shot to death in the room upstairs. The *News* was run by a politician named Brookers—and he was a rough rider. The administration he worked with had been the same one in power when Gary's father had been shot down by the hired killers. It was the same administration in power now. Brookers knew that Gary was alive, that Gary had started a clean-up of his own. Brookers was out to get him—and to get him properly, Gary knew that.

"My job's almost finished, Pete," he stated slowly. "Gorringe is still alive. And Sal the Dude. That's Callahan, I'm almost positive. But I've got to be sure. The gang's broken up—I'm pretty safe down here—"

"Safe!" Pete Ranning cut in sharply. "Like hell you are. Every side-walk pounder in the city has been staring at your photo. The dicks are out in force. And Callahan has his own special boys hunting you—you know that. The *News* states you're alive and wanted for "questioning." You know what that means. You've killed—and they know it. They'll get you—before you get *them*."

Pete Ranning stiffened in the chair opposite Gary's. Dillon came into the small room, smirking. He was short, red-faced. He was illiterate, and at times his mind wandered a bit. Sea men gave him trade. His graft toll was small— and the police didn't bother him much.

"Another toss-off, gents?" he muttered thickly. "Bad weather outside—"

Pete Ranning got to his feet. His face was pale; he stood stiffly, blinking his eyes. He started to say something, swore softly, thickly. His right hand moved downward, toward his right hip pocket. He swayed a little.

"I'm—feeling—rotten—"

Gary was staring at him. Dillon chuckled harshly.

"You need—another!" he stated thickly. "How about—"

He stopped. Gary was getting up unsteadily. He shook his head from side to side, swore thickly. He shoved a chair toward Pete's swaying body. Ranning dropped into it heavily. He started to speak again—his head fell forward, his body swung toward the dirty wall beside the chair. He breathed several times, heavily—then his body relaxed.

Gary Greer stood looking down at him. He chuckled foolishly.

"Can't stand the stuff, Touch." His voice was thick. "Damn strong, at that. It's got me feelin' rocky as—"

He staggered toward Touch Dillon. There was a little gleam in the shorter man's eyes. The liquor in both glasses that he had set before the men was gone—the liquor had been doped. One man was out. And the other—

He backed away from Gary Greer. He half turned away, toward the faded green curtain back of the door. He didn't see Gary's body stiffen—he didn't see the right arm swing.

"Touch!"

The voice was sharp. It was a warning. Dillon pivoted. He tried, in that last second, to rock his head. Gary had cried out sharply, and Gary was striking. His fist caught Touch Dillon under the left ear. There was a sharp crack— Touch groaned, his body collapsed. Gary caught him—there was no heavy thud to the wood floor.

He dragged him toward the chair he had vacated, eased him into it. He turned the back of the chair toward the door. His mind was working fast.

Ranning was pretty heavy—but the spot was a bad one. Gary got him in his arms—headed for the rear of the place. All speakeasy rooms were the same in one respect, along River Street. They had an easy exit to an alley. Dillon was motionless as Gary got Pete back of the small counter-bar, found the alley door. And he'd figured Dillon was dumb!

Rain splattered into his face as he reached the alley. A gust of wind rocked him off balance. He was forced to let Ranning down. A voice reached him— a half whisper.

"Got him, Touch?"

Gary Greer grunted. His back was turned to the speaker; he swung back toward the door.

"Come on!" he muttered thickly, and went in through the door again.

Inside, he swung around. Beyond the counter he could hear Touch Dillon groaning, trying to pull himself up. The man outside had mistaken him for Touch—he had given the game away. Gary's right hand fingers closed over his Colt—he felt the safety catch. The gun was locked.

Just outside the alley entrance he could hear the heavy breathing of the man who had spoken. He was bending over Pete—Gary heard him mutter grimly.

"Ranning! That makes—all three—"

The man was straightening—his form, soaked with rain, swung in through the doorway. He whispered hoarsely.

"Touch—where's the—"

Gary struck—he held the automatic by the grip. It was the barrel that battered down on the side of the questioner's head. The man's breath came out in a wheezing groan—he pitched forward at Gary's feet.

A faint light reached the floor near the alley door. Gary rolled the man over. He didn't recognize him. He had a fat, pallid face—and the gun metal had robbed him of consciousness. From beyond the counter there was a sudden crash as Touch Dillon, trying to pull himself up, lost balance and tumbled again.

Gary's fingers went through the pockets of the fat-faced man's clothes. In the first three he found nothing—in the fourth he found two sheets of folded paper. Voices reached him, from the rain drenched street beyond the main entrance of the speakeasy.

Gary straightened, headed for the alley. He got Pete Ranning in his arms again—moved toward Third Street. Pete was breathing heavily, but evenly. Across Third Street, deserted in the rain, a green light showed faded letters above it. The letters spelled the words *Jones Hotel*. Gary moved straight toward the entrance. Fear was driving him on now. The one he had struck down with the gun had said—"all three." The man had been wrong. But who was the third. Joyce Rawlings?

He swore fiercely. He was inside the narrow entrance of the hotel now. It was a mean corridor, badly lighted. He moved along it, swaying a little. Ahead was a dirty desk—a few chairs. A figure stood and watched him come. Gary dropped Ranning's form into one of the chairs, swore shakily. He grinned at a reddish face that held only one eye. The man had white hair—a dirty white. He chuckled.

"Booze?" he muttered.

Gary was getting his breath. But he managed to chuckle back.

"It's Whitey Leems," he stated. "He's been tossin' the bad stuff away for a week. One of the South Side boys. Want to put him away—and keep it quiet. He'll take plenty of sleepin'."

The red-faced man nodded. He and Gary carried Pete up two flights of rickety stairs. They dropped him on a bed. Gary pulled out a five-dollar bill. It was old, crumpled.

"Dig up a package of cigarettes any kind," he stated. "Whitey's got to smoke when he comes out of this. He's liable to wreck things, if he doesn't have 'em. An' he's out of 'em right now. Forget we come in, see?"

The hotel man flat-footed out of the room. Gary listened to him clumping down the stairs. The one bulb in the room gave a ghastly white light. Pete Ranning was out, but he was sleeping well enough. He'd wake up with a rotten head and bad taste. Gary got his shoes off, loosened his belt—eased up the tie pull around his neck. He went through his pockets, took away a small caliber automatic, a watch that looked too good, a check book.

It had been a narrow one. Touch Dillon had tried to dope him—had got Ranning instead, on the accidental switching of drinks. He'd made another mistake—thinking that Touch was dumb. It had been a bad place for the meet. But they were out of it. He wouldn't forget the face of the one he had knocked out with the gun—and Touch wouldn't forget him. The police were tagging him; Callahan and Elbow Gorringe were fighting hard. And the girl—

Gary swore thickly. That was the next job—to reach her apartment. If the gang had tricked her, trapped her—

The red-faced man was coming up the stairs again. He was humming in a hoarse tone. It was some sort of an Irish air. He rapped on the door, and Gary didn't tell him to come in. He walked three paces and opened the door. The red-faced one tossed a pack of humps on the chair nearest the bed. He grinned with his black teeth.

Gary nodded. He spoke thickly, but slowly.

"Don't be funny with Whitey. He's sittin' next to a certain Eyetalian guy. I've paid his board—an' when he walks out—just let him hoof it."

The red-faced one looked hurt. He swore in a mumbling tone.

"I ain't seen any Whitey," he stated.

"Sure," Gary grunted. "Open a window an' let a little air an' rain in. The only thing water or air can hurt is the bugs in here. I'll be in tomorrow, maybe—around noon."

The red-faced one shoved open a window. It wouldn't stay up, so he dug up a book from the shelf of a table—the one book in the room—and used it to prop open the window. The act seemed to amuse him. He chuckled a lot, but he didn't say anything.

Gary nodded his head. He tossed a dirty blanket over Pete Ranning, and went out. Down by the battered desk a cross-eyed gent was listening to the siren on a police car or an ambulance, and grinning. The siren was somewhere in the distance. Gary went on out. He turned up the wet street toward the center of town, away from the river. The siren's wail died.

Gary walked out near the curb, and he kept his eyes opened. Pete Ranning was out of things for twelve hours, at least. They had nearly gone down together. Touch Dillon had made a mistake, but maybe there had been a reason for only doping one whiskey. Maybe

Callahan knew that reason, or Elbow Gorringe.

They had used a ship from South Side Airport, for the bombing of Parson Jennifer's place. That had been Callahan's game. He had known that Frenchy Lamonte and Elbow Gorringe were meeting there. He had *fixed* the rendezvous. And the sky bombs had been dropped with the intention of blowing out two humans that might prove dangerous—to Callahan. He had failed. Gorringe had already rubbed out Lamonte. And Gorringe had got clear.

Gary had got clear, but Callahan had never known that he had been present. The detective with the beady eyes and the scrubby black mustache—was he Sal the Dude? Gary thought so. There was irony in the name—but there had been irony in many things since Gary's father had died on the muddy cobbles of a street only a few miles from the one Gary walked now.

And the squeeze was on. Gary was getting too close. Callahan was sitting inside police circles, inside political circles—and trying to smash the son of a dead man, before he was smashed. Gary had won victories—but they had cost him much. Ranning was in the fight now—and the girl Gary loved was in it. He had tried to spare them, and it hadn't worked out that way.

Two names remained on the list—two living names. Names of the death car "guns" who had battered down Sanford Greer, backed by a rotten city administration. Soapy Tyler had given Gary the names—and he had died. He had been dying when Gary reached him. Babe Lewis had gone down first. He had spoken of "Sal the Dude." Gary had tricked him; even as he had reached for his gun Gary had sent death into his body. Fifty Mile Liseman had been the second to die. His one bullet had gone wild. And now Gary had tricked Elbow Gorringe into sending lead through the skin of Frenchy Lamonte. Three names were wiped off the killer list. Gorringe was alive. Callahan was alive. And unless Soapy Tyler had failed to tell him everything—or had not *known* enough—one of the remaining two was Sal the Dude. And that man was the gang leader.

Rain dripped from the brim of Gary's soft hat. A night owl cab cruised by. Gary hailed the driver—got inside. He kept his hat brim pulled down over his face. The police were searching—cab drivers were often closely allied. They got around. He gave the address of a fashionable apartment building.

They had to cross the busy streets of the city. There was traffic. Gary Greer leaned back in the cab, tried to relax. Pete Ranning would be all right. His pulse had been steady enough; he had a strong constitution. Jensen would automatically take charge, out at the airport. It seemed ages since Gary had turned over the Field to Pete—had tried to make the world believe he had died in a plane crash. Many had believed it—but after the first two killers had died, the going had become too tough. First there had been suspicion. Now they *knew*, he was sure of that. Callahan and Gorringe—trying to get him before he got them.

He smiled grimly as the driver of another cab tried to cut his own driver off. The other man failed. They were ahead now, skidding on the wet asphalt, but ahead. A traffic signal held them up. They started again—were forced to slow down for a town car just ahead. And as they turned out— the cab they had got away from shot in from the left.

There was the squealing of brakes. For a second Gary Greer was stiff in the seat, his right hand fingers on his Colt. They were forced over toward the town car. They were squeezed. He got a glimpse of the other cab driver's head, half turned, a mocking grin on the prize ring face. His own driver was swearing grimly. The other cab went on—the town car, glistening in the rain, pulled out. They were motionless. The squeeze had been too tough—too close.

A slickered figure loomed up close to the driver's seat. A bull like voice sounded.

"What you waitin' for—three o'clock an' no traffic? You learnin' to drive—"

The cab jerked forward—the traffic cop's face swung behind. Gary was slumped low in the seat. He didn't look back. The cab driver continued to swear. Gary drew a deep breath. His fingers relaxed their grip on the gun. A traffic crash—police—recognition.

He laughed harshly. The cab driver heard him. He didn't like it.

"A lot of dirty crooks sittin' back of wheels in this town!" he stated. "A lot of ex-pugs tryin' to run things, squeezin' the decent guys out—"

Gary's voice, cold, sharp—cut in on the driver.

"Never mind that—watch your driving!"

The cab driver jerked his head to the front again. He muttered to himself. Gary's face was set grimly. He saw the apartment building ahead. It rose twenty stories high. He thought of Joyce Rawlings. He had told her he wouldn't come back until things were finished. But he had to know the truth. The one he had battered down had said "that makes—all three." For the first time since he had got control of himself, the night his father had been murdered, Gary Greer felt rage striking at him again. If they had touched the girl—

The cab swung up before the elaborate entrance. Gary gave the driver a bill, got out. He walked toward the corner. Fifty yards down the street was a delivery entrance. He went in. He had to be careful. Callahan knew about Joyce. If the place was being watched, on the inside, he would be caught. He had to go slow.

An elevator boy, off duty, came along the concrete corridor, smoking a cigarette. He was in uniform—Gary had never seen him before. He was young.

"Hello!" Gary smiled a little. "I'm from County Headquarters. Is Miss Rawlings in yet, do you know?"

The elevator boy's eyes widened. He stared at Gary.

"In yet? Say, they just took her out of here an hour ago. A gray haired guy is sittin' up above—waiting to see any of her relatives or friends. But they was City bulls that took her to jail."

Gary turned away. He didn't want the boy to see his eyes. Joyce—down at the detective bureau! Joyce Rawlings— mixed up with the police because of him. He swore grimly, faced the boy again.

"Didn't go around shouting about who they were and what they were doing, did they?" he asked. "Though the City boys always make a lot of racket on a pinch."

The elevator boy grinned. "I brought 'em down with her," he stated. "She was pretty quiet—but said something about getting some people on the phone. They said it would be all right to do that from the jail—that the chief just wanted to talk with her. That's how I know who they were."

Gary nodded. He forced a grin, lighted a cigarette.

"Beat the county to it," he stated cheerfully. "I'll go up and see who's sitting up above. Don't want him to see me, though. Give him a laugh."

The elevator boy nodded. "He's decorating the red plush nearest the entrance," he stated. "You can tell him by his big feet."

Gary went up above. He stood back near the elevators—and stared toward the ornate entrance. The red plush chairs were there—but no human with big feet decorated any of them. The police didn't have a thing on the girl— and she had too much money for them to fool with, unless they had plenty on her.

There was a tired look in Gary's eyes. He could guess what had hap-

pened. Someone known to the man he had battered down with the gun, back of Touch Dillon's speakeasy counter, had run the game. The gang had taken Joyce out, but they hadn't taken her to any police station. Maybe she had guessed that they weren't taking her— maybe she hadn't. The man who had remained in the lobby hadn't stayed long. He'd been playing the game, too.

Gary went out of the apartment delivery entrance slowly. He walked away from River Street for two blocks. He took a Green cab—rode a mile westward, got out and caught another cab five minutes later. He instructed the driver to drop him off at the corner that was fifty yards from the entrance of the *Jones Hotel,* then to drive to the hotel and leave a folded slip of paper with the clerk. He said there was a message he wanted to get to the clerk. There wasn't any message. He was playing safe. He had a trail to pick up, and he wanted to do it without getting squeezed.

HE cab slowed down as it crossed Bank Street, t h e avenue that ran parallel to River Street. Gary slipped out on the right side — he had paid the driver—fought for his balance on the slippery paving. He was out of sight of the *Jones Hotel*—the corner brick building cut off any chance of him being seen from the windows of the cheap hotel.

The cab rolled on; he could hear the wheels slush over the soaked street surface. The sound died—he heard the engine rumbling. He was close to the brick building on the corner now. He stared down Third Street. The driver was vanishing inside the entrance of the hotel. Gary waited. Then it came. From a window up above. A battering, tearing stream of bullets from what sounded like a sub-caliber machine-gun!

Glass in the cab clattered to the street. Splinters shot in the air—metal wanged as the lead tore against it. The car rocked under the impact of the machine-gun blast. It was shattered from engine hood to tail-light. The clatter died suddenly. A window slammed.

Gary Greer swore softly. From the direction of River Street men were coming—they came slowly, heading toward the cab. The driver didn't come out from the entrance of the hotel. From the direction of Second Street there was the sound of a car engine suddenly given plenty of gas, but not in gear. A police whistle shrilled, several blocks distant.

Gary swung around, headed toward Second Street. The going was tough—wind swept Bank Street, the rain cut against his face. The car engine was given the gas again, still out of gear. The driver was taking no chances—he had the machine ready for a quick getaway, warmed up. But it was clear that he was waiting for something.

Gary turned the corner. The car was near an alley that ran out back of the *Jones Hotel*, on Second Street. The wind-shield wiper was swinging; he could see the figure of a man behind the glass. He waved his hand, ran forward. It was his left hand that he waved—the right was in the pocket of his gray coat—the fingers gripped his Colt.

Gary moved out toward the street as he approached the car. He could see the driver's head, extended beyond the left side of the car. Gary was within fifty yards of the machine now. The shrill of a police whistle, on Third Street, came clearly. The man in the car blew the horn twice. He blew it sharply.

And then, suddenly, the machine jerked forward. It picked up speed rapidly. It sped straight toward Gary!

He jerked his body to one side. There was a short flash of red from the left of the wind-shield—he heard the hum of the bullet as it cut the air close to

his head. His own Colt cracked—the car swerved badly to the right, hit the curb sharply. A tire blew—the driver fought the car back into the street again. It was skidding badly as it rounded the corner into Bank Street, turning northward, and was lost from sight.

Gary faced the alley. There were muffled shouts from it—the sound of footfalls. A figure came into sight, then two more figures appeared. The second two seemed to be supporting a third person. Running—or the girl? It was one of the two, Gary was sure of that.

He was in an exposed position—the man in the lead spotted him right away. The getaway machine was gone. Gary saw the leading man jerk his head quickly, heard him mutter something. The two men behind him swung around with the third human between them.

Gary ran forward, zigzagging. He saw the man who had given the order, shifting his body to the side, move his left hand. There was the glint of metal. The right arm was curved at the elbow, rigid. Elbow Gorringe!

Elbow's gun spoke first. The bullet shrilled close to Gary's head. He dropped to his knees, braced his left hand on the wet asphalt. He raised the right, aimed carefully. Gorringe spilled a second shot as the wind rocked him. It gritted along the asphalt—wild.

Gary Greer was calm. He squeezed the trigger of the Colt—there was a sharp *crack!* Elbow's body jerked. He steadied himself, fired a third time. Gary didn't even hear the air-hiss of the lead. He fired his second shot.

Gorringe went to his knees. There was less than thirty yards of distance between the two men. But the light was tricky, and there was the wind and the rain. Gorringe was down, his gun arm was wavering. He collapsed forward, rolled over on his back. From River Street a car straightened out on Second, headed toward Gary. A siren was wailing again—blocks away.

Gary Greer straightened. He turned, ran toward a low wooden building that had been at his back. The building was some sort of a warehouse; steps led down to a basement entrance. He jerked his head below the level of the street as a hail of bullets nicked the iron railing above, the concrete wall back of the steps.

The car slowed down. Bullets continued to splatter above his head—for perhaps ten seconds. Then the car got into high gear again—he could hear it picking up speed.

He smiled a little. Gorringe had been hit twice. They had stopped, picked him up and got him in the car. He was sure of that. But it wouldn't do much good. Gary's right arm had been steady enough. Elbow was out of the game; he felt certain of that.

Slowly he raised his head. The street was clear. Rain streaked down—the wind swept up it from the river in gusts. From Third Street came the faint sound of voices, of shouts. A siren wail diminished, dying to a low growl. Gary stared toward the alley. His body stiffened. The figure of Elbow Gorringe was still lying there in the rain! Those in the car had not picked him up!

"Trick!" Gary muttered. "Maybe they did get him—someone else, waiting for me to walk out—"

He swore softly. That didn't seem possible. The police were too close. They might come down the alley, swing around the block any second. Those in the car had discovered that Gorringe was dead—they had high-balled out of the section. They had left him. A dead gangster never counted. Center City didn't go in for expensive funerals, like Chi.

Gary moved up the steps. He kept his right fingers on the Colt—and his eyes on the motionless figure. Sounds from Third Street had died. A river boat whistle sounded above the beat of the rain. Gary went up the steps—got out on the street surface. He moved toward the figure rapidly.

Suddenly he pulled up. The right arm was flung out. It was almost straight.

Elbow Gorringe had a crooked right arm. The figure lying just clear of the alley that ran through to the rear of the *Jones Hotel* wasn't that of Elbow Gorringe!

For several seconds Gary stood twenty feet distant, staring downward. Fear was striking at him. There was the strange limpness of death in the sprawl of the man's body. This was no trick. Those in the car had picked up a man—they had dropped another man!

Gary forced himself in nearer the man. There was something he recognized—the outline of the body, the build —even though the man was lying face downward. He dropped to his knees, rolled the man over.

It was Pete Ranning. Gary forgot the rain, the nearness of the police—as he stared into the white face of the man who had been his best friend. There was no expression on Pete's face. His shirt was opened at the front—he wore no shoes. Red stained the cloth of the shirt, over his heart. He had been dead for minutes.

Gary Greer got to his feet. He stood staring down at Pete Ranning's body, his lips twitching. They had found Pete, in spite of his efforts. They had found him up in the mean room of the *Jones Hotel.* And they had murdered him. Murdered him as they had murdered Gary's father.

He bent down again. He wanted to lift Pete in his arms as he had before, to carry him away from the alley, away from the rain and wind. There was no rage within him now. The hurt was too great. For the first time since he had started the fight against his father's killers the gangsters had struck back. Had struck back hard.

He thought of the girl. From between his lips came a fierce sound. They had the girl. The thought stopped him. Stopped him from lifting Pete Ranning, carrying him away.

He turned abruptly. He could be hard. He *would* be hard. The Colt he slipped into the pocket of his gray suit. He crossed the street, moved rapidly toward the river. He was fifty yards from the corner of River and Second Streets, when he heard the machine coming. An alley nearby was his only chance. He slipped inside.

The car was a detective's machine. It had the red-glassed side-light of such cars in Center City. It rounded the corner slowly, headed up the street toward Bank. The brakes squealed as it neared the alley. The sound of voices reached Gary indistinctly.

Pete Ranning—dead. Murdered as he had lain drugged up in the *Jones Hotel* room, perhaps. Or shot through the heart along the way. They had found him.

But he had not known of his death shot. He had seen no faces, felt no pain. That was the only consoling thought. The rotten part of it was that Gary had been to blame. He felt to blame. He had tried not to involve the girl, or Pete. The odds had been too great. The killers were ruthless. And Joyce Rawlings—

His body twisted, as he stood in the alley, listened to the beat of the car's engine as it waited for the men who were beside the body of Pete Ranning.

The girl had been tricked. She had been taken from her apartment. Gorringe was out of the fight. Gary could not be sure of it—but he felt that Elbow was dead. He guessed that the men behind him—the ones who had gone back into the darkness of the alley during the gun fight—had been carrying Ranning then. Had he been dead, or had they killed him after? And why had they not closed in on Gary as he had crouched on the steps of the warehouse?

The police had been too close. Perhaps Gorringe had not been dead—and they wanted to get him medical attention. Certainly they knew that Gary was still alive.

The voices had died now—the detective car was picking up speed. Gary stared toward Bank Street—watched the glow from the red light on the soaked street surface. His eyes went across the street, toward the alley. The body of Pete Ranning was no longer there.

Gary Greer waited until the detective car was three blocks distant, heading toward the center of town. Then he moved on to River Street, turned away from the direction of Third.

In the distance, over toward the city's business district, he heard the siren of the detective car. His eyes were narrowed to gray slits. Hurt slits in a pale, set face.

Callahan. His thoughts centered on the man. Callahan was the one he would have to find. It shouldn't be hard. Callahan was a crook sitting in the seat of a plainclothes-man. Callahan would know where the girl was—where they had taken her. There was only one chance now. River Street haunts were useless. There was no time to play stool-pigeons, to work inside from the outside of the circle. He'd have to get to one man—Callahan.

The gangsters had struck hard. They had tightened their grip. The girl had been taken—and Pete Ranning had died. Callahan was the only one who counted now. Gary knew less about him than he had known about the others. That was gangster creed—others always knew less about the big guy. But Gary knew that it was Callahan who had trapped Joyce Rawling, who had murdered Pete Ranning. It was Callahan who had ordered the squeeze.

 T was an hour before dawn. Casal Callahan walked from the entrance of the City Detective Building, slipped back of the wheel of the battered coupé near the curb. The battered coupé was Callahan's business car. Ten blocks distant, in a certain garage, he had a sporty green roadster. He kicked the self starter, the engine rapped

noisily. Callahan reached for the shift.

A figure slid up near the door—it swung open. Callahan stopped shifting. His right hand dropped toward a pocket of the coupé. A left hand struck it aside. The figure slipped into the seat beside Callahan. Something hard, metallic, pressed against Callahan's right side.

The detective's breath was sucked in sharply. There was a sickly grin on his face. His voice was hoarse, broken.

"Hello—Greer—"

Gary Greer smiled. It was a terrible smile.

"Hello, Sal!" he said grimly. "Take me for—a drive, will you?"

Callahan swayed a little in the seat. He was fighting for control, and he was gaining it. But it took effort.

"Sure, Greer," he managed shakily. "Which—way?"

His eyes went toward the entrance of the Headquarters Building. Gary laughed a little. The laugh was as terrible as the smile had been.

"One hand on the shift—the other on the wheel!" he ordered. "When you get through shifting—*both* hands on the wheel. Be very careful, Sal—we don't want an—accident."

Callahan smiled again. His eyes were narrowed a little.

"Which way, Greer?" he asked again.

Gary spoke very slowly. "Out Main —to Carlisle. West on Carlisle. Quiet street—we'll talk as we—ride."

The car jerked forward. Gary held the Colt pressed against Callahan's right side. He had the cloth of his coat over the weapon. He pulled his soaked hat down over his eyes. The streets were almost deserted.

Callahan drove carefully. The rain had become a fine drizzle. It was colder. They went west on Carlisle. Callahan was breathing heavily. The coupé was approaching the Italian section of the city now. Wooden shacks—jammed close together. Cars parked for the night, in side streets.

"Tired?" Gary asked grimly. "You're breathing—hard."

Callahan kept the smile on his face. His was a rather handsome face, though the man's body was short, thick-set. His black mustache was uneven, badly kept.

"Had a hard day—and night," the detective stated slowly, shakily. "Trouble —on River Street."

Gary said nothing. He pointed to the left, as they approached the next street.

"Turn—to the left. Go down half a block. Pull in at the curb, near Malletti's place. Get both hands on the wheel—keep them there!"

He saw Callahan's face twist—the man's thin lips were half parted. He pulled in near the dark, wooden shack beyond a ragged curb. He got both hands on the wheel. His eyes met Gary's. Fear showed in them.

"Listen, Greer—" he started— "maybe you an' me can get together on—"

"Maybe." Gary cut in sharply. "I ran into a wop named Conti about two hours ago. Out here, in this section. I was looking for Malletti, because I knew he was after you, Callahan. You sent up his brother a week ago. Conti was drunk. I fed him five hundred-dollar bills, and he talked. Among a lot of lies, he told me one truth. He said you were sometimes known as Sal the Dude. In this section—"

He stopped. Callahan's face was white—ghastly white. Fear was gripping him.

Gary laughed bitterly. It was a low, throaty laugh.

"Don't lie to me, Callahan!" he advised. "Your one chance is—straight talk."

"I ain't—lying—" Callahan's voice was pitched too high. Fear was driving his front away.

"Is Elbow Gorringe dead?" Gary cut in grimly.

Callahan nodded. He didn't speak. His eyes were wide with fear now.

Gary spoke again. "If I send lead through you here, Callahan," he said slowly, "Malletti will burn for it. They know he's out to get you. They know you made deals with him. They know you sent his brother up. *You* know something the other don't know, Sal. You know *I've* been working under Federal jurisdiction. *You* know you couldn't send me up for the murder of your crooked pals. That's why you didn't come after me, *that* way. You wanted to kill. You killed Ranning tonight. I got **Gorringe**. Working under a rotten administration, you ordered my father—put on the spot, Sal the Dude!"

Callahan tried to speak. His words came out hoarsely.

"I swear to God, Greer—I didn't have a chance—"

"You're going to get one!" Gary's voice was like ice. "You're going to take me to Joyce Rawlings! You know where she is. If she's hurt—or if you try one trick—"

He shoved the gun muzzle deeper against Callahan's side. The man back of the wheel spoke shakily.

"I'll—play the game—Greer! She isn't—hurt. I swear to God—"

"Drive!" Gary's voice was grim. "And listen to what I'm telling you—"

The car engine raced. The engine rapped again. But something else was rapping, too. It was clattering. Beating like a steam riveting machine. A repeater rifle!

Callahan screamed. Just one word. "Malletti!"

And then the bullets were ripping into the car. Battering against the hood. Tearing at the metal and wood, the fabric!

The car was rolling. Gary bent forward. Irony. He had brought Callahan out to Malletti's place—to drive him on. To make him realize that Gary could kill—and get in the clear. Malletti hated Callahan. And now the Italian had heard the detective. His high pitched voice had carried to the frame house. And Malletti was battering down lead to get the man he knew was in the car.

Something struck Gary heavily across the top of the head. He straightened, his body jerking. The machine-gun fire had died—the car was picking up speed. Weakness was gripping Gary. Waves of dizziness swept through his head. He tried to fight it off. Callahan was staring at him, puzzled. The expression faded.

Gary tried to tighten the grip on his Colt. But he failed. He saw Callahan's right hand streak back from the wheel—it caught him heavily under the right temple. He pitched forward.

It was minutes later when he recovered consciousness. The car was on a country road. There was a gag in his mouth. Callahan was driving slowly, a smile on his face. He glanced at Gary, but he said nothing. Instead, he started to hum. Gary tried to move his arms—his wrists were cuffed back of him, and the steel was fastened to something that wasn't movable.

The car bumped along the road. Callahan drove with a yellow-white smile on his face, and hummed. There were two bullet holes through the wind shield. The metal at Gary's right was torn. His head ached terribly. His whole body ached. He picked out a few words of the song Sal the Dude was now singing.

" '*Sure do love to hold you Honey—
Sure do love to—squeeze—'* "

Callahan jerked his head toward Gary's. He broke off. He chuckled.

"I'm a good guy, Greer!" he muttered grimly. "You want to get to that kid of yours. By God—I'm *takin'* you!"

He started humming again.

SAL, THE DUDE, by RAOUL WHITFIELD
The smashing wind-up of the Gary Greer series in
OCTOBER BLACK MASK

Bar Nuthin', Puzzle Buster

By EUGENE CUNNINGHAM

Dodging bullets and trying to solve a robbery-murder mystery at the same time is pretty nearly a man's sized job.

AR NUTHIN' half-slid off the bed, to land sitting up between bed and wall, with long-barreled, white-handled .44 Colt menacing the darkness. He let go the big hammer, driving a bullet toward that tiny *creak-creak* of the ancient floor which had waked him; which had warned of someone moving stealthily toward his bed.

With the roar of the shot something fanned his very cheek; something pinked his ear and thudded into the wall behind him. He flinched instinctively with the sting and before he could recover and fire again he heard

the door into the hall slam. He came erect like a cat and leaped clear over the bed. He shot across the room and jerked open the door to look up and down the hall. But it was pitch-dark. His man might have been within arm's length, yet invisible.

For perhaps sixty seconds there was thick silence in the Thomville House. Then doors began to open and matches were struck; kerosene lamps and candles were lit and into the lower floor hallway poured the guests of the hotel. They found Bar Nuthin'—who had covered the hall in the dark—bending beside a lighted lamp, staring at a trail of red spots on the floor.

"What's the matter?" demanded the

landlord calmly. Then he recognized Bar Nuthin' and his eyes narrowed a bit.

"Yuh got some prowlin' hairpins around," Bar Nuthin' grunted, moving now to follow the blood-trail and with the dozen-odd of male guests at his heels. "Somebody come into my room an' I let go at him an' he heaved a bowie at me. It's a stickin' in yo' wall in the room. Hmm! He skipped out the window . . . "

And over the sill he slid, Colt in hand, a tall, muscular figure, looking even bigger in his underwear. He came back in a couple of minutes and regarded the gathered men—cowmen and freighters, a couple of drummers, traders and punchers-in-town—with a keenness masked by the habitual indifference of brown face and narrowing blue eyes.

"He's curled his tail an' lit a shuck," he grunted to the landlord. "Wonder who he was. . . . Well—no matter now! I'll meet up with him eventual an' then—" He twirled the Colt absently on the trigger-guard.

"I'll git the sheriff," the landlord said, scowling.

"Well, I'm not waitin' for him!" Bar Nuthin' said emphatically. "I'm turnin' in again—but this time it'll be in yo' corrals I reckon."

Then the strained, tallowy face of a drummer aroused his sardonic amusement. The fellow was pop-eyed and open-mouthed with excitement. Solemnly Bar Nuthin' stooped and set his lamp on the floor. He bent his red head and sniffed loudly at the blood-spots. Then he nodded to himself, got up and went into his room. The drummer's large mouth sagged lower still.

"My stars!" he gasped. "He's a blame' bloodhound?"

"Well," the landlord drawled, judicially, "jist about! You squander around Texas a spell an' you'll hear tales o' Sergeant George Washington Ames —more usually called Bar Nuthin' Red

—that you jist cain't believe. They'll be jist half-true. The prize puzzle-buster o' the Texas Rangers, they call that long coupled hairpin. He's on red-striped wheels, fella!"

Bar Nuthin' came out of his room dressed. Again he said that he intended to sleep in the corrals. But once outside he went silently around the old frame hotel. He came back then to the window of the room adjoining that in which the visitor had found him. Gently he raised the unlocked sash and slid inside. Having placed a chair against the hall-door, he went to bed.

He was out at dawn. On Thomville's main street, he looked up and down with a serene, if watchful, blue eye. And as he whistled, he wondered if the attack of the night had any bearing on the errand which had brought him here the evening before. He had received Captain Hewey's order only two days earlier—but that did not mean that nobody in Thomville knew that President Bob Horton of the Stockman's Bank had arranged to have a Ranger investigate the bank robbery of three weeks before.

He went over to Wo Lee's restaurant on the far side of Main Street. He was just beginning his breakfast when a wizened, battered and scowling man came in; a little man who wore upon his buttonless vest a golden badge. This Bar Nuthin' reflected, must be Sheriff Mark Sones. He nodded colorlessly to Sones.

"Where in hell was you last night?" snapped the sheriff. "Andy Platt rousted me out at one o'clock to come find the fella that was tryin' to knife you. I couldn't find nothin'—not even you. Then, when I was just gittin' good to sleep, be damned if Andy never sent for me ag'in—dead Mex stableman out in Andy's corral! I swear I do'no' what Thomville's comin' to!"

"How was the Mex killed?" Bar Nuthin' inquired, lifting his coffee cup calmly. "For when yuh find who downed him, I'd like to meet up with that hairpin. He's the one who tried knifin' me. . . ."

"He was smacked over the head with a singletree. But what makes you think 'twas the fella that was after you?"

"I made it right plain I was sleepin' in the corral. But—not bein' altogether a dam' fool, I never slept the' . . .'"

"You come up about the bank robbery, didn't you?" Sones frowned. Bar Nuthin' wondered at the unfriendliness of his tone. He nodded indifferently and Sones slid off the stool and shrugged.

"Le's go then. Bob Horton'll be in the bank now."

Bar Nuthin' followed him outside into the early June sunlight. A handsome, swaggering six-footer, as yellow-haired and blue-eyed as Bar Nuthin' himself, came loafing down the line of plank-floored verandas toward them. It seemed to Bar Nuthin' that Sones' face tightened even more than was habitual to him at the sight of this good-looking cowman in his immaculate white shirt and fifty dollar Stetson and expensive gray pants and shopmade alligator boots.

"H'lo!" cried the yellow-haired young man. "How's the Long Arm o' the Law this bright, sunny mawnin'? Got them bank robbers yet? Nah? Too bad! An' election only a few months off an' a rival candidate comin' up. They'll have you out on a limb yet, Sones—an' saw off the said limb."

He was past before Mark Sones seemed to find adequate reply. Bar Nuthin' grinned as under-breath the sheriff muttered impotently about "damned smart Alecs." He asked gently who the vocal young man might be.

"Lace Burney—got the Bridle-Bit outfit east o' town! He thinks he's quite somebody. But if ever I git a chance at him, *he won't be nothin'!* I reckon—" a sudden maliciously-amused grin stretched the sheriff's ill-tempered mouth "—he ain't so cheerful as he makes out.

He wants to hook up wi' Marian Makewn, but ol' Cass Makewn ain't got much time for Burney. I hear Cass tell him last night he don't want no wild-ridin', harum-scarum hairpin into his family! Lace used to raise plenty hell!"

"Girl don't seem to figger like her pa," drawled Bar Nuthin', who had glanced over his shoulder. "If that's the girl yuh been talkin' about. She's right full o' lovin' kindness, seems to me. . . ."

Sones whirled and stopped dead still. In front of the general store beyond Wo Lee's restaurant, Lace Burney had stopped before a slim girl and she was smiling up at him.

"Yeh, that's Marian Makewn," Sones growled grudgingly. "But ol' Cass'll be back from the ranch an' *he's* runnin' that outfit. They're a-livin' in town now—the Makewns. An' Lace don't see Marian so much as when they was out on the Wrench."

But he was snarling as if that meeting down the street were a personal affront, as he and Bar Nuthin' turned into the low, one-story stone building which housed the Stockman's Bank. It was a single, long room with three-quarters of its space fenced off by a woven-iron grill. The ancient vault—which had been so easily opened by the robbers of three weeks before—was set in the back wall. Sones led the way to a door in the grilled partition and a big bulldog of a man got up and opened the door for them.

"Bob, this-here's Ames, the Ranger," Sones mumbled.

Bob Horton stuck out a hamlike hand. His fierce gray eyes narrowed a little as Bar Nuthin's hand closed like a steel hook upon it, easily countering the bear grip of the banker.

"Set down!" he grunted and returned to his chair, to look a shade contemptuously up and down Bar Nuthin's shabby puncher outfit.

"He's come to settle up the bank robbery," Sones grinned. "But somebody like to settled *him* at Andy Platt's last night."

"Didn't scar up yo' vault door much," Bar Nuthin' commented, glancing at the vault. "Or did yuh have it fixed?"

"This gang never worked that way," Horton scowled, following the Ranger's glance. "First time a bank was ever robbed in Texas—so far's I know—this away. They done some o' that fancy combination-jigglin' I have heard about bein' done back East. Put a kind o' doctor's stethoscope to the door an' listened to the tumblers fallin'. Jiggled the knob around—an' opened her."

"Huh! I never took much stock in that before. I do'no' a thing about yo' robbery, so le's start from the beginnin'. I was in Liffy a couple days back, just goin' through. Got a letter from Cap'n Hewey. He says to come to Thomville an' see what I can find out about yo' robbery. Here I am."

"Well, the's nothin' much to tell. Three weeks ago we went to bed one night with thirty-odd thousands in that vault. Ten thousand in unsigned currency. We got up the next mornin' an' the vault door was open, swingin' wide. The bank door had been jimmied. We was shy twenty-nine thousand seven hund'd—all the currency an' gold. Sones picked up a sheet o' the unsigned twenties an' this stethoscope-gadget I told you about lyin' in back o' the bank where the robbers'd got on their hawses."

"You couldn't trail these fellas," Sones said gloomily. "They had the devil's own luck. A bunch o' stock had been on the road before we started lookin' for 'em. Tracks was wiped out. I set the wires a-buzzin', o' course. But nobody'd seen a gang that might've been ours. You might think the scoun'els had hooked wings on to their hawses. An' none o' that money's showed up, neither, so far's we can tell."

Bar Nuthin' sat staring blankly at the wall. Horton still glowered at the big, careless-seeming Ranger. Now the grilled door in the partition opened and a pale, well dressed young man came in. Bar Nuthin' saw him from the corner of an eye. Sones nodded. Horton lifted a hairy paw to stop the newcomer who was going on past the president's desk with his papers.

"Walt, this here's the Ranger—Ames," grunted Horton. "He aims to clear up our robbery for us. Boly's the cashier, Ames."

"We'll hope he does," Boly nodded jerkily. "You told him what we know, Mr. Horton? You might believe that an eastern gang had descended on us, Mr. Ames. Nobody in this section of Texas had ever known of this sort of robbery."

Past the windows of the bank now came the big Lace Burney with Marian Makewn beside him. Lace was talking earnestly and the girl's face seemed to Bar Nuthin'—in the one glimpse he had of it—more than a trifle worried. He chanced to glance up sidelong at Boly. What he saw in the cashier's pale face rather explained to him the manner in which Boly had come into the bank. Bar Nuthin' thought that Boly was another admirer of the girl, and that he had seen the two together before coming off the street.

But he pulled his thoughts back to this robbery. He had heard of working combinations of safes until they opened. But, as Horton and Boly said, it was a new thing in Texas. Bank robbers in the cow country usually depended on blasting powder to persuade safe doors.

"Well?" Bob Horton demanded pointedly. Bar Nuthin' shrugged.

"Looks kind o' foggy an' blind," he grinned. "Reckon all I can do is squander around some an' see if the's any sign o' this gang havin' holed up around anywhere. For—"

Through the outer door of the bank burst a lean young man with a badge on his shirt. He looked quickly around then came running back to the partition.

"Hey, Mark! C'm'on out. Ol' Cass Makewn's lyin' out beside the road to

the Wrench. Been dead since sometime last night, Snukes Acree says.
Snukes found him a while ago an' split
the breeze into town. Shot in the back
an' dragged off the road a piece. I
got Pancho saddlin' our hawses!"

"My Lord!" cried Boly. "I wonder
if Marian's heard!"

Sones came to his feet, glaring at his
deputy. Bar Nuthin' was standing, too.
Sometimes he was moved by impulses
he could not explain. So it was, now.
His work in Thomville was connected
entirely with the robbery of this bank.
The murder of a more or less prominent cowman, interesting as it might
be to a Ranger sergeant whose life was
made up of dealings with crime, had
no real meaning for him. But something stronger than curiosity pushed
him out of the bank at Sones' heels.

"I'll ride out with yuh, if the's no
objection," he said.

He ran across the street—now beginning to fill with men and women
converging upon a point where—he
guessed—that Acree who had brought
the news was standing by a horse. Bar
Nuthin' shot into the corral behind the
Thomville House. He snatched down
his swellfork saddle from a peg. He
threw the blanket upon King Solomon's
back and was cinching with flying fingers when old Andy Platt the hotel
keeper came up to lean on the bars and
chew his reflective cud of Star Navy.

"Goin' out to look at ol' Cass Makewn, huh?" he drawled. "Goin' to be
hell on that pore kid, Marian. . . . Her
pa murdered like this an'—Lace Burney
goin' to be charged with murderin'
him. . . ."

"Burney?" Bar Nuthin' snapped,
turning where he was about to swing
up. "Now how come Burney'll be
charged?"

"Him an' Cass was rowin' before
Cass rode out o' town. They had rowed
before, but not quite so hefty. An' Lace
was s'posed to be sleepin' here last night.
When that knife-throwin' gunie woke
us all up I looked into Lace's room.

The bed hadn't been slep' in. An' his
hawse was s'posed to be in my corral.
But when Mark Sones found my Mex
stableman dead out the', this mawnin'
early, Lace's hawse wasn't in the'. . . .
Mind you! I like Lace. But Mark
Sones'll have him throwed into the cala-
boose by noon. Mark's nobody's
fool!"

Bar Nuthin' pressed his knees against
the zebra dun's barrel and went out of
the corral a screw-tailed thunderbolt,
mulling this new angle to the murder.
He saw Sones and three or four other
riders going out of town on a road that
pointed south, riding fast. From the
corner of an eye, as he pushed Solomon
after the sheriff's party, he saw Lace
Burney on a saloon-veranda, staring
that way. Burney whirled at the thut-
tering drum of Solomon's hoofs. Bar
Nuthin' frowned. Of course, he conceded, it might be imagination tricking
him, but Lace Burney's face seemed to
be very worried of expression.

He overtook the posse and reined
in a bit to keep alongside of the sheriff.
They went at the gallop for seven or
eight miles, then drew in upon the murder scene and swung down. Snukes
Acree led the way off-trail to a dry
arroyo close by, in which the body lay.
But Bar Nuthin' lagged behind.

He was not so much interested in seeing the dead Cass Makewn as in visual-
izing the crime, here on the spot where
it had been committed. There was a
boulder ten feet off the trail. Behind
it a horse had stood for a good while,
and when he had poked about for a
time, Bar Nuthin' found trodden into
the dust a .44 shell smelling of powder.
He looked down at the prints of a
booted foot. Nothing about the tracks
that was individual. Nothing about this
.44 shell—

"Huh!" he grunted and at a sound
of men coming back to the trail from
the arroyo, popped the shell into his
pants pocket. It was an impulsive
move. He had lone-wolfed it so long
that he disliked taking any one into his

confidence; even discussing a mystery with another.

"Find anything?" called Mark Sones. "Cass was shot twice an' both was hits, plumb center. Damn neat job o' murder!"

"Hawse-tracks an' some bootprints," shrugged Bar Nuthin'. "I don't see a thing about 'em to tell us anything."

He went up to where the deputy sheriff and Snukes Acree were looking down at the sprawling figure. Cass Makewn was a man of middle height and rather slender. Carelessly dressed, like any old time cowman. His face was strong featured, but good humored. Looked like a man—Bar Nuthin' reflected—who could either make or take a joke.

There were two bullet holes in him, as Mark Sones had said. One had struck him in the breast and split the heart. The other was on the right side —and it, too, had plowed up to pierce the heart. Doubtless Cass Makewn had been a dead man before the .44's echoes had ceased reverberating.

"Ol' Coaly, he come in the ranch-yard before daybreak," Snukes Acree said thoughtfully. "Cook found him tryin' to git into the corral. The' bein' blood on the saddle, I come on to see what the matter was. An' I found Cass here."

The same bootprints—about a number ten size—showed dimly about the body. The murderer had calmly dragged the corpse off the road and gone on. Perhaps to town; perhaps on into the hills by a stock trail, of which there were many. There was nothing to show just what he had done.

"Lefty," said Mark Sones to his deputy, "you stay right here an' keep folks away until I go back to town an' handle some odds an' ends. I reckon the coroner's jury'll just ride out here an' look things over. Comin' back wi' me, Ames?"

On the road in Mark Sones suddenly and dramatically put a hand into his pants pocket and drew out a flattened

.44 shell. He held it out to Bar Nuthin', who took it quickly and stared flashingly at it. Then he looked up blankly at Sones.

"Scratch on it," he grunted. "What d' yuh make o' that?"

"He stepped on it an' scratched it when he smashed it," Sones said carelessly. "But it's a .44 an'—Lace Burney is a .44 man. Dam' fine shot, too! I tell you, Ames, I have been sher'fin' a long time. In this country, a murder's goin' to be in one o' two corrals:

"It's either done for robbery or somethin' like that, by some saddle-tramp, or it's among our own folks. An' in *that* case, you got to look for a reason. Well this'n was done by Lace Burney, you can lay yo' last peso on that. An' I got the reason!"

His wizened face was so bitter-lined now that Bar Nuthin' easily understood the venomous dislike Sones had for Burney; understood what the younger man's sarcastic tongue had made the slower-thinking sheriff suffer.

But Bar Nuthin' wondered. Wondered if a man of Burney's apparent type *could* have committed a cold-blooded murder, in order to marry the victim's daughter. It seemed incredible. How could a man face the prospect of living with a woman, knowing all the time that if she guessed what he was, she would turn on him with utter horror and disgust? He spoke his thoughts aloud.

"Huh! He never downed Cass just to hook up wi' Marian! Ol' Cass was a rich man. Marian's his only relative. Now, if Lace can marry her, he'll have the money he's been a-needin' a long, long time to pull the Bridle-Bit out o' debt!"

Bar Nuthin' nodded absently. But he was thinking that while the sheriff's theory about the scratch on that .44 shell was fairly plausible, it was plausible only when you looked at the bent shell. Now that .44 in his pocket was not bent. But it, too, was scratched. A faulty ejector in a particular .44 was responsible for the scratch. Bar Nuthin' intended inspecting .44's.

"There's Lace's hawse," the sheriff said grimly, as they rode into the main street of Thornville. "That curly iron-gray in front o' the New York Saloon. An' the's Lace Burney!"

Bar Nuthin' gave the wizened little man credit for courage. He turned his horse and, with Bar Nuthin' trailing, rode straight up to where Lace Burney, very grave of face, now stood against an awning post before the saloon. They reined in and Burney looked up at them with narrowed blue eyes.

"Lace," said Mark Sones metallically, "where was you last night—all last night—from the time you saw me last until plumb daylight? I'm warnin' you, I know you wasn't in the bed you hired at Andy Platt's."

"You don't say so?" Barney drawled with attempt at the sarcastic manner of the earlier morning. "You look under that bed, Mark? Aha! That's where I was. When I get a few drinks into me, I'm scared somebody'll bite me. So I always crawl under the bed an' sleep on my gun."

"Lace Burney"—it was the sheriff's official tone now—"I'm arrestin' you on suspicion o' murderin' Cass Makewn—"

How that big fellow could go into action! Bar Nuthin', irritated as he was at being so fooled, had to give critical praise to Burney's technique. He had a Colt out from under his open shirt in a blurred twinkle of movement. Its muzzle moved in a short arc and covered both Sones and Bar Nuthin'.

"Either o' you look like you're goin' after a hawleg an' I'll drill you—so help me!" Burney rasped. "Grab yo' ears! I'm leavin' you. I do'no' a thing more'n you-all do, about who killed Cass. But I ain't bein' arrested, today!"

Still covering them, he backed across the porch and inside the saloon. With his disappearance, Bar Nuthin' rammed the hooks into Solomon with a vicious abruptness that brought an outraged squeal from the zebra dun. He whirled

Solomon and ran him along the hitch-rack, then jumped him almost sidewise across it. Down the side wall of the saloon they raced and around the corner. Bar Nuthin' jerked Solomon to the left, then. He swung down deftly with long Colt-barrel, cracking Lace Burney across the temple as the big man came out of the back door.

Sones came quickly behind him and hurled himself from the saddle. He had Burney handcuffed before the Bridle-Bit owner opened his eyes. Bar Nuthin' grinned a little as he looked down.

"Couldn't let yuh get away wi' that, fella—if I could help it," he said. Burney sat up and lifted a hand mechanically to his temple. The handcuffs jingled. He scowled.

"Don't try nothin'!" Sones said grimly. "We're goin' to the lockup right now an' if you make any breaks, I'll bust you one myself. I got no use for a lowdown murderer!"

Bar Nuthin' watched them go upstreet toward the jail. Then it occurred to him that the bank robbery had not been in his mind for some hours. He shrugged his big shoulders impatiently.

"Way things happen around here, Hewey ought to send up a couple Rangers!" he said grimly.

He was passing the bank when he remembered that Burney's horse was still at the saloon hitch-rack. He turned back and stood looking at the Winchester carbine in the saddle-scabbard. The town's idlers had been lured by sight of sheriff and prisoner toward the jail. Bar Nuthin' took out the carbine and sniffed the barrel. Seemed clean. He worked the lever, throwing a brazen spatter of cartridges behind him. He picked up a couple and examined them. No scratches on them, or on any of the remainder.

"Reckon he killed Makewn with that gun?" a nervous voice inquired, behind him. He was Boly, the cashier.

"I don't reckon *yo're* more'n three-eight's sorry to see Burney with the jewelry on," Bar Nuthin' grinned.

"Why, I've nothing against him!" Boly denied indignantly. "But if he committed a coldblooded crime like that, he ought to swing for it. Cass Makewn was a fine old fellow."

"Boly! Hey, Boly!" someone called from the doorway of the New York Saloon. Boly whirled with an odd sound. Bar Nuthin' looked flashingly at him, then turned to the red bear of a man now coming out to the veranda-edge, a shaggy and angry figure.

"What do you mean, turnin' back a hawse in that shape?" the red-haired belligerent demanded hotly. "By Godfrey! If I'd be'n in the stable last night when you brung him in, I swear I'd likely have messed up yo' haircut a plenty! What'd you do, anyhow? Both his knees skinned up like he'd been turnin' summersets! An' the Mex says he was just a-drippin' sweat!"

"He—he ran away with me," Boly said in a small voice. "But I'll pay for it! I—I have been busy this morning and I intended hunting you up. I'll pay whatever's right!"

"You're—dam'—right—you—will!" the liveryman drawled grimly. "Stovin' up a good hawse like that! An' you needn't tell me he run away wi' you, neither. I do'no' what the hell you was chasin', last night, or what was chasin' you. But I know that black hawse o' mine. He wouldn't run away if a flock o' engine whistles was tied to his tail."

"Well, anyway, I tell you that he did run away with me; got the bit in his teeth and ran over most of the county before I could control him. But I said I'd pay damages, Shea!"

Bar Nuthin' was listening, eyes narrowed and beginning to show, far back, an odd, cold light. He projected himself, now, into this conversation, but with the gentlest of drawls:

"How's this black hawse shod, Mr. Shea?"

"All around," the liveryman said surlily. "Boly, you come down to the stable right after dinner an' settle up."

Bar Nuthin' regarded the cashier steadily. His brown face was like stone in which his eyes blazed, frosty blue. Boly tried to look him down, but could not. He moved restlessly and finally muttered something incoherent about the bank. He turned away. Bar Nuthin' let him go a half-dozen steps, then:

"Come back here," he said levelly, hardly raising his voice. *"Come—back —here!* Or—"

Boly whirled, with a gasp. His face was chalky pale. He licked his lips. But desperately, he tried to be angry:

"What do you mean by this?" he demanded. "I—"

"Come — back — here!" Bar Nuthin' said again. His hand had gone under the flap of his jumper. Boly came on dragging feet.

"So 'twas *you* splittin' the breeze back toward town, from the arroyo where Cass Makewn was lyin'," Bar Nuthin' drawled. "Fella, how-come yuh never told about Makewn, last night? How-come yuh was out th', anyhow? Fella —yuh better talk fast!"

"I don't know what you're talking about!" cried Boly. "I wasn't on that road at all! Just because Shea rented me a horse is no reason for insinuating—"

"Fella, I'm not insinuatin' . . . I never do such. . . . I speak right out in meetin'! How-come yuh never told the town, last night? What took yuh down that road?"

He reached with left hand into a hip pocket and brought out a pair of handcuffs. His right hand slid from under the jumper-edge, with a white-handled Colt. Boly gasped. His mouth worked:

"I was afraid to!" he burst out. "I have been practicing riding. Nights were my only opportunities. Last night I started out for a ride and when I got close to where Makewn was killed, I thought I heard two shots, close together. But I had been thinking of something and hadn't been paying attention to anything around me. I wasn't sure that I heard the shots. I turned off the road and went quietly that way."

He seemed to gain control of himself as he talked. He even shrugged indifferently.

"I've been in Thornville long enough to know that it's not wise to go rushing into affairs that don't concern one. It might have been Cass Makewn shooting at a wolf. I got to that boulder—almost to it—and I saw a horse standing there. In the road a man was bending over, dragging something. Mind you, in that hazy moonlight, I couldn't be sure of anything. I turned around and rode very quietly away."

"Never come to yuh that it was a murder yuh'd run on to?"

"I didn't know! And if it were— well, to be frank with you, I didn't want to mix in! If it were, someone would stumble on to the corpse; and he or they could do the reporting! I wouldn't be marked, perhaps, by an undiscovered murderer, as the man who'd reported his crime."

Bar Nuthin' shook a slow head. It was quite plausible—looking at this pale "pilgrim" in gun-toters' country. But he was disappointed. He had mechanically noted the tracks of that hard ridden horse and filed away the discovery to be used, if and when it seemed to apply to the murder. But the only hookup he had stumbled upon made a kind of .22 caliber noise.

"A' right!" he grunted. "Keep yo' mouth buttoned up an' so will I. Unless I *have* to tell somebody. . . ."

He watched Boly go somewhat waveringly, but very quickly, on toward the bank. His wide mouth curled a little. Then he turned. In the saloon doorway was a tall, very lean man; a cowpuncher by the look of him; but a salty specimen. He was towy haired with faded little gray eyes under colorless brows. His nose was like a hawk's beak, over a lipless mouth and a pointed chin. He looked as if he had slept in his clothes for weeks; they seemed as much a part of him as his skin.

Bar Nuthin' let no shadow of his thoughts show in his face. He seemed to regard this lounging one without interest. But to himself he was saying that if ever one man had *all* the earmarks of a killer, this fellow was a walking collection of them. And he felt that, while he did not know him, he should. He wondered how much of Boly's talk this man had heard.

Someone inside the saloon called "Cranch!" and slowly the man turned, keeping the door frame at his narrow shoulders in a way that seemed habitual. He disappeared inside and Bar Nuthin' frowned a little as he looked after him.

"He almost rings a bell wi' me," he said aloud. "Almost."

He went moodily upstreet to the jail, which was a narrow two-story stone building behind the courthouse. Bar Nuthin' Red Ames, "prize puzzlebuster of the Texas Rangers," owned two qualities which made of him a detective—ability to wait patiently until bits of evidence formed into handcuffs or the rope, and flashes of intuition which came sometimes to illuminate seemingly meaningless objects and incidents.

In his own term, he "messed around and watched until something turned up." Just now, he had the feeling that he was in darkness; in the very center of movement. If he could only snatch out swiftly and surely, he would have the solution of this murder.

He saw Mark Sones and a body of men riding out of town. Coroner and jury, he thought, with some thrill seekers. Small doubt as to the verdict they would bring in! He went to the jail and found a wooden legged man in the office, with a sawed off shotgun across his knees and a frayed *Police Gazette* in his hands. He asked to see Burney and the man hesitated:

"Do 'no,' . . ." he drawled. "Me, I'm jist the jailer an' Mark says not to let nobody see Lace. But, hell! I'm not takin' that to mean you, Ranger.

Not when if it hadn't been for you, Mark wouldn't have no prisoner to be snippety about!"

He unlocked the jail corridor door and Bar Nuthin' went down to where Lace Burney sat on a cot in the end cell, head on hands. He looked up suspiciously, through the bars.

"What's Boly practicin' ridin' about?" Bar Nuthin' grunted.

"Huh? Boly?" Burney stared. "Dam' if I know, unless he thinks *that* would make a girl look at him! Why?"

"Saw the coroner's jury squanderin' out to the scene o' the crime. What d' yuh reckon the verdict'll be? 'Person or persons unknown—' or—'Lace Burney' . . . Guess how I'd bet!"

"You wouldn't bet with me! For I'd be bettin' the same way. They say you're a whizzer as a puzzle-buster, Ames. Well, how come you cracked me over the coco when, if you amounted to a hoot in hell as a detective, you'd know I never killed Cass?"

"I never gathered yuh in because o' Cass Makewn," Bar Nuthin' grinned cheerfully. "I done that on general principles. Yuh mustn't never throw down on a Ranger, fella, unless yuh aim to go on wi' the motion. It spoils yo' speed: A halted motion is always a slow motion. Spoils yo' looks, too—yuh ought to see yo'self! How many .44's yuh know right well, in this country?"

"Oh!" said Lace Burney. "So he was downed with a .44, was he! Well, so far's hookin' anybody up to that murder is concerned, he might's well have been downed with a rock! For there's just plenty .44 saddle-guns in this country. Ever' other cowboy's packin' one. I got one—as you know."

"Yeh, I know. An'—well, yuh look like yuh need somethin' to stiffen yo' back, so I'll tell yuh, I'm right sure yuh never killed Cass Makewn. But I do'no' *who* done it—yet."

"Thanks!" Burney grinned. "But if that little devil, Sones, can't get to hang me, he's goin' to be most awful disappointed. An' I swear, *I* do'no' who'd

have killed the old man. I had more interest in doin' it than anybody else could have. For Marian is goin' to marry me an' she's his sole heiress. Now, I'll tell you somethin', Ames: Sones is makin' a lot o' the old man tellin' me last night I couldn't marry Marian. Well—"

"I can't prove this, mind you, but after he told me how wild I'm supposed to have been, I got hot under the collar. I followed him off from where Mark Sones was listenin'. I reminded him o' some little things he never thought I knew. Things he'd done when he was a young squirt down in the Frio country, that my dad had told me about. I told him I was settled down now, an' I wanted to marry Marian. *An' he told me I could!*"

"A' right. Then where'd yuh go? Fella, I'm easy convinced. But yuh're up against Mark Sones now an' he's not a bit fond o' yuh. Yuh got to show an alibi that'll hold water — about an ocean o' water! Yuh got to talk to me if I'm helpin' yuh!"

"I reckon I'll have to stick to what I told Mark—about bein' under the bed," Burney said slowly. His reckless face set in grimly stubborn lines. "I can't embroider the tale."

Bar Nuthin' said nothing; merely watched him—and whistled.

"Ames, I was helpin' out a good friend o' mine. At what, I can't tell you. It's not my secret. I'm sorry for I certainly do appreciate your tryin' to help me."

"It's yo' funeral!" grinned Bar Nuthin'. "Yuh see, if I believe yuh never killed Cass Makewn, the only thing I'm after is the murderer. Yo' gettin' free really don't concern me any!"

With which cheerful thought, he turned away. The one-legged jailer let him out of the cell block and remarked that Marian Makewn was in the office, wanting to see Lace Burney. Bar Nuthin' went on in and stood looking at the girl. She was on the verge of a breakdown, he thought. Her face was pale and tear-streaked; her slim hands were clenching and unclenching.

"If I was yuh, Miss," Bar Nuthin' said slowly, "I would try to make Lace Burney tell where he was, last night. But—"

He checked himself. He had been about to say to her that he did not believe Lace had killed her father. But the jailer would be quick to relay this opinion to Sones and Bar Nuthin' was not ready to have the sheriff and the town know what he believed.

"Let her see him," he grunted to the jailer and went out.

After a belated midday meal, he drifted down to the New York Saloon and went inside. It was a big place and apparently very popular with both townsmen and men from the ranges roundabout. The mahogany bar was enormous. There was an arch-top mirror in the center of the back-bar, and on each flank of it displays of weapons that reached clear to the ceiling. Four bartenders were on duty, though this was not a busy hour. Bar Nuthin' looked curiously about.

At the end nearest the door a squat man was counting money from a cash drawer. He had shoulders enormously wide, by contrast to his height—which was no more than five-seven. His head was close-cropped—which made more apparent the way the skull above the small, flat ears went up almost to a point. His jaws were tremendous. He turned as Bar Nuthin' came up to the bar and revealed a brown, hairless and stonily expressionless face, in which black eyes shone dully—like bits of coal.

"Howdy, Sergeant," he nodded. "Have one on the house. I'm Barto Freed. Glad to meet you."

His thin mouth twitched oddly as he talked. He seemed to flip the words out of one corner. Somewhere, sometime, Bar Nuthin' thought, without letting his thoughts show, Mr. Barto Freed had known the inside of a prison—and for no short term, either. A man does not

develop that habit of talking in six months. . . .

"Glad to meet yuh," he nodded colorlessly.

As he drank, he was conscious of a steady snarling down the bar. Barto Freed looked with his stony stare that way, then seemed to dismiss any interest in the noise. He grunted to Bar Nuthin', then picked up his canvas bag of money and went out. To bank, Bar Nuthin' guessed. He turned sideways and listened to Cranch snarling about a rifle which the man said had been stolen from his saddle two days before, in front of this very saloon. He had drunk enough to be ugly of temper and it seemed that this rifle was his special pet.

"That ol' .45-.90?" a young puncher inquired scornfully. He too, had drunk a good deal, or misread Cranch's character completely. "Hell, I wouldn't gi' ye two dollars for a corralful like it. Ye ought to be dam' glad somebody was drunk enough to sneak it. Gi' ye a good excuse to buy a real gun."

"Is that so?" snarled Cranch. "They don't make a better gun than a .45-.90! An' that ol' Betsy'd plug a man plumb center at seven hund'd yards. And yo' mouth is too en-tire-ly loose, fella! Too —loose!"

He slid along the bar and smashed the puncher in the face. Two terrific blows and the indiscreet one sagged to the floor and lay still. Cranch looked down at him savagely, then hooked an elbow on the bar and called loudly for another drink. When it was put quickly before him by a worried looking bartender, he poured it down in a gulp. A freighter's gold piece, passing over the bar at his left, caught his wandering eyes.

"Gi' me that—an' a couple more yellow boys like it!" he demanded. "C'm' on! Tell Barto Freed to charge it up to me."

The bartender objected, nervously. He asked Cranch to wait until Freed came back from the bank. Cranch caught him by the arm and the bartender's face writhed. He let go the gold piece.

"Fella!" Cranch growled, with face rammed into the bartender's. "If Freed ain't told you fellas that what Ery Cranch wants around here, he gits— then it's time he done it. Or I'll tell you myself! Now, you fork over four more like this. Then I can go buy my liquor any place I feel like."

The bartender opened the cash drawer and took out the required amount. Cranch pocketed the gold pieces, with an ugly, triumphant grin. He had another drink and then for the first time noticed Bar Nuthin'—who was watching him in the bar mirror while seeming to study only the racked weapons beyond it.

"Speakin' about that .45-.90 o' mine," Cranch said abruptly, "I reckon it's no wonder it was stole. . . . Gittin' so, a man can't keep a dam' thing— what with Rangers around. You know, them scoun'els'd steal the fillin' out o' yo' teeth, you leave yo' mouth open. . . . I'm beginnin' to have a right good idee about where my rifle went to. Some dam' Ranger stole it!"

All eyes in the barroom went to Bar Nuthin', during a sudden, intense hush. He turned, grinning, to look at Cranch. Then he turned back to a trembling bartender and demanded pencil and paper. It was given him, quickly. He began to write, looking up from the paper to Cranch; writing a brief sentence; looking up at the puzzled one again. He nodded after a moment:

"I'll just look yuh up in my List o' Fugitives from Justice," he said calmly. "I halfway remember yuh, now. But —not by the name o' Ery Cranch. But I'll find yuh in the book."

He laughed in Cranch's scowling face, then, and shoved the paper into a shirt-pocket—letting his hand remain under the Booger Red jumper, on the butt of a white-handled .44. Cranch was crouching, down the bar ten feet. His gun-

hand was like a claw—and creeping up his shirt-front. . . .

"Cranch!" Barto Freed called metallically from the front door. "Don't you pull a gun on a Ranger, in my place! Don't!"

He came in and passed Bar Nuthin'. He stopped before Cranch, the pulses pounding in his thick neck as he stood sidelong to the bar.

"You come on back an' I'll tell you a few!" Freed said in the same motionless, yet compelling voice. He drew Cranch with him—by sheer force of will, it seemed. They disappeared through a door beyond the bar.

Freed came back within five minutes —alone. He nodded to Bar Nuthin' and expressed himself apologetically concerning the trouble. The bartender whom Cranch had manhandled reported the taking of the hundred dollars. Freed shrugged carelessly.

"He can have it—but he'll hear about the way he took it!" he said grimly. "I owe him some money for handlin' some stuff for me, but he can't come hellin' around because o' that!"

Here was another small puzzle. Bar Nuthin' knew that Barto Freed was a power in Thornville; that his money was in more than one enterprise; that, in addition to other activities, Freed had a ranch—the Ace of Spades—southwest of town. Of course, Ery Cranch might have been doing perfectly honest work, or trading, or something of the sort, in connection with the ranch.

But it was funny. . . . Such as Cranch would not work except under the strongest sort of compulsion. Compulsion such as penitentiary guards would provide, Bar Nuthin' thought grimly.

He had no line on Cranch. He knew his Fugitive List from cover to cover, so far as hefty gentlemen were concerned. Ery Cranch, by that or any other name, was not in any list submitted to Austin by a sheriff, for Ranger information. Not among the major criminals, at least, and it was not likely that *he* would be a man charged with chicken stealing! Yet—there was something in the back of his head that slid away aggravatingly, like a drop of quicksilver, when he tried to catch it. Something about that lanky, pale-eyed, lipless killer there.

While it might have nothing at all to do with either the murder or the bank robbery, his only official interests in Thomville, Bar Nuthin' thought he would have given half a month's pay to know what Freed had received from Cranch, in the way of service. One such as the saloon-keeper would be mixed in many deals—all of interest to a peace officer. Or so Bar Nuthin' believed.

He talked idly to Barto Freed, hunting for some lead in this maze. He talked of Burney's connection with Makewn's death. The coroner's jury —so Freed said—had charged Burney with the murder. A boy had ridden in hellbent, anxious to be first to publish the news. Freed expressed himself as openminded. He liked Burney, but if Lace had done the murder it was a peculiarly coldblooded business, demanding quick hanging.

"Well, the murder's Mark Sones' business," Bar Nuthin' said indifferently. "I'm here on the bank robbin' —an' it looks like I might's well be some'r's else! But I'll stick so long's the State pays my way. Yuh never can tell when yuh'll stumble on to somethin' an' Thomville's not a bad place. I see worse."

He talked about the old weapons on Freed's wall, pretending an interest he felt not at all, trying to get back to the subject of Ery Cranch. He handled an English derringer which was supposed to have been the property of that famous outlaw of the Mississippi Valley —Murel the slave-stealer.

"Somebody steal a gun off yuh?" he asked, returning the derringer and nodding toward two empty hooks on the wall. Barto Freed almost grinned as he looked that way.

"Folks don't steal off me—much. . . ." he drawled out of a mouth-corner. "I stick on a thief's trail till I get him an' that's regardless o' what he took. Folks know that. No-o, I took a Dechart squirrel-rifle down from there to have the lock fixed. I'm goin' to show some folks around here what that ol' flint-lock'll do, when she's right."

Bar Nuthin' drifted out. It was late afternoon, now. Bob Horton came out of the bank and hailed him. Bar Nuthin' hummed audibly and waited for Horton to come across the street to him, instead of obeying the banker's imperative hand-motion. The small defiance reddened the big man's face. He stopped and glared. Bar Nuthin' humming, looked at him calmly and waited for Horton to speak.

"Well! What're you doin' about the bank robbery? Seems to me all I see you doin' is ridin' around the country with Mark Sones an' bellyin' up to the bar in Barto Freed's! That yo' idee o' how to catch bank robbers? If 't is, then I do'no' what the hell I ever sent to get a Ranger, for! I got a Mex errand-boy that could do that much. I tell you, fella! I want some action on that robbery! An' if I don't get it, I'm sendin' a hot telegram to the Governor—an' he's a personal friend o' mine, too!"

"He's a right good friend o' mine, too," Bar Nuthin' said sweetly. "So that ought to make *us* friends—but be damned if it's doin' it! Trouble with yuh, Horton, yuh been a sizable frog in a li'l bitsy puddle too long! Now, yuh may be ten foot high in Thomville, but yuh don't mean a thing to me! I'll handle this robbery my own way in my own time. Meanwhile, how come Barto Freed's hirin' dyed-in-the-wool killers like Ery Cranch to ride on his Ace o' Spades? Yuh know so much about ever'thing, tell me that will yuh?"

The expression of near-fury on Horton's face struggled, now, with mirth. The latter emotion finally conquered.

He stood there and laughed tremendously.

"I certainly will!" he wheezed, at last. "Barto never hired Cranch to punch cows on the Ace o' Spades. He had some cows stole, a spell back. Cranch recovered 'em for him when peace officers wouldn't have hankered for the job. Cranch come up, then, to collect his pay. I know what you're thinkin'—an' it is what I might've *expected* you to think:

"Cranch is maybe a gunman. I reckon he is, or he wouldn't have been recommended to Barto Freed on this stock business. You got to fight the devil with fire! But because he's a tough nut, is no sign he's a bank robber—an' anyhow, he wasn't around till four-five days ago. An' Barto was playin' poker with Mark Sones an' me an' some others, the night the bank was robbed. So I reckon you got to start all over again, to hang the robbery on to somebody. You can't hang it on to Barto an' Ery Cranch! Which is what you was thinkin'. . . ."

"Yuh take a lot for granted," Bar Nuthin' said with a sudden, flashing grin. "Yes, sir, yuh certainly do. I do'no's I mind, though—for yuh'll find out plenty soon enough what I do think. Meanwhile, yuh might's well believe that I'm tryin' to pin a bank robbery on to Barto Freed an' Ery Cranch an'—oh, throw in fo'-five others, just for luck! As well believe that as anything: It'll keep yo' mind from strayin' too far out. . . ."

And he moved off, leaving Horton to glare after him, with big shoulders shaking. But his amusement was not long lived. This was as knotty a puzzle as he had tried busting in a long while. He considered the theory advanced by Horton, Boly and Mark Sones—that a skilled gang had struck, here in the cow-country.

But Sones was a good sheriff. He had done the natural and efficient thing, in setting the telegraph wires to humming with messages all around. It seemed incredible that a gang of strangers could have hit this bank and then vanished. For the country roundabout was thinly populated. Strangers were highly interesting to the natives. They would be observed and word of them would travel far and quickly.

Bar Nuthin' knew that Cass Makewn's body had been brought into town. It now lay in the Makewn house and Marian had many women of Thornville in the house with her. He thought that the girl must be there, overcome by the tragedy—which for her had two faces, since Lace Burney lay in jail charged with the murder. So he was surprised when, at dusk, wandering aimlessly about, he saw the girl come quickly up the dusty side street from Makewn's toward the main street.

"I've been looking for you!" she said quickly. "I slipped away from the house. It's almost more than I can bear, anyway; all those good women tiptoeing about and looking sad. It makes his—his death seem worse. And I know that Lace couldn't have done such a thing. Couldn't! And Dad would rather have me help Lace, now, than just sit and cry over *him,* when that is useless, anyway."

"He tell yuh where he was, last night?" asked Bar Nuthin'. He gave credit to the girl's strength of mind, and her sensible view of the situation. "I'm—scared he's got to tell. . . ."

"He won't, though! He's mule-stubborn when he thinks he is right. He was helping a friend. He says he can't tell who that friend is, or what they were doing. Because it would get his friend in trouble. If the mysterious friend wants to tell, to help Lace, that will be different. Oh, I argued with him! But he knew all the while that I didn't believe him guilty; that I wouldn't believe it no matter what the evidence might seem to show. So he just told me to be patient; that it would be all right eventually. But, Mr. Ames—

"Our Mexican houseman saw Lace

with a man named Monty Cane, after Dad rode out of town. He says that Lace and Monty were talking very earnestly, in a corner of Villareal's *cantina* in Lower Town. Pedro went in for a drink and saw them there. Monty is a kind of harum-scarum boy. More weak than wicked, Dad always said. He has a little ranch—the Lazy-M—ten miles west of here, just off the Flatus-Thornville road. I don't know why I think so, but I do believe that you could find out where Lace was, by learning where Monty Cane was, last night!"

"Lace an' Monty good friends?" Bar Nuthin' said slowly.

"Yes and no. Lace is a simpleton about friendship. He always has been. Any dead-beat can get his last dollar by claiming friendship for Lace. I know he thinks Monty is shiftless. He doesn't approve of some of Monty's associates and—habits. But if Monty Cane needed help in something, Lace would be just the idiot to get himself into trouble by giving the help—and keeping quiet about it, afterward, for fear of hurting Monty."

"Yuh don't reckon Lace Burney'd help Cane in a deal such as might throw him up against the law? Because, if he would—if he did, last night, Cane *might* figure to save his own skin at the expense of Lace Burney!"

"I wouldn't put it past Lace! So— I am trusting you. . . ."

"Well, I'll see what I can find out," Bar Nuthin' promised, if uncomfortably. "But all this is a long way off the trail I'm s'posed to be ridin'—the bank robbers' trail."

He watched her go back toward the house in which Cass Makewn lay. Irritably, he mulled over this new angle to the murder. He was so concentrated on thought of Monty Cane that almost he was forgetful of all about him. Almost—for Bar Nuthin' did own a habitual alertness like that of a wolf.

So when a rifle barked three times from the corner of a dark building across the side street from him, and a bullet tore through the crown of his Stetson so close that it moved his hair, automatically he hurled himself to the ground. But before he had more than begun the motion, another bullet burned his arm. He had two guns out as he sprawled in the dust and he slammed five bullets at the corner from which he had seen the rifle's flash. The firing ceased, but he lay there until presently, from the main street, men came running curiously.

Only when they neared him did he get up and go at a crouching, short-stepped gait to where the assassin had sheltered. It was a deserted house, by which the man had stood. There were his bootprints in the soft earth. Bar Nuthin' studied them—about a Number Ten size. . . . The same size as those which had showed around the scene of Cass Makewn's murder. But even in this land of small rider's feet, there were plenty of men who wore boots as large. He went carefully over the ground and grunted suddenly at sight of the ejected shells.

Three of them he found and at discovery of a scratch on each, he made a savage, disgusted sound. For it was too much of a coincidence, to believe that there were in this narrow region two .44 saddle-guns with faulty ejectors; ejectors that scratched the cartridge shells as they were flung out. Too coincidental, also, to believe that Cass Makewn's murderer and this bushwhacker were different men, merely using the same weapon. No. . . . He had fired five shots at the murderer of Cass Makewn. And the fellow had got clean away. It was maddening.

He snarled impatiently at those crowding up behind him and asking fifty questions about the meaning of the shots. He growled the briefest of explanations to Mark Sones, who came running up as he tried to follow the prints of those Number Ten boots.

"Well," Bar Nuthin' said grimly to Sones, when the tracks disappeared in a welter of hoofprints before a corral,

"I reckon we got to give it up again! But I aim to meet up with that gunie before we settle the cat-hop. An' when I do—"

He got away from the crowd as quickly as possible and went prowling about the edges of town. His rage had become a cold and deadly determination, now, to meet that dry-gulcher face to face and settle this business in a blaze of shots.

He prowled through the darkness, as silent and as ready for swift battle as a wolf. He found nothing suspicious; saw nobody in the gloomy section of the town off the main street, but one man riding out of town. But there was nothing odd to be marked about this rider—which was disappointing.

He went by back ways, finally, to the New York Saloon. He came in through the rear door, into a short hallway that reeked of whiskey. Raucous snoring attracted him to a doorway on the right. The ill-fitting door was half open. Bar Nuthin' looked in and saw that it was a kind of storeroom, with a cot in a corner. A kerosene lamp burned smokily. Ery Cranch was sprawled on the cot, flat on his back, mouth open. An empty quart bottle was on the floor by the cot.

Bar Nuthin' slid on into the barroom from the hall. It was crowded and the men clustered along the great bar were gabbling about the attempt to kill the Ranger; recounting the attack on Bar Nuthin' in the hotel room and the murder of the Mexican stableman in the corral, the night before. Evidently, Mark Sones had let out Bar Nuthin's theory that the stableman had been killed in the belief that he was the Ranger. For it was argued soberly and drunkenly, pro and con.

Barto Freed was at the bar's end, near the door. A rather handsome young cowboy was talking to him, a slender, dark, loose-mouthed youngster, who moved his shoulders and hands a great deal as he talked. Bar Nuthin' came unnoticed the length of the room and

pushed in to the bar beside this cowboy. Freed nodded to him and pushed bottle and glass his way.

"Certainly after you, Sergeant," he said. "Better be careful. Third time's the charm, you know!"

Bar Nuthin' grinned cheerfully. He poured himself a small drink and emptied the glass. His eyes wandered and upon the leather cuffs of the cowboy at his elbow, he saw the letters "M.C." in brass spots. So this was Monty Cane— He answered the description that Marian Makewn had given of him—harum-scarum; more weak than wicked— An idea formed in Bar Nuthin's alert mind. But he hardly knew how to set his plan in motion.

"Well, see you some more, Barto," Cane said at this moment. From the corner of his eye, Bar Nuthin' watched him go somewhat unsteadily to the front door.

"Reckon I'll sleep in the jail, tonight," he grunted to Freed, with a thin smile. "Safest place."

He followed slowly after Cane. He saw him moving up the line of verandas ahead and quickened his pace. So silently did he move that he was at Cane's elbow before the Lazy M man heard him. Cane whirled with a startled gasp.

"Yuh're Cane," Bar Nuthin' drawled genially. "Like to augur wi' yuh a li'l bit. Yuh know this country well an' I don't. Will yuh help me out some, fella? I do'no' even who I can talk to—safe."

"Why—sure! Anything I can tell you I'll be glad to. Where do you want to go?"

"Reckon the's nobody in the sher'f's office now. We won't be bothered the'. Let's try it."

He talked aimlessly of the ranches roundabout; of rustling; of the bank robbery, which he called a mystery not likely to be solved; of Cass Makewn's murder. More and more easily, Monty Cane replied. They came to the jail. The wooden-legged jailer was in the office, as in the afternoon, with his shotgun and his ancient *Police Gazette*.

"Let's in the cell block," Bar Nuthin' said to him. "We want to augur a spell an' don't let anybody bother us."

Cane seemed a little nervous, now, but Bar Nuthin' grinned reassuringly. The jailer let them in and locked the door behind them. There was an oil lamp at the end of the narrow corridor and Bar Nuthin' scratched a match. He looked in through Lace Burney's cell door and Burney asked what he wanted.

"Cane!" called Bar Nuthin'. "Come here!"

Lace Burney sucked in his breath swiftly and stared at the big, grinning Ranger. Then his face set in stubborn mold. He began to whistle softly.

"What—what is it?" Monty Cane said shakily. "Hello, Lace."

"Hello, Monty, ol' timer!" grinned Lace. "You been shootin' up the town, or somethin'?"

"He come in to tell yuh that he's not such a lowdown skunk as to let yuh lie in jail on a murder charge, when he can clear yuh by tellin' where yuh was last night," said Bar Nuthin' quietly.

"Didn't yuh, Cane? C'm'on, now, speak yo' piece! Burney has covered yuh like a li'l man, but I know the two o' yuh was together all last night. Yuh know what Burney's up against. Yuh was into somethin' last night; yuh needed help an' Burney gi' yuh a hand. Ordinary, he wouldn't say a thing about it. But he's due for the rope if yuh don't speak up. I do'no' what yuh was doin'—yet. But 't wasn't murder, anyhow. So if yuh got to lay yo'self liable to a li'l trouble, to save Burney's neck, it's up to yuh as a man to *lay* yo'self liable!"

"I—I don't know what you're talkin' about!" Monty Cane said, in a voice hardly above a whisper. "I—I never saw Lace but once last night. That was just for a minute. I would be glad to help him out, if I could. But I don't know where he was. I don't an' that settles it!"

Sidelong, Bar Nuthin' was watching Lace Burney's face, as seen with the shadows of the bars upon it. So he caught the tiny flash of contemptuous surprise upon Burney's features.

"That go for yuh, Burney, too? Yuh back him up?"

"If Monty says he never saw me but that once, you oughtn't to doubt him," Lace Burney drawled inscrutably.

"Reckon not— He has certainly throwed yuh down. Yuh never thought he would, did yuh? Yuh thought he'd speak up like the *friend* he'd always claimed to be. But he's goin' to claim he never ask' yuh for help, last night; that yuh wasn't with him at all. Fine kind o' hairpin *he* turned out to be! Yuh think, now, that yuh ought to bust a girl's heart an' go on wi' yo' mouth buttoned up, for the sake o' such as—as this?"

Monty Cane's white face was shining with perspiration. His weak mouth twitched as Bar Nuthin's lazily stinging drawl arraigned him. But he clenched his fists desperately and shook his head:

"I—I don't know a thing to tell! I— I would help him if I could. But he wasn't with me, last night. He wasn't with me!"

Stubbornly, he looked up at the low ceiling of the corridor, evading both Bar Nuthin's contemptuous eyes and Lace Burney's twisted grin.

"Come on, then," Bar Nuthin' grunted. He took Cane's arm and led him back along the corridor, toward the door into the sheriff's office. But when they reached the end cell, by that door, he halted Cane.

"Got any hardware?" he inquired, producing a Colt flashingly and ramming its muzzle into Cane. "Le's see . . . Uh-huh, .38 double-action under yo' arm. . . . We'll just take that. Can't let our li'l prisoners have weapons, yuh know."

"Prisoner?" gasped Cane. "Why— you can't arrest me! What is the charge?"

"Resistin' an' officer," Bar Nuthin' informed him solemnly. "That will hold yuh plenty until I can squander around an' find out what yuh was up to, last night. An' don't worry about my not findin' out! I have got plenty ways to do just—that—thing!"

He ignored the desperate protests of Cane and called the jailer. Between them, they searched the Lazy M owner thoroughly and shoved him into the cell. Bar Nuthin' turned the key and grinned at him sinisterly; then he turned to the jailer.

"Hold him *incomunicado*. Tell Sones, if yuh happen to see him before I do, that this *como se llama* —what d' yuh call it—is right valuable. For if Lace Burney killed Cass Makewn, Monty Cane had a hand in it. An', Mister Cane, yuh want to remember that! It's come to fixin' up an alibi, not just for Burney, but for Monty Cane!"

"Sigall!" cried Cane desperately, to the jailer. "You send word o' this to Barto Freed, will yuh? Right away! Freed'll fix it up. You tell him what happened here. He'll say where I was last night. He knows an' he'll attend to this Ranger that has come mixin' in Thomville affairs, he will!"

Bar Nuthin' grinned amusedly at the defiant threat. But he recalled how he had found Monty Cane leaning so confidentially against the bar, so close to Barto Freed. How the two were talking in low tones. Remembered, also, his original thought about the saloonkeeper with sight of the convicts' way of talking. Now, he wondered, had Cane and Lace Burney been occupied with some shady deal in which the saloon man figured? If so, and Barto Freed were going to furnish an alibi for Cane, why hadn't he furnished one for Lace Burney, who undoubtedly had done as much for Freed, on this mysterious errand, as Cane?

"Well, well, well!" he grunted to himself, standing outside of the sheriff's office door in thick shadows. "If this ain't the *boggiest* ford! Wonder if Freed'll come right out an' tell what Cane was doin', to alibi him? If he does—hell! It has to let Lace Burney out, too— But Freed said to me that

he'd always liked Burney, *but* if he did a cold-blood job like that murder, hangin' oughtn't to be a week off—"

AKEN by a sudden impulse he went toward what Thomville called Lower Town and hunted the *cantina* of "Big Antonio" Villareal.

Bar Nuthin' had a way with Mexicans. Speaking *"pela'o,"* or lower class, Spanish as fluently as any native, he was treated by Mexicans almost as one of themselves. So he drew "Big Antonio" off into a ducky corner of the little drinking-place and looked at him thoughtfully—a regard which Villareal returned frankly.

"Are you a friend of Lace Burney?" Bar Nuthin' demanded frankly, in the Mexican language.

Villareal nodded quickly, but his eyes narrowed and shadowily his wide brown face seemed to harden. Bar Nuthin' had his own notion concerning the reason; he was almost sure that the *cantina* owner had heard some of the talk between Monty Cane and Lace Burney the night before; that he knew Burney had not killed Cass Makewn because of being elsewhere. But—knowing that Villareal knew this was *not* gaining the information!

"Do you wish to see him hanged by the neck? When you could take the rope from him — and none be the wiser concerning your friendly action? Not even Burney himself, unless you desire?"

"You talk riddles," Villareal lied glibly. "I do not wish to see him hung, no! But that *I* can do anything to save him—absurd! What has a poor, ignorant *cantinero* to do with this? The sheriff has said that he murdered my other friend . . ."

"What do they say, among your people—who are almost my people, also —of Bar Nuthin' Red Ames, who is a sergeant of Rangers?" Bar Nuthin' was leaning across the pine table, hard blue eyes boring into Villareal's face.

A faint smile came to the *cantinero's* heavy mouth:

"Truly, they say that he is a tall devil!" he answered with paunch shaking amusedly. "They say that not the old gray lobo of the plain is more wolf than is Bar Nuthin' Red. They say that, to him, nothing can be hid; from him, none escapes."

"*Sí?* Yes? And what else, my friend? What do they say of his word, once passed? Does he keep it, always?"

"Always! *I* believe that—my friend."

"Then tell me something I need to know! I promise you to use what you say as if it came to me from the winds that blow. I promise that your name shall never be mentioned. I already *know* the most of what I need to know. But I must be sure—by testimony of one who heard. Tell me this and besides what I have promised already—silence—I promise that the name of Big Antonio Villareal will be kept in my memory as that of one to whom I owe a favor; one to whom that favor is to be repaid when repayment is possible."

"What is it you want to know?" Villareal said slowly. Then he grinned in the manner of one dropping barriers to a brother:

"You want to know where Monty Cane took Lace Burney, of course— Well, I know! They sat in this very corner here and I listened from the next room. A length of pipe is in the wall here, its end masked on this face of the wall. So I heard Monty—who is no good, Sergeant — beg Lace Burney to help him in a matter which he could not handle alone, but in which he was afraid to get help from anyone else:

"He told Lace that stolen Mexican cattle—we call them 'wet cattle,' as you know—had been brought to the Lazy M. He must move them quickly to the Ace of Spades—to the ranch of Barto Freed. He said that the sheriff was suspicious of him and, because Mark Sones does not like Monty Cane, he

would be quick to pounce upon the Lazy M, where the mere rustling of Mexican cattle by another would not rouse the sheriff's office.

"But—my friend! *There were no wet cattle on the Lazy M!* Not last night. I was sure there were none. Today, I know it beyond a doubt. Lace Burney and Monty Cane drove a hundred of Lazy M cattle through the night to the Ace of Spades. I—took the trouble to learn this, through a man of mine. For if wet cattle are coming into this country through such as Monty Cane, *I* wish to know it. But I had better say no more about *that.*"

Bar Nuthin' mulled over this. Cane had wanted Burney out of Thomville; he had drawn him out with a promise of secrecy that still held Burney. Why? It seemed logical to believe that it was to pave the way for the murder charge under which Lace Burney lay. To destroy his alibi. Cane was now denying that Burney had been with him. Even if Burney said that he had helped Monty Cane drive wet cattle, Cane's denial of this would be more weighty than Burney's affirmation. For Burney was the man on trial. It was to be expected that he would try to wriggle out of the rope.

"Why would Barto Freed want Cass Makewn killed?" he demanded suddenly of Villareal. The *cantinero's* expression told him instantly that there was no answer here, to such a question.

"I can think of no reason. Makewn had nothing that Freed could get; had nothing to do with Freed. Now, if the cashier of the bank—Boly—had killed him— But *he* has not the stomach for killing anyone. Nor would he kill the father of the girl for whom he is mad, I think. No, I do not know."

"Who is tryin' to kill *me?*" Bar Nuthin' grunted, voicing a thought that popped into his mind. "He who tried to drive a knife through me, in the hotel; he who killed the stableman mistaking him for me; he who fired three times at me this evening?"

"That, also, I do not know—or I would gladly tell you. But, speaking as one man of sense to another—you were ordered here to find the men who robbed the bank. Is it not truth? Well, just suppose that your coming on that errand was known. You are the man, my friend, who is famous for solving such mysteries. Suppose those robbers were here and you came into town. Well? Would it not be a good thing to kill you before you found out anything? I would think so! If I were one of those robbers, I should have a good killer slip into your room with a knife."

"What think you of that robbery? Was it, then, men from somewhere else? Professional robbers who could put the listening thing, the stethoscope, of a doctor to the vault door and hear the tumblers?"

"A boat! Give me a boat!" Villareal grumbled ruefully. "You get me into waters of the deepest. You persuade me to tell you things which I had not thought to say to anyone— My friend, that listening thing, which the sheriff picked up on the morning after the robbery, was no strange device to me. Not so! When Gonzales the physician of the Mexicans died, he left his tools to his widow. She put them all in a room of her house not a mile from here.

"I saw all the things and that strange device was among them. When she died, cousins, nephews, grandchildren, descended upon her house like grasshoppers. All the things vanished. I have seen a seventeenth cousin earmarking his cattle with what Gonzales called a scalpel!"

"Could you trace for me the trail of that stethoscope-thing? Find out who had it and, if possible, how it moved, to come to lie there behind the bank with the stolen money!"

"I will try. But I cannot promise to succeed."

Bar Nuthin' vanished from the *cantina* by a back way shown him by Villareal. In his mind the facts concerning the murder were milling about, all jumbled with such meager information as he had on the bank robbery. But most prominent in his thoughts was that stethoscope. If he could only trail it from the home of the widow Gonzales to the bank's door!

He went to the jail and Sigall grinned at him, over the shotgun and the *Police Gazette*.

"Lace Burney is right sore at Monty Cane!" he chuckled. "I went in a spell back an' took it on to myself to get sorry for Lace not havin' no exercise. I let him out in the cell-corridor an' ambled out. Then I *sneaked* back an' listened—an' *hombre!* What he was tellin' Monty through Monty's cell door you couldn't put in no kind o' book, without you took an' fireproofed the pages! Him an' Monty was up to some devilment last night an' he wants Monty to come clean an' tell what."

"Cane never figured her just that way, though, huh?" Bar Nuthin' grinned, but absently, for he was looking for the stethoscope.

"Not ex-act-ly. He kept sayin' that Barto Freed'd fix 'em both up with alibis. Got no more prisoners? Reckon Mark Sones is in a poker game. He ain't been around."

"Where's that stethoscope jigger he picked up behind the bank? I kind o' want to look at that."

"Slick as hell, way them robbers worked it," said Sigall, unlocking a wall cabinet door. "Here she is—an' dam' if *I* see yet how they could hear a thing through it. I have put her up to the safe door here and jiggled the knob a half hour at a spell an' I can't hear a thing."

Bar Nuthin' looked thoughtfully at the snaky tubes. Then he went over to the small office safe and with the ear pieces in his ear tried to hear the tumblers clicking when he moved the combination knob. He could hear nothing but the pound of blood in his own ears. He squatted frowning before the door, with the thing in his hand. There were scratches on the small hard rubber funnel of it—*A. de G.* Was that for A. de Gonzales? Plausible.

"I have always been kind o' proud o' my hearin'," he grumbled to Sigall. "But dam' if *I* can hear any tumblers clickin', or anything else. I always understood that these jiggers made sounds louder."

He turned it over and inspected the funnel. It was an old-fashioned binaural stethoscope and the rubber tubes from funnel to ear pieces were brittle and cracked: Mechanically, he tried to blow through it—and could not. He looked hard at the funnel and saw something cottony far up in it. A match poked into the funnel produced an ancient spider's cocoon with a dried larva still in it.

"I'll be damned!" grunted Sigall. "No wonder you couldn't hear out o' that. An'—listen! That spider never got into that after Sones found the stethoscope. Not any! For why? Because it has been tied up in that paper all the time since it's been in the office. I monkeyed with it a while, day after the robbery. Then I tied it up. Now, what good was it to them robbers?"

"Why, it *was* heaps o' good, Sigall," Bar Nuthin' grinned from the doorway. "But—it ain't a speck o' good, now!"

He vanished, leaving Sigall to repeat mutteringly the sentences and shake his head with a puzzled frown.

Bob Horton's big house was on the edge of town. Bar Nuthin' reached it at a trot. There was a light in the lower floor. He looked through a window and saw the bank president and Boly sitting comfortably with a bottle and glasses on a table between them. He hesitated. He *knew* now that the dropped stethoscope had been left for Sones to find—to indicate that this robbery had been done by experts who could work a combination. And he knew, too, that actually the vault must have been unlocked by either Horton or Boly. But that was to be proved—a very different matter.

He went up to the door and knocked. Horton himself opened the screen. Bar

Nuthin' slid inside and was whispering frantically before Horton could call his name. Horton gasped:

"Got him? Where is he? In jail?"

"No. If I'm not crazy, the one single robber o' yo' bank is settin' in that room right now. It's Boly," Bar Nuthin' whispered. "Come on in an' le's see if I'm right!"

Boly looked up quickly at sight of Bar Nuthin'. His pale face seemed to grow paler still. But he smiled and nodded. Bar Nuthin' merely stood looking at him stonily, then smiled in his turn, but a contemptuous, tolerant smile. Boly's slender hands drew into claws.

"Boly," Bar Nuthin' drawled, "what did yuh do with the money?"

"Money? What are you talking about?"

"The twenty-nine thousan', seven hund'd, yuh took out o' the vault the other night—before yuh heaved down old Gonzales' stethoscope where Sones could find it, an' yuh could tell him what it had been used for. No use lyin', Boly! Jig's up an' we're just sweepin' up the scraps! Yuh got one chance—come clean!"

"I don't know what you're talking about!" the cashier persisted in a whisper. "I—I had nothing to do with the robbery."

But Bob Horton had been watching him and now he turned to Bar Nuthin' with a snarl, as he went to the wall where a quirt hung.

"Step outside a minute! His face gave him away. The lowdown skunk! I'll have a confession out o' him in ten minutes—with this quirt!"

"Find out what he was goin' out the lower road for, too," Bar Nuthin' said in conversational, uninterested, tone. "He was the' last night when Makewn was killed. Maybe he downed Makewn, too, *I* do'no'. Have him tell yuh."

He slid out into the hall with mouth tightened grimly. He heard Bob Horton's snarling voice and a shrill, womanish cry from Boly, then the whistle of the descending quirt. It did not continue long. Horton called harshly and Bar Nuthin' went back.

"He'll talk, now," grunted Horton, looking down at the cowering cashier, whose cheeks were furrowed by streaks of tears.

"Barto Freed deviled me till I agreed," Boly whined. "He made the scheme. Even to planting the stethoscope. He used to be a safe-cracker. He did a long term in the Missouri penitentiary for it. The money is in the safe at the New York Saloon. I was going out to his place—the Ace of Spades—last night. But I don't know a thing about Makewn's killing. I swear I don't! I was so scared, when I ran into that, that I came straight back to town. Freed had told me to come out there for division of the money. We'd quarreled about it. He wanted eighty per cent, and I'd taken all the risk. He was angry this morning, because I hadn't come."

"Was it Freed that tried to kill me?" Bar Nuthin' demanded, smiling like a man who looks forward to a pleasant meeting.

"I don't know! But he knew that you were coming to Thomville. He warned me to be careful of you. He said you were the devil!"

"Let's heave him into jail an' drift downtown," Bar Nuthin' grunted to Horton and the banker nodded. On the way to the jail Horton made strange rumbling sounds, which translated at last into a very complete apology. Bar Nuthin' growled impatiently. Even though he had done the job he had been sent to do, there remained another unfinished. Since it was a personal matter, it worried him the more by its mystery. He wanted to meet the bushwhacking gentleman whose thrown knife was now in his pocket.

"Heave this hairpin into a cell, will yuh, Sigall?" he called to the jailer, thrusting Boly into the office. "Drunk an' disorderly; disturbin' the peace; lyin' to an officer."

Then he and Horton moved quickly away, going toward the main section of town. It was not yet eleven; the lights of saloons were bright on the main street. They went into the New York and ran into an excited group, in the center of which was Mark Sones and a rough looking cowboy.

"Hey, Bob!" Sones called excitedly. "Tobe Keeney, here, he has just come in from Liffy. He says they told him up there that our robbers—or some fellas that likely are our robbers—are back in the chaparral there. He heard the Liffy folks was makin' up a posse to go out an' look. I reckon Ames an' me ought to high-tail down an' take a look, huh?"

Bar Nuthin' trod upon Horton's toe. The banker merely shrugged at Sones, and looked sidelong at Bar Nuthin's smiling face.

"Le' me talk to this Keeney boy a minute, outside," Bar Nuthin' grunted, then led the cowboy out and away from the light.

"Now, yuh lyin' son o' somethin' or other, yuh spill it!" Bar Nuthin' snarled furiously, shoving Keeney up against the wall with the muzzle of a Colt. "I saw yuh ride out o' Thornville, not two hours back, an' yo' hawse ain't travelin' sixty miles an hour! Who put yuh up to tellin' that story? Fella, I'm plumb sick o' lyin' pups! Yuh're crowdin' Gates Ajar so close yuh'd ought to hear 'em squeak in the breeze! Talk up, or I'll blow a hole in yuh a two-hawse wagon could go through! *Talk up!*"

"*Barto Freed!*" gasped Keeney, shrinking back from that .44 muzzle and the equally deadly tone. "He told me to ride out a piece an' come in wi' that story. Don't shoot, Captain!"

"Get aboard yo' nag an' leave this country in a cloud o' dust!" Bar Nuthin' commanded. "Don't come back this year, neither!"

He watched Keeney plunge toward a horse at the rack and go down the street like a madman. Then he went inside, smiling gently. Sones and the crowd looked at him expectantly.

"Keeney'll be back, after while," he said. "Le's have a drink an' augur this over."

Breasting the bar, mechanically, his eyes traveled to the racked weapons and he stiffened a little. The bartender was putting bottles and glasses along.

"Huh?" said the bartender mechanically, at Bar Nuthin's question. "That .44? Oh, Ery Cranch borrowed it from Freed, the other day. Fetched it back a while ago. No, I never *saw* a squirrel rifle there. Whiskey for ever-body, gents? Huh? Shorely yuh can see it. But it's just a common .44."

Bar Nuthin' took the carbine. From the pockets of his jumper he produced some .44 shells. He loaded it while the crowd watched curiously. Then he began to work the lever. Out flew the golden stream of cartridges. He pocketed them again with a swift glance at each —though he had never doubted finding a scratch on them. He grinned shadowily at the man of drinks:

"Just a common .44?" he drawled. "It's the uncommonest one I have run into in quite a spell! Where's Cranch?"

But out of the corner of his eye he saw Cranch coming in the front door, beside Barto Freed. Bar Nuthin' let the carbine stay on the bar and moved as if he had not seen them—across the barroom, until he was ten feet away from the bar and there was nobody behind him; nobody in the line of fire from that door.

"Well, well, well!" he drawled, turning now to face them. "Here he is hisself, in person; ol' Killin's-Done-While-Yuh-Wait Cranch. I aimed to save yuh trouble, this time, Cranch: I come lookin' for yuh, so's yuh wouldn't have to sneak into my room, or kill sleepin' Mexicans, or dry-gulch me from behind a corner, to find me. An' now I'm here —I wanted to ask' yuh—

"What kind o' reputation yuh reckon yuh'll be havin'—yuh goin' out an' killin' ol' man Makewn, when Barto Freed told yuh *so* careful it was that greedy cashier, Boly, yuh was to down? Boly wantin' half o' the bank money that Freed had put him up to stealin'."

The occupants of that barroom were like men turned to stone. Even Freed and Cranch, stopped there just inside the door, seemed paralyzed as the war-grinning Bar Nuthin' went breezily on with his revelations. But it was no more than momentary. Cranch and Freed, after a lightning glance around, at the men by the bar, reached for hide-outs. Bar Nuthin' had been expectant of this. Neither was of the type to be taken easily. He shot Cranch neatly through gun-arm and shoulder, with a single bullet.

Some inspired one at the bar hurled a bottle. It caught Barto Freed in the face and he staggered, fumbling with a heavy pistol. Mark Sones streaked the five feet to the door and cracked the saloon man over the head, as Bar Nuthin' ran in on Cranch.

"Fella," said Sones awkwardly, when upon the bar lay the money from the safe, and the arm and shoulder of Ery Cranch had been dressed, "I do'no' how you done it, yet! How you figured Makewn was killed by mistake for Boly. I *sabe* that he was. But not how you figured it. But—anything I can do for you, why—"

"The's one li'l bitsy thing. . . ." Bar Nuthin' said solemnly. "Let Lace Burney out o' jail in company with Monty Cane. Leave 'em to themselves a spell. An' then—stand up with Lace at the weddin', when he goes marryin' a fine girl name Marian Makewn."

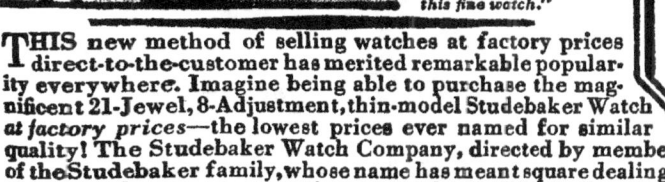

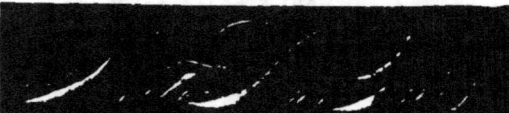
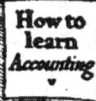

ANONYMOUS—
but it changed her entire life

Her charm and good looks weren't getting her anywhere. She found herself on the shelf at 33—and unable to account for it.

Then, one morning she received that bleak white envelope with its anonymous enclosure—a national advertisement across which was written in bold masculine hand,"Wake up."

She took the hint. And it brought her happiness and popularity.

,   ,   ,

Halitosis (unpleasant breath) is the damning, unforgivable, social fault. It doesn't announce its presence to its victims. Consequently it is the last thing people suspect themselves of having—*but it ought to be the first.*

For halitosis is a definite daily threat to all. And for very obvious reasons, physicians explain. So slight a matter as a decaying tooth may cause it. Or an abnormal condition of the gums. Or fermenting food particles skipped by the tooth brush. Or minor nose and throat infection. Or excesses of eating, drinking and smoking.

Intelligent people recognize the risk and minimize it by the regular use of full strength Listerine as a mouth wash and gargle.

Listerine quickly checks halitosis because Listerine is an effective antiseptic and germicide★ which immediately strikes at the cause of odors. Furthermore, it is a powerful deodorant, capable of overcoming even the scent of onion and fish.

Lambert Pharmacal Co., St. Louis, Mo., U. S. A.

★   ,   ,   ,

Full strength Listerine is so safe it may be used in any body cavity, yet so powerful it kills even the stubborn B. Typhosus *(typhoid)* and Staphylococcus Aureus *(pus)* germs in 15 seconds.

LISTERINE

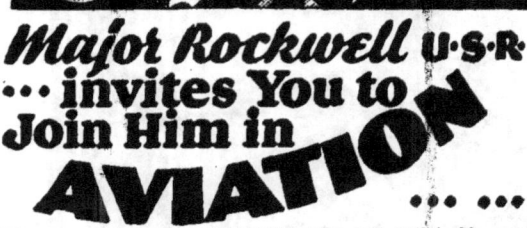

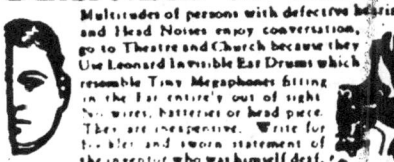

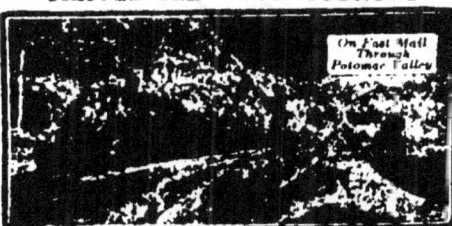

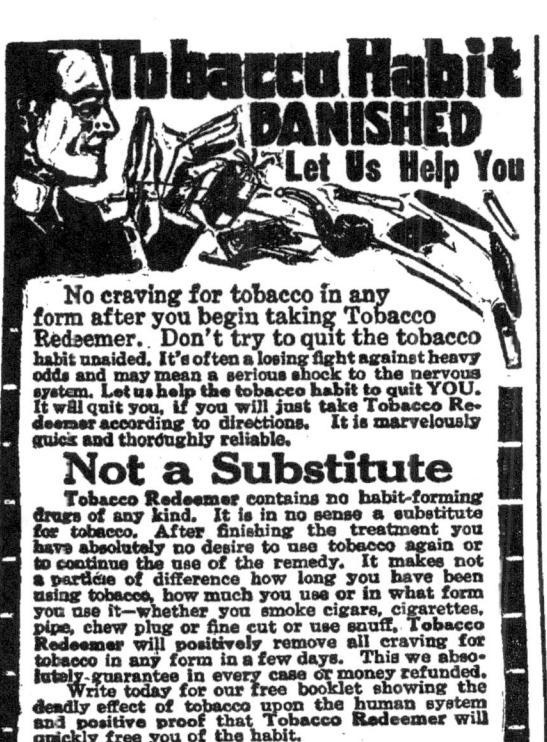

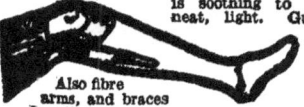

Please mention NEWSSTAND GROUP—MEN'S LIST, when answering advertisements

Kill This Man!

THERE'S a devil inside of you. He's trying to kill you. Look out for him! He tells you not to work so hard. What's the use? The boss only piles more work on you. He tells you not to bother with your body. If you're weak—you always will be weak. Exercise is just a lot of rot. Do you recognize him? Of course you do. He's in us all. He's a murderer of ambition. He's a liar and a fool. *Kill him!* If you don't he will kill you.

Saved

Thank your lucky stars you have another man inside of you. He's the human dynamo. He fills you full of pep and ambition. He keeps you alive—on fire. He urges you on in your daily tasks. He makes you strive for bigger and better things to do. He makes you crave for life and strength. He teaches you that the weak fall by the wayside, but the strong succeed. He shows you that exercise builds live tissue—live tissue is muscle—muscle means strength—strength is power. Power brings success! That's what you want, and gosh darn your old hide! You're going to get it.

Which Man Will It Be!

It's up to you. Set your own future. You want to be the Human Dynamo? Fine! Well, let's get busy. That's where I come in. That's my job. Here's what I'll do for you:

In just 30 days I'll increase your arm one full inch with real live, animated muscle. Yes, and I'll add two inches to your chest in the same time. Pretty good, eh? That's nothing. Now come the works. I'll build up your shoulders. I'll deepen your chest. I'll strengthen your whole body. I'll give you arms and legs like pillars. I'll literally pack muscle up your stomach and down your back. Meanwhile I'll work on those inner muscles surrounding your vital organs. You'll feel the thrill of life shooting up your old backbone and throughout your entire system. You'll feel so full of life you will shout to the world, "I'm a man and I can prove it."

Sounds good, what? But listen! That isn't all. I'm not just promising these things. _I guarantee them!_ It's a sure bet. Oh, boy! Let's ride.

EARLE LIEDERMAN, The Muscle Builder
Author of "Muscle Building," "Science of Wrestling," "Secrets of Strength," "Here's Health," "Endurance," Etc.

Send for my new 64-page book  IT IS FREE

"*Muscular Development*"

www.ingramcontent.com/pod-product-compliance
Lightning Source LLC
Chambersburg PA
CBHW080910020726
47502CB00008B/2415